EDWARD
TOVEY

Island
OF Courage

The dark shadows of history threaten a
blossoming romance on a Greek island

Mereo Books

2nd Floor, 6-8 Dyer Street, Cirencester, Gloucestershire, GL7 2PF Tel
An imprint of Memoirs Book Ltd. www.mereobooks.com

ISLAND OF COURAGE: 978-1-86151-965-8

First published in Great Britain in 2020
by Mereo Books, an imprint of Memoirs Books Ltd.

The address for Memoirs Books Ltd. can be
found at www.memoirspublishing.com

Memoirs Books Ltd. Reg. No. 7834348

Typeset in 11/15pt Century Schoolbook
by Wiltshire Associates Ltd.
Printed and bound in Great Britain

Contents

Historical note: The gods of ancient Greece
Historical note: the massacre at Anoegeia

Historical note: the gods
of ancient Greece

HERCULES was the gatekeeper of Olympus and the god of strength, heroes, sports, athletes, health, agriculture, fertility, trade and oracles, as well as divine protector of mankind and hero of Greek mythology. He was born out of wedlock, the result of an affair Zeus had with Alcmene. He arrived in Crete to slay the troublesome Minoan bull as the seventh of twelve labours put upon him by King Eurystheus. Hercules was the god of all Cretans, and following his capture of the Minoan bull, the animal became the symbol of the strength of the Cretan people.

EUROPA was the first Queen of Crete and mother of King Minor of Crete. Zeus, transfixed by her beauty, pretended to be a large white bull to attract her to his loins. Whilst playing with her nymphs on the seashore, the bull appeared and befriended her. She stroked it and climbed onto its back and together they ran into the sea, swimming to the island of Crete. There he turned back into a man and made love to her under a cypress tree.

KING MINOS OF CRETE: The ancient Greeks had a number of legends about Crete. The most famous tells of a

Cretan king named Minos, who kept a minotaur (part man, part bull) in a maze on the island and sacrificed young Cretans to feed it. Bulls became very important in Minoan religion and the horns of bulls are common symbols in Minoan art and architecture.

The Minoan civilisation, the first to appear on European soil, developed on Crete from about 3600 to 1400 BC, establishing a great trading empire located midway between Egypt, Greece, Anatolia and the Middle East.

Historical note: the massacre
at Anoegeia

❧

On an island within a country, with its own history as the birthplace of Europe's oldest civilisation, the Minoan culture flourished 4000 years ago. Over the centuries the Greeks, Romans, Byzantines, Saracens, Venetians and Turks all came to Crete, and each built their own fortresses, palaces and places of worship. This was where Hercules was revered and Queen Europa's beauty outshone all others, and the Cretan Bull left a nation with a legacy of honour and strength of character, and great respect for their homeland. Together the story excites the imagination and makes it possible to believe that they existed.

In more recent times, another nation arrived, bringing death and destruction to the island. In 1944, one village suffered more than others – Anogeia. On the village war memorial is a plaque with a copy of an order issued by the then German commander of the Crete Garrison, H. Muller:

ORDER BY THE GERMAN COMMANDER OF
THE GARRISON OF CRETE

Because the town of Anogeia is the centre of the English intelligence on Crete, the people of Anogeia committed the murder of the Sergeant Commander of the Yeni-Gave, as well as the garrison under his orders because the people of Anogeia carried out sabotage of Damasta because in Anogeia the guerrillas of the various groups of resistance find asylum and protection and because it was through Anogeia that the kidnappers of General Van Kreipe passed using Anogeia as a transit camp, we order its COMPLETE DESTRUCTION and the execution of every male person of Anogeia who would happen to be within the village and around it to a distance of one kilometre.

As a result of this order, the village was completely destroyed. A total of 117 people from Anogeia were executed by the Germans during the occupation. Anogeia was not the only one to suffer.

After the war, Kommandant Muller was executed by the Greek government for war crimes.

Of all the resistance movements who fought the Nazis in World War Two, few had the tenacity, courage and love for their homeland shown by the Cretan andartes (guerrillas). Their bravery when facing the firing-squads became legendary. Before they were shot, they would raise their heads to the mythical figures above which had been so revered by their forefathers.

CHAPTER 1

Crete, April 2017

'All rise!' the penal court official called out as the elderly judge walked into the chamber, resplendent in his red robes, which oozed authority and status. This was the main courthouse in Heraklion, the ancient city and capital of Crete. The atmosphere was tense. The public gallery was full, the faces of the public showing their anticipation of what was to come. This was a trial which had held the attention of the whole population, their interest pumped up by the front pages of the press and social media for weeks on end. You could have heard a pin drop.

Straightening his robes, the judge took his seat and banged the desk with his gavel.

The clerk of the court spoke. 'The court is now in session. Will the accused please stand.'

Two young Germans dressed in Nike shirts and black jeans

stood up, looking smug. Each raised a single finger in the air. This did not go down well with the people in the gallery, who shouted obscenities at the pair.

'Quiet!' shouted the judge. 'Quiet, or I will clear the court.'

Addressing the jury of four men and women and three professional judges, he asked the spokesman if they had reached their verdict.

'Yes we have, your honour.'

'And to the charge of murder in the first degree on both accused, what is your verdict?'

There was a hushed pause. Clearing his throat and with a nervousness which everyone in the room felt, the spokesman said, 'Guilty, your honour.' There was a huge cheer from the gallery, many standing on their feet.

'Quiet... quiet! I will clear the court if this disruption continues,' said the judge. Turning back to the jury, he asked, 'And is that the verdict of you all on both the accused?'

'Yes, it is your honour.'

'And on the second charge of rape. How do you find the accused?'

In a stronger voice this time, he said, 'Guilty, your honour.'

More thunderous applause and the whole gallery standing, shouting and applauding. The judge, realising what the verdict meant to those in attendance, let the noise subside before continuing.

'And is that the verdict of you all on both the accused?'

'It is, your honour.'

'Thank you, you may stand down.' After studying his

papers, he said to the accused, 'You will be taken to the cells and brought back to the court in three weeks' time for sentencing. Please clear the court.'

On hearing the verdict, the two accused stared at the judge and raised their arms in Nazi salutes.

CHAPTER 2

The previous summer – 2016

Tom had read somewhere that Crete 'wraps itself around you'. What did that mean, he wondered? Did it refer to the island, its history or the people? Maybe an amalgamation of all three.

The largest island in the Greek archipelago, Crete was one of at least one hundred and seventy inhabited islands, but it had always held a mystique above all others in Tom's inquisitive mind. When he was a young boy, his father had taken him to see *The Guns of Navarone*, a film starring Gregory Peck about an attack by British special forces on a Greek island where much was made of the love the Cretan people had for their place of birth. Now, having opted to study classics at university, he was excited by the culture, and although all the Greek islands had different stories to tell, he felt that Crete maybe had more to offer than the others. His last visit when he was in his early teens had been all about playing on the beach and roaming the hills and mountains. Thoughts of the past were not considered, only the present.

There was a considerable amount of excited chatter in the cabin of the Airbus 320 from Athens headed for the island in the sun. This was the height of the summer of 2016. The excitement of those jetting off had been dulled somewhat by the constant crying of a baby almost all the way, regardless of the efforts of the parents to stem the noise. The usual saviour, the dummy, appeared to be having little success. Added to that there were a few young lads who seemed intent on showing off, having had quite a few beers even before the plane had taken off. When one of them was refused more alcohol by the stewardess and objected, the senior steward had to be called. His mates fortunately made him see sense.

The buzz in the plane quietened a little when the whine of the turbofan engines increased in pitch as the undercarriage was lowered. This was followed by the reassuring thud of the wheels locking into place. Heads in the cabin could be seen turning to look out of the porthole windows, some with slightly anxious looks on their faces, as the plane was being buffeted by the wind on its approach to the runway. But with the sun pouring in from the starboard side, the prospect of beautiful weather seemed assured.

'Wow – just look at that view!' Tom Richardson was peering out into the sunshine as the aircraft dropped on its approach towards Heraklion Airport. The rugged White Mountains in the distance as they approached the island gave way to a dramatic coastline which, in some respects, reminded Tom of the holidays he had spent with his family in Cornwall when he was much younger. His friend Charlie, who was in the middle seat, leaned across Tom to share the view, already dreaming of throwing herself into the clear, warm, crystal blue water of the Sea of Crete.

There was a little tension among the passengers as the plane approached its landing. Crete was living up to its reputation as 'the windy isle', and the breeze was making the plane rock from side to side, with passengers gripping the arm rests a little more tightly than usual. But with a slight bump and some cheering and applause from a few of the more vociferous passengers, the plane safely touched down with the brakes full on.

Tom and Charlie had met at Cambridge University, where they had been part of a large group of students who regularly went clubbing. But unlike many of the others, they had kept their relationship strictly platonic.

Tom's father, Neville Richardson, a career diplomat, was the British Ambassador to Greece and had suggested some months earlier to his son that he might like to use the family holiday home in Crete for a short break during the summer recess. It had been a stressful period in the latter period of his second year studying classics, and the offer was a very welcome one.

Since his father's appointment to Athens, it had also been a stressful time in the embassy. Following the financial crisis of 2007 and 2008 which had been triggered by the Greek recession and a structural weakness in the Greek economy, Greece was in serious financial difficulties once more. Revelations that the size of the Greek debt had been grossly undercounted by the Government meant that diplomatic relations with the rest of the European Union, including Great Britain, were not as cordial as he would have liked, to say the least. Out of the blue, the EU had demanded that Britain should join the Greek rescue fund, but as Britain was not in the Eurozone, it stated its position that it had no responsibility for bailing out the Eurozone. This did not go down well with the rest of Europe, particularly with Germany, but the EU was losing patience again with the regime in Athens and tempers were getting frayed. Continuing financial assistance was the order of the day, whilst at the same time there was no discernible improvement in taxable income into the Greek treasury. The old ways of the Greek people and their desire to avoid paying their taxes at all costs continued.

When Neville had made the offer to his son, Tom had not been of a mind to go on his own, but he did not have a regular girlfriend at the time, so, knowing that Charlie was desperate for a break and had no plans, he had asked her if she wanted to join him. She had jumped at the opportunity and felt flattered to be asked. There were five weeks to go before returning to university, and a holiday in the sun was exactly the tonic she needed. To spend a week on a Greek island wearing T-shirts and shorts and soaking up the sun was, in her eyes, the nearest thing to heaven. Unlike Tom's, her parents were not well off and her job as a barista at Costa in Harrogate during the summer break had come to a premature halt, so money for holidays was a bit tight. Although she had been at home with her parents in their three-bedroom semi for most of the summer, the job was not well-paid, and she had not managed to save as much as she would have liked. She felt obliged when at home to 'pay her way', which did not leave a lot in her purse for large items of expenditure like holidays.

When Tom said that all she had to find was her airfare and some money for the bare essentials, like food, suntan lotion and alcohol, the picture got even better. Her parents were always prepared to help her out as their only child, even though not blessed with much spare cash themselves. In return she was determined to get a good degree, something neither of her parents had ever been in a position to consider.

Charlie was an attractive brunette who invariably set men's pulses racing, but she never used her looks to get a man she found appealing. She had always waited for the right man at the right time. She could afford to. Too many of her girlfriends played the field and slept around, but that was not her way.

With Charlie staring fixedly out of the window at the landscape, Tom rested his eyes as the Airbus taxied towards the long, low-rise terminal. They passed planes parked up to disgorge their passengers onto buses, which made Tom think about just how important tourism was to Greece as a nation. If for any reason the flow of tourists stopped or even slowed down, particularly at this time, it would be a disaster. There would be even more pressure on the Greek government, and his father, if that were to happen. The Greek people were an ancient and proud race and had welcomed visitors to their country for centuries – although not all were embraced as friends.

Having arrived on terra firma, Tom felt that he could relax properly for the first time. A few deep breaths, a long look up to the mountains and he could already feel the tension dropping from his shoulders. The last few weeks at university had been tough; he had been concentrating hard so as not to let his parents down and had rarely gone out. He now truly felt as though he was distancing himself at last from the pressures of doing well in the eyes of his mother and father, who expected so much of him. His tutor had given him a really hard time – and if he was honest, he deserved it, to some extent. He knew his father would be furious if he let him down, so he gave it his all – and had survived. Just. But his grades were not something to be immensely proud about.

When the plane had come to a complete stop, the passengers unclipped their seat belts and leapt out of their seats to get their bags down from the racks – something Tom never quite understood, as you never got off the plane any quicker. Over-eager anticipation to get into the sun, perhaps. After five minutes or so, the stewardess would open the door and that wave of extreme heat would hit you as you walked towards the steps leading down to the boiling tarmac. That was the moment when you knew you had finally arrived at your holiday destination. And this time they had touched down bang on time, the journey taking just over an hour.

In order to get as much out of their first day as possible, they had arranged an early start from Athens. Tom's father had arranged for the embassy car to take them to the airport, and his mother had been up and fussing around, offering to make them sandwiches and making sure they had everything. She had taken an instant liking to Charlie and was keen to make her feel welcome in the Richardson household.

'Have you got the keys to the house, Tom?' she asked.

'Yes, Mum. In the bum bag where you put them last night.' He gave her a wry but loving smile.

There was a seventy-mile bus ride from the airport to Chania (pronounced 'Hania'), where the Richardson family owned a delightful old terraced house in one of the town's narrow and very Venetian streets, not far from the harbour. Chania was the prettiest town on the island, and as Neville had once said to Tom, 'you visit Chania and you will want to stay forever'. It was a real picture-postcard town; one Tom's parents had visited when Neville was on a diplomatic visit to the island some years earlier and had fallen in love with.

As Tom and Charlie left the transfer bus to walk into the terminal, Tom said, 'The last time I came to Crete, the bus we caught was boiling. It was so old it had no air conditioning. Not a great way to start a holiday! Hopefully this time it will be different.'

They went through passport control without any difficulty. The British always seemed to be welcome here; something to do with the war, his father had intimated. The British Consul to the island, unbeknown to Tom, was waiting discreetly just to make sure there were no hitches, having advised passport control of their impending visit. The Consul had been briefed that this was a private visit, so a low-key presence was the order of the day. His father had told him to read up a bit about the modern history of Crete – not just the classics they studied at university.

As they walked out through the double doors of the terminal, it seemed hotter than ever. They had read that it had reached 33 degrees the day before, and this felt like more of the same. Still, that was why most people came here – the sun and sand first, the partying, and then perhaps for the culture, of which there was plenty to enjoy on the island. Wearing a Jack Wills outfit specially purchased for the holiday, Tom felt the part. He was ready to chill and have a good time.

To Tom's extreme pleasure, given the heat, there was a gleaming new coach in the bus park waiting for passengers from the flight. Its first stop was Rethymno, but the whole journey to Chania was scheduled to take only two and a half hours, so they should arrive early in the afternoon. They were first on the coach, so they grabbed the two best seats at the front.

Charlie leaned over and gave Tom a big kiss on the check. 'This is so good of you Tom, to ask me. I am very grateful to you and your parents. Without this, I'd be spending another week in Harrogate. Not that I've got a lot against Harrogate, it's a very pretty town, but you know what I mean.'

The driver kept the engine running to keep the coach cool whilst waiting to see if any other passengers were about to come on board. After ten minutes or so, it was obvious that no one else apart from Tom and Charlie and half a dozen others were coming, so the coach moved off. It was a spectacularly beautiful day and all they had to do was sit back, relax, enjoy the scenery and look forward to chilling out with good food and drink and the sea and sand.

The coach took the ring road around Heraklion, not the most attractive of towns. It had suffered colossal damage in the last war and was suffering now with damage of a different kind – an overload of graffiti. Once away from the capital, they headed inland until the Sea of Crete appeared again on their right, just before reaching Rethymno. This was Crete's third largest town, with a strong Venetian and Turkish influence in its architecture. A very tall minaret dominated the skyline. This appealed hugely to Charlie.

'If you like Rethymno, you'll love Chania,' Tom told her.

The coach pulled into the central car park to allow passengers off and to visit the cloakrooms before setting off on the last leg of the journey to Chania. This was a flashback from his childhood that Tom remembered well. Whenever they had come to the island as a family, they were treated like royalty. The CD plates on the car supplied by the Consul alerted everyone to the importance of the occupants. Today they were just ordinary tourists, and Tom had no problem with that. In fact, he welcomed it.

'Fancy a quick beer?' Tom asked Charlie. 'We can get a cold one in the café over the road.'

He remembered that he had promised his classics tutor that he would visit the archaeological museum at Heraklion or Knossos in order 'to improve his knowledge of the Minoan culture'. When they got back onto the coach, Tom said to Charlie, 'Whatever we do, we must visit the museums while we're here, or next term will be made hell for us by Old Badger [his nickname]. That's a condition of the holiday.' He gave her a big grin.

'It'll be interesting to see whether any of the ancient Greek and Latin we have learned can be used and understood today,' she replied. 'Can't wait to try it!'

It was after lunch when they pulled into Chania, and fortunately the family home was not far from the drop-off point outside the central market. Looking at the beautiful old buildings, Charlie said, 'Oh, Tom, this is gorgeous! Can we have a look round? The market looks so interesting, I just love looking at all the different fruit and vegetables and fish. Please Tom!'

'I think we had better drop the bags off first and by then it may have cooled down a bit,' he replied. 'Then we can walk back to the market and then on to the old Venetian harbour, and with any luck we'll find another cold beer.'

Walking along the narrow streets with their cases dragging behind on wheels wasn't easy, and it became more difficult as they approached the house. The alleyway leading to it was stepped and cobbled, which meant that they had to carry their cases. It was lined with pots of all shapes and sizes with striking plants growing up the sides of the houses, which made for a classic picture-postcard scene. Ancient overhanging balconies added to the interest.

Charlie was taking everything in. They passed tiny cafés where men appear to sit all day smoking and playing cards, without seemingly a care in the world. The general stores, the car hire offices, everything was so laid back – and, of course, as the notices on the doors warned, most shut in the early afternoon and did not re-open until three or four o'clock.

As they approached the Richardsons' house, Charlie's jaw dropped.

'Tom, this is so beautiful!'

She gazed at the whitewashed walls, the well-tended hanging baskets which brought a splash of colour, and the aged front door, redolent of years long gone.

'I can't wait to see inside,' she said. 'This is nothing like I imagined. You must give me a guided tour.'

Having unlocked the house, they dropped everything in the hallway and Tom showed her 'Chania House', as it was affectionately known by the family.

'Oh Tom, this is delightful,' Charlie said. 'So full of character. I can see why you all love it so.'

The marble floor made the house feel cool, even though it was baking outside. Charlie could sense that it had been furnished with considerable care, with touches of modern mixed in with old Venetian influences. The upstairs windows were open to let a breeze filter through the house.

'Our rooms are on the right at the top of the stairs,' said Tom. 'I'll carry your case up and then we can go and take in the town and harbour.'

After coming down, Tom wandered into the kitchen and noticed some fresh fruit in a bowl, a sure sign that a member of the Papadakis family had been in to clean and stock up. Locking the front door, they wandered down to the one-hundred-year-old municipal market at Sofoklis Venizelos, where fruit, vegetables, fish and meat, as well as bits and pieces for the tourist trade, were in abundance in the beautiful old iron building.

'Come on, we can shop later,' said Tom. 'If we go through the market and out at the other end, we can walk past all of the classy clothes shops in Chatzimichali Daliani – you'll love those – and then on down to the harbour. You'll be amazed by what you see when we get there.'

CHAPTER 3

Mainland Greece
March/April 1941

The beauty of the rocky landscape belied the disaster taking place. In northern Greece, against a backdrop of tall, rangy cypress trees stretching up towards an unbroken blue sky, British troops were dropping back down the side of a rugged mountain range. The roads were no more than farm tracks at best, causing irreparable damage to vehicles and to the marching foot soldiers. With the platoon harried by the Luftwaffe from the air and chased by German armour and infantry on the ground, it was suffering serious casualties. Sergeant Bob Neame of the Rangers Battalion, King's Royal Rifle Corps, which was attached to the First British Armoured Brigade, was exhausted. And so were his men.

'Hey Sarge, when are we going to rest up for a bit?' said

Corporal Weeks. 'We've been on the move for almost two days with no rest and bugger all to eat.'

Neame was aware how tough it had been for his men, but there was little or no choice. 'If we don't keep going, Corp, we are going to end up in the bag,' he replied. 'I managed to avoid it at Dunkirk and sure as hell they're not going to get me here. So, let's just follow orders and get a move on.'

Bob Neame had landed with the Rangers at Piraeus in early March, part of a rescue mission by 60,000 Empire soldiers, mainly Australian and New Zealanders. They had been ordered to head off an invasion by German and Italian forces from the north. After a month of serious fighting and falling back, he was almost relieved that they were going to be withdrawn. He was, first and foremost, an infantryman. Promotion had been offered early in 1941 when he had been in the Western Desert with the 6th Infantry Division up against the Italian army. It was tough fighting in the desert – it wasn't just the enemy you had to contend with, the sand got into everything and the flies were a constant pain in the backside. And the heat had been unbearable at times. He had enjoyed being with his mates in the Royal West Kent Regiment, but the promotion was conditional on transferring to the Rangers, who were desperately short of experienced NCOs. He wasn't sure how he felt about being an infantryman attached to an armoured brigade, but the Rangers enjoyed a good reputation in the army and if his main job was to support and protect the tanks, then that was good enough for him. And the pay of a sergeant was vastly better than that of a corporal – his first promotion. The cruiser tanks had fought courageously in Greece, but the terrain was not on their side and tough as he was, Neame, like everyone else, needed his sleep.

Bob Neame had been a Territorial before the war and had signed up in Maidstone when war was declared in September 1939. Having spent his youth in his home town of Ramsgate working as a labourer on building sites, he had yearned for a bit of excitement. He had married young and had a young family, so being a part-time soldier fitted the bill well, as he could be flexible with his working day and family, and he enjoyed the companionship of army life. He had been away to a couple of summer camps at Shorncliffe Barracks in Folkestone and enjoyed every minute of it. He had been seriously considering joining as a regular before war broke out. After some further training, he had been sent to France to join the British Expeditionary Force and had said goodbye to his wife and children. But after the euphoria of marching through Belgium to head off the German advance, they were soon in full retreat and heading back towards the coast.

Neame was with the 1st Battalion Royal West Kent Regiment, part of the 4th Infantry Brigade, which had been stranded on the beach at Dunkirk for days waiting to be taken off. It had been a terrifying experience. Not only were the Luftwaffe strafing the beach almost constantly, but they were being shelled by heavy artillery. They had dug in deep into the sand dunes to try and get some cover, but it was a false hope. If any explosions came close, the sand would offer little or no protection, as many of his friends had found. The RAF had tried their best to cover them, but by the time they had flown across the Channel, they had only had a few minutes over the beaches before they had to return.

The criticism levelled at them was grossly unfair. They had fought courageously over the fields of Northern France, unseen by the soldiers on the beach, and had accounted for many German aircraft. Neame and thirteen surviving members of his platoon had stood for hours in the water, after being called forward by the beachmaster, waiting for a boat to take them off. A pleasure steamer, the *William Allchorn*, had been their saviour. It was carrying far more than it was registered for to provide day trips along the south coast, and there was a serious concern at times that it would capsize. But after a relatively uneventful journey, they had tied up some three hours later in the harbour of Ramsgate, Neame's home town. Volunteers with blankets, tea and 'wads' were waiting for the troops as they came ashore. A more welcome sight they had never seen. Many broke down in tears, for it had been a terrible ordeal. Neame's wife had shed her own tears when she had found that he was safe and well.

After the long retreat from the mountains in northern Greece, it was Wednesday, April 23rd when they arrived back at Piraeus, this time for the evacuation. Here we go again, thought Neame. The Greek government had surrendered to the German forces three days earlier and it was time to go. To him, it seemed like a colossal waste of both men and equipment to come all this way to fight for a month against overwhelming odds, and to achieve what? Was it just a gesture, or did they seriously think they could stop the German army?

After an uncomfortable night's rest, another beautiful day dawned. The sun was partly obscured by palls of smoke from burning ships in the harbour. The acrid smell permeating the atmosphere was extremely pungent, making the men's throats sore and their eyes water. Reporting to the harbourside, they were confronted by indescribable devastation, so bad that they were told to get ready to head for Porto Raftis, some considerable distance away. It was obvious that Piraeus had suffered severe damage from the German bombers, but worse was to come just as they were leaving. The bombers returned and three ammunition ships exploded, almost completely flattening everything which was still left standing. The tremors and shock waves almost knocked them off their feet. Neame's platoon stood in awe and amazement a few minutes later at the sight of British civilians, mostly women, walking down towards the waterside to be evacuated. They were dressed in their Sunday best, holding umbrellas to protect them from the sun, carrying suitcases and holding the hands of young children. God bless the British spirit, he thought.

'Corporal!' Neame shouted as they arrived in Porto Raftis some eight hours after leaving Piraeus. 'Get those men under cover. We won't be able to get away yet, so let's try and get a bit of rest before the call comes to embark. Rustle up some char and grub if you can. And we need to take a roll call for the record.' Thinking about the wounded, he said, 'We may have to leave Thomas behind if there are no nursing facilities on the boat. He's in a bit of a bad way. I must report to Captain Turner when the roll call's complete.'

Neame's platoon, or the remnants of it, had arrived at the port after a forced march from Piraeus which had seemed to go on for ever. The journey had started in British army trucks, but when they ran out of petrol, it was on foot for the rest of the way. Long before they arrived, they could see huge palls of smoke billowing across the sky and anti-aircraft fire directed at the Luftwaffe overhead. Passing through the streets of the town, he noticed civilians staring at them with a great sadness in their eyes, realising that they were being left to their fate. The light was beginning to fade, a benefit in that it would keep the Luftwaffe at bay and the temperature would drop a bit, but logistically it was more difficult to work out what on earth was going on.

Corporal Weeks had located a mobile kitchen which had been abandoned, and the unit enjoyed one of the best meals they had had for some while.

'Sir, get some of this inside you,' said Weeks. 'There's enough here for a whole regiment.'

Neame grabbed hold of a plate laden with tinned sausages and beans. He had never tasted anything so good. Anchored out in the bay were the Royal Navy anti-aircraft cruiser *Calcutta* and the assault ship *Glengyle*. Lifeboats began transporting troops from the beach as soon as it got dark, while the Australian cruiser *HMAS Perth* waited offshore as cover for the embarkation. The New Zealand Brigade had formed a perimeter defence around the town at Porto Raftis, in order to keep the Germans at bay for as long as possible. Neame could see the beachmaster running backwards and forwards trying to get some organisation into the long lines of soldiers. Memories of Dunkirk came flooding back. There was frantic activity in trying to get the men and equipment aboard and away out of the harbour as quickly as they could. The heavier arms and all the vehicles had to be left on the beaches or in the streets of Porto Raftis.

In a matter of a few hours, almost six thousand troops had been embarked and Neame and his unit were still waiting for the call. He noticed smoke starting to appear from the funnels of both ships and the anchor chains being lifted. He thought with horror that they were going to be left behind. His best mate, Corporal Henry Weeks, who was on duty whilst the rest of the unit were getting some rest, sat with his head in his hands. 'Those bastards, leaving us in the shit,' he muttered.

Suddenly Lieutenant Commander Clark, the beachmaster, appeared out of the gloom. 'The rest of you are to make your way immediately along the harbour wall, where boats from the *Perth* will pick you up,' he told them. 'But you'd better get a move on because the *Perth* must slip anchor by two a.m. to get well away from the mainland before daybreak. Let's move it!'

Weeks, his whole demeanour now changed, shot off to round up the men. 'Come on, or we'll miss the boat,' he said with a chuckle. The news that they were leaving had given him a new lease of life.

As the *Perth* weighed anchor in the dark, they could

make out the silhouette of the *Calcutta*, which was sailing with them. The sheer size of the two vessels gave them considerable comfort. Both ships could wield considerable fire power if attacked from the air. Yet Neame's first thought when boarding the cruiser was that he was sailing even further away from England, a place he had not seen for a very long time. His commanding officer, Captain Turner, had told him that their intended destination was either Egypt or Crete. Neame was beginning to feel homesick and depressed.

'It's a very odd feeling, this,' he said to Weeks as the warship pulled away at some speed. 'I feel relieved that we've got out of that disaster, but I get the feeling we're sailing straight into another.'

Their fate had not yet been decided – or if it had, they had not been told. Before being sent to Greece, they had seen action in the Western Desert, and that had been very different. They had fought well and given the Italians a damn good account of themselves. He had been brought to his senses when Captain Turner had shouted at him to carry out a roll call. They had managed to keep together during the withdrawal, but they had lost some good men during the retreat. The walking wounded had managed to stay with them, but the more badly wounded, like Thomas, had sadly had to be left behind.

They were only a couple of miles or so away from the coast and twinkling lights could be seen from the distant shore when the shout went up, 'Take cover!' Neame heard the scream of a Stuka dive bomber in the half-light heading straight for the cruiser. Thankfully, because of the concentrated anti-aircraft fire from both cruisers, the plane veered away and the bombs crashed into the sea, missing the boat by a hundred yards or so. It was a warning that all was not going to be plain sailing.

They headed in a south-easterly direction past the Cyclades and the next few days were spent taking evasive action whenever enemy aircraft appeared overhead. Luckily the *Perth* avoided any damage, but during the evacuation from Greece, they heard that twenty-six ships had been sunk with great loss of life.

CHAPTER 4

Chania, summer 2016

'Come on,' shouted Tom up the stairs, 'it's time to get out of the pit.'

Having risen early, he had pulled up the blinds on a beautiful morning. The university clock in his head had still not reset itself. Charlie had earlier looked at her phone and decided that another hour in bed was definitely what she needed. Then she remembered that Tom had a full itinerary lined up for them both, so she staggered down in a short nightie, gratefully accepting a refreshing glass of orange juice from Tom.

'One thing's for sure,' said Tom at breakfast. 'We are just going to chill and explore today and tomorrow we're going to the museum, then the lecture from my tutor won't be playing on my mind for the rest of the holiday. I don't know why he didn't insist that you did some cultural trips as well while you were here.'

He knew very well why – it was because Charlie had, as she had put it, worked her butt off and not left her studies till the last minute like Tom. She had done well in her exams, and you could tell that their tutor thought she was highly intelligent as well as being a stunner.

'That's cool,' Charlie said. 'I'm happy to do that, as long as we can get in the sea some time today.' Going back upstairs, she shouted down, 'By the way, how are we going to get the museums tomorrow?'

There was a knock on the door.

'That must be Maria,' said Tom. 'She'll be looking after us while we're here. I haven't seen her for ages. She's the one who left the fruit and bread for our breakfast.' Tom opened the door full of anticipation at meeting the young girl he remembered from family visits many years before. Just seeing her standing there on the threshold took his breath away. He wasn't even sure that it was the Maria that he used to play with and have fun with. She was a couple of years older than Tom, so grown-up and so pretty. Her long black hair and dark eyes were a trademark of Cretan women.

Tom gazed at her in amazement. 'Maria? Is that really the little girl I used to play with in the school holidays? I can't believe how you've changed!'

Maria smiled and gave Tom a big hug and a kiss on each cheek. '*Poly kala*, Tom. It is so very good to see you again. You have grown up so much since I last saw you as well, I can't believe it! You have become a very handsome young man!'

Maria was the daughter of Nikos and Melissa Papadakis,

who had looked after the house since Tom's father had bought it years ago when Tom was not even a teenager.

'Those days playing in the hills and on the beach seem such a long time ago now. I know you should never ask a lady how old she is, but…?'

'I am twenty- two now. Going on thirty, my mother says!' she said with a wicked smile.

Tom stared at Maria, thinking of the young girl he had spent so much time with during his early family visits to Crete. He had been only twelve when they had first come to the island and fourteen the second time, and she was a couple of years older. His parents were more than happy when they used to go off together and for two weeks a year, she had been his surrogate sister. Her parents, Nikos and Melissa, had often come for lunch or dinner when they stayed there. It was a very happy and trusting relationship.

He gave her another kiss on each cheek. 'It really is so good to see you again. Our holidays were such good fun when you were around.'

She was glowing with the attention from this attractive young Englishman. 'How are your parents, Tom?' she asked.

'They are well, thank you. Father is obviously busy in Athens – the economic situation is not good. The diplomatic service has its work cut out trying to keep the warring parties happy.'

Maria's father Nikos was a history teacher in Chania and when Tom's family came to stay in the summer, he was generally around to help. His wife Melissa was a tour guide working in Chania and Rethymno, and the summer was a busy time for her. Maria had studied at the university in Athens, and had returned to Crete to help her parents, as jobs on the island were scarce, irrespective of grades. As their only child, Maria was pleased to help her father supplement the family income by looking after Tom's family and house whenever they came to the island. The introduction had originally come by way of Nikos's brother, Yiannis, who worked for the Greek government in Athens and had met Tom's father at a function for European diplomats. It had all worked out really well and Maria felt a special connection with the Richardson family, having spent some of her youth with Tom when they were younger. Secretly Tom was, in her mind, her first love, and her heart would flutter whenever she saw him. Now it was positively thumping.

'It's probably five or six years since we were all here last,' said Tom. 'I know my father has been here a few times on holiday and once on business.' Realising that Charlie had just come down the stairs, he said, 'Maria, can I introduce you to a friend of mine? This is Charlie.'

'Of course,' said Maria, but her face could not hide her disappointment as Charlie entered the room. '*Chairo pol'y*, Charlie. *Parakalo*.' Speaking Greek, she murmured quietly to herself, 'I thought Charlie was a boy's name, but you are most definitely not a boy!'

Charlie turned to Tom to ask what she had said. Sensing a slight tension, he was careful with the translation. 'Oh, Maria was saying welcome and that she was very pleased to meet you.'

Charlie shook Maria by the hand and smiled. 'Thank you Maria. I am sorry that I cannot speak your language, but I will try and learn a little while I'm here. My ancient Greek will probably not help!'

Maria took Charlie's hand and said, "My parents, with a little help from me, have been looking after the family for some years now so I know a little English. I like to talk to Tom in our language so it will encourage him to talk Cretan. I have always had, how you say, a soft spot for Tom!' Then, after a short pause, she asked, 'Are you two lovers?'

Startled at such a forward question, Charlie looked at Tom for an answer, but neither of them responded.

'So, Tom, you might have some time for me then,' said Maria, laughing. She turned towards the kitchen, and began to sing as she carried out her tasks.

Charlie turned to Tom and said quietly, 'She's got the hots for you, you'd better look out!'

'What's wrong with that? I'm very flattered,' said Tom, happy to wind Charlie up.

'Stop that. You're here with me. And you never know, I might want to become a little more than a friend!' Going back up the stairs, and knowing that his gaze was following her, she gave her backside a tempting wiggle.

Tom thought it was time to change the subject, so he shouted up, 'In answer to your original question, Dad leaves an old car, with no air-conditioning, in the garage round the back and I'm insured to drive it. I'll just make sure it's running, and then we can go out on foot when you're ready.'

All Charlie wanted to do was explore. She loved walking around looking at the markets, shops, buildings and people, and seeing at first hand the civilisations she had read about in books. To her this was heaven. The bonus was that it was hot, and she was on holiday with a good-looking guy.

Before they left Athens, the good-looking guy had sat with his father one evening whilst Tom's mother and Charlie were getting supper ready, talking about how and why Greece had got itself in such a mess financially. 'It's important for you to understand what has happened here in recent times, Tom, and why the Greek Government has no love for the EU and particularly the German administration,' said his father. Pouring them both a beer, he continued, 'As you may have read in the press, the Greek people do not like paying taxes. The same applies to many Latin countries including Italy and Spain, but Greece is perceived to be the worst.'

In order not to appear totally ignorant about the situation, Tom said, 'But I thought the main problem was successive socialist governments promising the people the world in order to get elected and not worrying how it was going to be paid for.'

'Well, there is considerable truth in that, like final salary pensions for life,' he said with a smile. 'But I believe that the problem started a long time ago, in the 1830s when the first king of the new state of Greece was a German.'

'How on earth did that come about?' asked Tom.

'It was decided that a regency council was needed to

'Europeanise' the country, and the Bavarian, along with two others and thousands of German-speaking advisors, was sent to start work. The first move was to introduce a policy of heavy taxation, which as you can imagine, didn't go down too well. They were trying to reform the country and change the mentality of a nation without taking into account its customs and ways of thinking back to ancient times. It was unrealistic. Greece was an insecure nation at the time, stuck between eastern and western cultures, with Germany trying to 'Germanise' it.'

'But if a German influence has been here for over one hundred and fifty years, why is there so much acrimony towards them now?'

'The Greek people feel that Germany has been responsible for making life so difficult for them over the EU bail-outs, with the German people giving vent to their feelings in the press questioning why more and more money is being poured into Greece when their tax receipts are so low. Hard-working German ethics against lazy profligate Greeks has become the norm in the press. And of course, there's the war. That's a big story.'

'Do you mean the occupation?'

'Yes. Germany didn't just occupy, they allowed hundreds of thousands of Greeks to die of hunger, took all the gold out of the banks and killed a hundred and thirty thousand people as reprisals when they were just protecting their homeland. You'll see evidence of this when you get to Crete. There's still a lot of bad feeling, particularly amongst the older generation.

They feel that Germany never paid full and proper reparations for all the damage and misery they brought to the country and the islands over the four years of occupation. And now the country is having austerity rammed down its throat and they don't like it. Protests in the streets have been going on for years and the main target of their anger is Angela Merkel. They are told no more tax avoidance, no more salaries for life, no more retiring at fifty.'

'I had no idea it was that bad. Does it make your job more difficult, having to deal with your German counterparts when there is so much bad feeling?' asked Tom.

'That's a good question. And yes, I know Kurt in the German Embassy very well, but they're aware of the antagonism and shrug it off. They can talk from a position of strength, and being diplomats, they know how to deal with it – most of the time. Now let's go and see how the ladies are getting on. I'm hungry!'

CHAPTER 5

Crete, April/May 1941

Standing at the stern of the ship enjoying the blasts of warm air from the eastern Mediterranean and watching the ship's wake disappear over the horizon, Captain Brian Turner was deep in thought. Then his musings about being a long way from home were interrupted by a call over the Tannoy for him to attend a meeting in the boardroom of the ship.

Taking a seat in the smoke-filled room, he was advised that his Rangers unit would be attached to the 14th Infantry Brigade, who also happened to be on the cruiser. Until that moment, he had not known whether it was Egypt or Crete they were heading for. He was advised that they were sailing at full speed for Crete to join the 14,000 British troops who were stationed there.

The birds circling above the ships were hopeful of an easy meal, but for the troops below decks, the motion was causing many to throw up as the ship sped its way across the waves. Captain Turner had been told that about half of those leaving Greece would be sent to Crete and the remainder to Egypt. This would bring the strength of the garrison in Crete up to around 40,000 men from the Empire, with around 10,000 soldiers from the Greek Army. Once they had left the waters around Greece and the Stukas were out of range for the time being, things quietened down and everyone could relax a little.

When they were about a day's sail from the island, a German E Boat approached them, but once the cruiser opened fire with her forward guns, she quickly disappeared. It was obvious that the Germans were looking to extend their territorial ambitions even further in an easterly direction.

Shortly after the sun was up the following morning, Crete came into view. It was a majestic sight with the White Mountains forming a backdrop to Suda Bay, an important harbour and home of the Royal Navy Eastern Mediterranean fleet. The natural harbour was five miles long and guarded by a peninsula on the north side and an escarpment on the south. There had been constant air attacks by the Luftwaffe and the sad sight of the cruiser *York*, which had been beached after being repeatedly bombed, was an ominous sign of things to come. As they were arriving, JU88 Stukas were attacking shipping in the bay and in quick succession they had sunk two merchant ships carrying vital supplies. The anti-aircraft fire from the *Perth* and others soon drove them off, one trailing smoke. The bay was becoming littered with sunken and damaged shipping.

After negotiating their way along the bay, they moored up alongside the quay on the northern side of the inlet. Turner located his senior NCO, Bob Neame. 'Sergeant, gather your men and equipment and line up ready to disembark,' he said. Whilst still on the Greek mainland, they had been ordered to keep hold of their rifles, ammunition and side arms but leave all other heavier equipment behind. Transport was waiting on the quayside to take them past Chania towards an airfield at Maleme. 'When you arrive, report to the New Zealanders who are moving east to defend the airfield. You need to dig in and take up your positions on the high ground known as Hill 107. Get details of your duties and support when you arrive. Good luck to you. I have to report to the Area Commander in Chania, then join you later.'

It was a beautiful day, and as is quite normal in Crete in the early summer, there was a warm southerly breeze blowing to cool things down a bit. As they moved away from the bay, it occurred to Neame that the roads were every bit as bad as those in northern Greece, if not worse; they were really no more than dirt-tracks. The men chatted among themselves, not quite sure what the future held, but they were content to let others make those decisions.

The lorries transporting the Rangers drove through the outskirts of Chania and British troops who had been on the island for some while threw chocolate and biscuits to them as they drove past. They were digging in in key positions, just wearing trousers, boots and their helmets, having removed their shirts due to the heat. Captain Turner had told Neame that senior officers on the island had been told by the intelligence services to expect an aerial attack at any moment. The Commanding Officer of the British forces was already talking of a retreat from Crete almost before they had arrived.

Not knowing exactly where he was supposed to be going, other than heading for Maleme airfield, Neame asked a military policeman who was directing traffic at a busy junction. He advised him that the Area Commander was based in the airfield operations office adjoining the main hangar. Making his way through streams of infantry heading in the same direction, he eventually found the New Zealand commander's office. Coming smartly to attention, Neame was instructed to take up positions with the 21st New Zealand Maori Battalion on the west side of Hill 107 overlooking the airport.

Keen to make a good impression on the Kiwis, Neame made sure that they marched to their positions as though they were on the parade ground at regimental HQ. As they made their way towards the hillside overlooking the airfield, a wonderful smell of wild thyme permeated the air. Although combined they made quite a formidable force, he realised that they were only armed with Lee Enfield rifles, Bren guns and a couple of Vickers machine guns, plus a few mortars and not a lot else.

Corporal Weeks said to Neame, 'If it wasn't for the war, this would look like a nice place to spend some time. You could come here with the missus on holiday when this lot is all over!'

Thoughts of his wife reminded Neame, as if he needed it, just how far from home he was. He wondered how she was, looking after their house in Maidstone with his young son and daughter, who he hadn't seen for over a year. The photo in his wallet was a distant reminder of happier times, and he was missing them hugely. Hopefully those times would come around again before too long.

Taking up their positions in the sweltering heat, Weeks shouted, 'Come on Hemmings, put your back into it or Jerry will be here before you've dug a hole big enough to sit in, let alone stand.'

This was an anxious time, but it was good to be busy, taking their minds off a possible invasion. They had arrived at the end of April and for the next two weeks all they could do was prepare the ground while the officers worked out a plan of action and waited for the inevitable. It was comforting that they had a first-rate infantry regiment alongside, having proven themselves on the Greek mainland.

Captain Turner returned the day after they arrived and took Neame and the other NCOs aside to advise them what was expected. Having left Greece with little in terms of equipment, they had to beg, borrow and steal what they could. Ammunition for their .303 rifles had been secured, but there were only about a couple of hundred rounds per head. That would not get them very far in a fire fight.

At a quiet moment later in the day while they were resting and smoking a couple of their ever-dwindling supply of cigarettes, Captain Turner asked Neame, 'Have you heard from home recently, Sergeant?'

'Not since the post that arrived when we were in the mountains in Northern Greece, sir – that was probably three or four weeks ago now. I suppose we were quite lucky; some guys haven't heard anything for months. It's a job for the post to keep up with us. I guess it will be even more difficult now.'

Turner reflected for a while, thinking about his own family. He and his wife had not been getting on too well since war had been declared. She couldn't understand why he felt that he had to go and 'do his bit'. He and his wife ran a farm in the Suffolk countryside which was regarded as a 'reserved occupation'. Because he had been a territorial reservist for five years, he couldn't understand why she felt so surprised by his decision. When they had said goodbye many months ago, it was not a happy occasion and he had only heard once from her in all that time.

'How are things at home?' he asked Neame.

'Well, my Pamela is a one-off and I have two wonderful kids,' he replied. 'They will have forgotten what I look like. They are only two and four and I've only seen Elsie, our youngest, Elsie once since I joined up, and that was when I was evacuated from Dunkirk. What about you, sir?'

'Unlike you, we're not blessed with children yet. We only got married a couple of years ago and running a farm puts a bit of pressure on our relationship. My wife couldn't understand why I felt I had to enlist. It's been a bit difficult,' he said, looking sad.

Neame thought it best to leave the subject and said, 'I'd better make sure that the men have been fed and watered before we change watch, sir. I'll catch up with you at roll call.'

In early May, the weather was as good as it gets with warm, if not hot, days, wonderful blue skies and balmy evenings. It seemed a shame that there was a war on. Neame had been told by Captain Turner that an invasion was expected any day, but they were as ready as they could be. The positions had been well dug in on the hill overlooking Maleme airport where the invasion from the air was expected; however the rocky ground made it really hard work to get deep protective cover. Capturing the airport would give the Germans the opportunity to bring in substantial reserves following the initial waves. They had to hold it at all costs.

On May 20th, the inevitable began. Intelligence had got it spot on. From the hillside they witnessed the heavy bombing of Chania followed by the arrival of hundreds of Luftwaffe transport planes, some towing gliders which filled the sky overhead. Neame, who was second in command of his platoon, had been positioned on the slopes of Hill 107 on the edge of Maleme airport, which everyone knew would be the first target for the invaders. It was the only substantial airport on the island. The Rethymno and Heraklion airfields were smaller and would not be able to take transport planes. Captain Turner had impressed on Neame the importance of securing Maleme. It was of the utmost importance for the Germans, so holding it was equally vital for the Allies.

As the German parachutists floated down, they were mowed down in their hundreds before they had reached the ground. As they landed, Neame saw civilians, including women and children, running from their houses and attacking the fully-armed German soldiers with knives, axes, scythes and anything they could lay their hands on. They systematically stripped uniforms and weapons from the dead and dying soldiers, running away to hide them for another day, he guessed. He had to shout an order to his men to aim away from the locals, as he certainly did not want the killing of innocent children on his conscience.

Neame heard the radio crackling away to say that troops were also landing by sea. It was looking a bit grim, but they had given the Germans a bloody nose and with the casualties inflicted by the civilians, this was a day they would not forget in a hurry. He felt that there would be a heavy price to pay later.

Maleme airfield was surrounded by olive groves and dry stone walls which afforded little cover. In mid-morning the Stuka bombers arrived, screaming down to drop their lethal loads. As the Royal Air Force had by and large been withdrawn to Egypt, the Germans had the skies virtually to themselves. Only the warships out in the bay showed them that they weren't going to get it all their own way. The anti-aircraft effort on the ground comprised a light battery which put up some resistance, in addition to three antiquated

Italian field guns and nine light tanks which were in such a poor state that they were being used as mobile pill boxes. However, the combination of anti-aircraft fire and small arms fire from Hill 107 accounted for many German planes. Neame's platoon could claim to have damaged one transport plane, and he watched it flying low away from the island with smoke pouring from one of the engines.

After an hour's respite when ammunition was replenished and water was brought round, eighty gliders carrying seven hundred and fifty men landed on and around Maleme airfield. Neame's platoon could only stare in awe as the waves of aircraft came over towing their charges. They were sitting targets to those Allied soldiers who had survived the bombing and were positioned around the town and on the hill. Captain Turner, who was standing on the first-floor terrace of an old farmhouse with their radio operator, was directing his platoon to fire on the gliders, but he was aware that a small group had landed safely near the airfield blast pens and were starting to pour fire in their direction. He sent a message to Neame to alert him and instructed the men on their right flank to get the mortar in action to silence them.

'Lob those mortar rounds at three hundred yards,' shouted Neame. 'Make every one count. And Corporal, get the men to concentrate their fire on the soft under-belly of the gliders as they descend. We must get them before they hit the ground.'

The first waves of attack in the west of the island, concentrated in the Maleme and Chania area, had been almost annihilated. The rifle and Bren gun fire from the high ground on Hill 107 had caused massive casualties; one unit from the Air Assault force lost 112 out of 126 men. The glider troops were almost completely wiped out by the New Zealanders and Neame's Rangers. Reports were coming in that parachutists and glider-borne troops had also attacked Rethymno, where the mainly Australian garrison had fought ferociously and driven them back. At the end of the first day, not one German objective had been secured, but everyone knew that this was just the start.

'Well done men,' said Turner. 'We've given Jerry a bad time. He won't forget today in a hurry. Sergeant, carry out a roll call and report on our casualties. Any walking wounded must stay here, we'll need them. Evacuate those more seriously wounded by Jeep to the Medical Corps tent.' Walking over to the front line dug outs, he could see that the men were exhausted emotionally and physically and needed to be fed, watered and rested. 'Sergeant, arrange for some chow and water for the men and post look-outs so some of them can get a bit of shut-eye. There are still some German units that have survived who might want to make life uncomfortable before reinforcements arrive.'

'Yes, sir,' said Neame, coming to attention. 'Corp!' he yelled. 'Get a working party together to go to the mess tent and sort some grub for the chaps. And plenty of water or they'll dehydrate in these conditions. Look sharp now and tell them to keep their heads down, we don't want any more casualties.'

That evening the temperature dropped, which was very welcome after a hot and difficult day. Surprisingly, the order was given to withdraw from Hill 107, leaving the airfield undefended. Turner couldn't quite understand why this was when they had won the day, but orders were orders. It transpired that a complete misunderstanding between senior officers had led to this tactical mistake, and the following day the Germans walked in unopposed. By mid-afternoon on the second day, Maleme was in German hands and reinforcements were starting to arrive.

In addition to the terrible casualties the Germans had suffered on the first day, a sea-borne landing due at Suda Bay had gone badly wrong when a whole battalion of the 5th Mountain Division were drowned after being attacked by the Royal Navy. This news was relayed to the men as a way of helping to keep their spirits up. A second landing did take place with 7,000 more troops, reinforcing the paratroops that remained. All Neame's men could do was sit and wait until orders arrived.

The British Commander in Chief on the island, Major General Freyberg, realising that the position was hopeless ordered all troops to make their way over the mountains to Sfakia on the south coast. Captain Brian Turner and what remained of his platoon left their positions with the New Zealanders to face another evacuation, this time to Egypt. This would be Bob Neame's third evacuation in a year.

CHAPTER 6

Athens, 2016

'Are you sitting comfortably Kurt? Some of what you are about to hear may not be to your liking. The speaker is a Greek history professor.' Neville Richardson and Kurt Schreiber were attending a lecture at the central library in Athens, along with other ambassadorial staff and business people.

The room went quiet as the speaker took to the rostrum. He started by welcoming everyone. 'I would like to try and explain how I see the Greece of today and how events from the past may have contributed to some of our current difficulties. The relationship between Greece and Germany in recent months has taken a serious nose-dive following the economic recession in the early 2000s, with Greece blaming Angela Merkel and the EU for being obstructive when it came to further bailouts. But the mistrust of each other goes deep, back to the post-war period and way before.'

Taking a breath, he looked across at the German Ambassador. 'In 1832, the first king of the new state of Greece was a German, Otto of Wittelsbach. I wonder how many of you here were aware of that? This young Bavarian arrived with thousands of German-speaking advisors whose brief was to 'Europeanise' the country.' The audience smiled, chattering among themselves. 'The first move was to set up a regency council of three Bavarians to govern Greece. They introduced a policy of enforcing heavy taxes, which did not go down too well with the local people. Nothing has changed then.' It was his turn to smile. 'It wasn't long after that that German archaeologists started to excavate the most famous sites, including Olympia, and German scholars started publishing the best of the classical Greek authors. They were trying to reform the country and change the mentality of the nation without taking into consideration its customs and ways of thinking, going back to ancient times. Greece was at that time an insecure nation, stuck between the cultures of east and west, with Germany trying to impose its northern European thinking. So, for over a hundred years, Germany had been trying to 'Germanise' the country. And then came World War Two.'

Kurt turned to Neville and said, 'I was rather hoping they wouldn't be bringing this up tonight. We're not proud of what happened. Many of us still feel embarrassment about what our forefathers did in the war, particularly here in Greece.'

The speaker carried on. 'As many of you here know, Greece suffered hugely following the German occupation of the mainland and the islands during the war and Germany would not entertain paying the war reparations that were demanded after hostilities had ended. In 1953, Germany signed an agreement which effectively cut her debts with other countries, including Greece, by half. Yet now Germany insisted that Athens must agree to more painful austerity before any sort of debt relief could be put on the table. They demanded that Greeks be made to pay for past profligacy, when Germany had benefited not that long before from more lenient terms than it was now prepared to offer.'

This made Kurt wince, something noticed by Neville Richardson.

'Another issue which rubbed further salt in the wounds was that Germany was the first EU country to violate the Stability and Growth Pact, running up a budget deficit of more than 3% in 2002 and for each of the following three years. No sanctions were put upon Germany for its transgressions. So why was there one rule for one and another rule for the other?'

Kurt sat watching the others in the audience. Some were sharing his discomfort, while others were enjoying the moment.

'But Greece didn't help herself,' the speaker continued, looking up as if searching for support. 'We persistently ran a budget deficit exceeding the 3% limit after joining the EU and the hard-working Protestant work ethic in Germany, who thought that the Greeks were lazy, greedy and don't like paying their taxes, has some measure of truth.'

He then paused, as if coming to an important moment. 'In 1941, Germany invaded Greece after their allies, the Italians, had failed in their attempts to occupy the country. They occupied the mainland, including many of the islands, for over three years, during which time they carried out mass killings against the civilian population, something which has never been forgotten. Around 300,000 Greeks died of hunger and 130,000 were killed in reprisals – 150 Greeks for every German soldier. More than 1.2 million Greeks were made homeless. The Jewish community was almost exterminated. Gold stock was taken from the vaults of the Central Bank of Greece to fund Hitler's campaign in North Africa. In Crete, the villages of Alikianos, Kandanos and Kondomari bear testament to the bestiality of the occupying German forces where hundreds of civilians were executed. In 1941, when the German paratroops landed, it was the first time in the war that German troops encountered mass resistance from a civilian population. And they paid a heavy price for it in the months and years which followed. Could this be Germany today, embarrassed by its past, and coming on strong as they did seventy-five years ago?'

At this point Kurt stood up and walked out of the hall with a face like thunder, leaving many thinking deep thoughts about the past.

At about the same time as the meeting was going on, a radical far-right group of a few hundred youngsters were holding an evening meeting in Frankfurt at which Greece and the ongoing bail-out issue were top of the agenda. 'Freunde,' began the leader of the group. 'Our Finance Minister, Wolfgang Schäuble, has been depicted in the Greek media as an ogre dressed in a Nazi uniform. What does this tell you about these lazy, good-for-nothing Greeks who are destroying our euro? They just want something for doing nothing. The time has come for us to say in their language – OXI! That means NO!' Huge cheers came from the floor. 'We as a hard-working nation are pouring billions into the euro pot. There are those of our so-called friends, like the UK, who are hiding behind the fact they are not in the euro to avoid paying their contribution. Their economy is doing well, they can afford it. And it's partly because they are not paying their share that they are doing well. They should pay up so we pay less.' More roars of approval from the audience. 'I urge you who are considering holidaying in the Greek Islands, don't! Let them stew in their own olive oil!'

The British Embassy in Athens received a report from the Foreign Office of the adverse comments regarding the UK and the anti-Greek hysteria in some German cities. The Secretary to Neville Richardson suggested that a communication be issued at a low-key level so as not to concern those journeying to the islands but making them aware.

CHAPTER 7
Crete, 2016

The sun was filtering through the blinds as Tom opened one eye to look at the time on his phone. His room was at the front of the house, facing east, and as a result it got the full blast of the early morning sun. It was another of those glorious days where any early mist gave way to a stunningly beautiful morning. The day before had been spent settling in and walking around the town sight-seeing and doing a little shopping. Today, they would be a bit more active.

After a healthy breakfast of fruit and yoghurt prepared for them by Maria, who was used to rising at dawn and had let herself in, Tom and Charlie were getting ready to pack up the car ready for the off, as it was a couple of hours' journey to the museum. Tom had heard Maria moving around downstairs and noticed that she was not quite her normal self; she seemed a little quiet and subdued. He was still waiting for the appropriate moment to ask if all was OK when she broke the silence by asking him if they had seen the protest march in Chania the day before.

'No,' said Tom. 'What was that all about?'

'Everywhere in Greece and also here in Crete, people were protesting against Germany not agreeing to pay money owed from the last war. Many felt that they should stand up and say something – especially as they are being very difficult with Greece with heavy demands in return for the bailout money. Many are very angry.'

'Did you take part then?'

'Yes, I did,' she said. 'Just to support my family really. They suffered greatly in the war. We lost our home, as did many in our village, and we received nothing. We had to start again. But I am not against the German people – just their government. They strut around saying they are the driving force in Europe, calling us a lazy nation. The Greek politicians don't help, they just don't want to do anything to upset the German tourists. But the Cretan people wanted to let the world know the truth about what has been owed to us for over fifty years. I'm sorry but I got carried away with the anger on the streets and went drinking afterwards, so I feel a bit worse for wear this morning.'

Tom and Charlie looked at one another, slightly embarrassed at seeing Maria getting a little emotional. Charlie went up and put her arm round her. 'I am so sorry, Maria. It must have been very hard for your family.'

'They were very dark days,' said Maria. 'Not only did they occupy the island, but they were hard on the population, executing people and burning down their homes, particularly those who had helped the British soldiers who had come to our aid. So the German government's attitude now is a bit hard to take. We love the British people. The same can't be said about the German government. But I am from a different generation, so I don't feel quite the same about Germans as my parents, and certainly my grandparents.'

Tom wondered how he could lighten her mood. 'Would you like to come out with us today? We're going to the museum at Knossos.'

'That is very kind of you,' said Maria with a shy smile. 'But you have come here to have some time on your own. I am meeting a friend later for lunch. I shall be fine, but thank you for listening.'

While Tom and Charlie were preparing to set off, Maria sat at the kitchen table for a moment of quiet contemplation. She was feeling more than a little ashamed about what had happened the night before. She had got carried away with the whole excitement of the march, the anger, the noise, and the young Germans appearing to be on her side shouting for Greece. She had drunk too much, and been offered and smoked weed, and she had gone too far with one of them on the beach. She didn't even know his name. If her parents found out that this had happened, and with a German, they would be extremely angry and would find it hard to forgive her. But what had really hit home after Tom's arrival was that he was her first unrequited love, and seeing him again sparked the reality of that. All these years it had been Tom she had really wanted, and she had dreamed of him so often for so long. And when he had arrived, this handsome young Englishman had simply taken her breath away. What Tom didn't know was that she had replaced a photo she had in her bedroom of them playing on the beach all those years ago with one she had secretly taken on the morning she had met him again.

She got up from the kitchen table; there was something she wanted to say to Charlie before they left. As they were about to drive off, she opened the front door and ran to the car, tapping on the window. 'Charlie,' she called, 'it can be quite windy on the island, please make sure you're covered up from the sun – especially if you're going to the beach on the way back from Knossos.'

'Thank you, Maria. I will.'

Tom was trying to work out how to get the antiquated green Fiat with a sunshine roof into gear. He smiled up at her. 'You're looking particularly lovely today,' he said.

'Thank you, kind sir! It's amazing what a bit of make-up will do.' The gear stick found its slot and lifting the clutch the car started to move. 'Come on, let's hit the road.' Charlie was keen to get away; she was feeling a little jealous of Maria, who obviously had deep feelings for Tom. She wondered why she felt that way. Tom was handsome, polite and good company. He was the one guy most of her friends used to fancy like crazy. And now she had him all to herself.

When they had left Chania on the road heading east, Charlie turned to Tom. 'Shall we stay in tonight and I'll cook you something a little special?' she asked. She wasn't going to tell him, but having Maria around had made her want to get to know Tom a little better. She couldn't help wondering what he was like in bed. Perhaps some time soon she would find out.

'What did you have in mind?' Tom asked. 'I really fancy something like pasta with chorizo and a side salad chased down with a nice little red. Would that suit you?' A peck on the cheek indicated that this was the right answer.

They reached the town of Rethymno quickly, as there was very little traffic on the roads. Driving through the town, they could see the vast expanse of the Sea of Crete to their left, and the sight of it made Charlie want to stop and throw herself into the deep blue ocean.

As they were making good time, Tom said, 'How about if we take a slight detour and visit the Sfendoni Cave? It's not far off the beaten track and maybe we can get a coffee there. How are you about going underground – you don't suffer from claustrophobia?'

'No, I'm fine. I read something about this cave. Magnificent stalactites and stalagmites apparently – I can never remember which is which. Good job I remembered the camera!' The thought of the sea had been put to the back of her mind temporarily, but she knew that by the end of the day a swim was a must, and not just because of the intense heat.

Before they arrived at the cave, they pulled up in the

village of Zoniana. 'It will be better and cheaper to get a coffee here,' said Tom. 'This is real Crete, off the tourist track.'

He went around the car and opened the door for her. She was impressed. How many times had a man done that for her in her life, except her dad? Very few, if any. She liked it; it made her feel special.

'Thank you, Tom. This looks just the ticket.'

Sitting outside a traditional Cretan café was an old man relaxing in a wicker chair. He had a wonderful set of whiskers, and a smile to go with it. He beckoned them over.

'I can tell you are English,' he said. 'You are very welcome here.' He shook Tom warmly by the hand and shouted behind him, 'Nico, come and look after these people from England.' He turned back to Tom and Charlie. 'Nico is my grandson,' he said.

A boy appeared, wiping his hands on his apron. '*Parakalo*, what can I get you?' he asked.

'*D'yo o kafes, efcharisto*,' said Tom.

Nico, obviously pleased that Tom had made the effort to speak his language, invited them into the air-conditioned bar to cool down. In a frame on the wall behind the counter was an old poster with 'WANTED' in Greek above the image of a bearded warrior.

'Do you know what the story is behind that poster?' asked Tom curiously.

'Yes, of course,' said Nico. 'That is my grandfather, the man you have just spoken to.' He pointed proudly at the poster. 'He fought with the British in the mountains in the last war, and the Germans put a price on his head. They did some terrible things to the Cretan people and many of your people came here to help us, so the English are always welcome. We cannot say the same about the Germans.'

'But it was so long ago now, and we Europeans are all one nation – well, almost.'

'I was not born when this took place, but if you talk to anyone, especially in the mountains, they will tell you the same. It was not warfare, it was murder.'

Tom was trying to understand this deep-seated hatred. After a short pause, Nico broke the silence. 'Have you been here before?'

'Yes, to Crete, but not to this village,' said Tom. 'My father loves this island so much, and the people, that he bought a small house in Chania. He works in Athens and he's had a long connection with the Greek people.' He looked at Charlie, conscious that she was being left out of the conversation. 'Charlie and I are staying here for a short holiday. We are studying classics at university, so a visit here is part holiday, part work.'

'I am studying the Minoan civilisation,' Charlie said, 'so visiting Crete is very important. You can read books and go on the internet, but you can only really get the feeling for it by coming here.'

They left the cool of the bar to sit outside. Nico brought out their coffees, and Tom thanked him. 'You are very welcome,' said Nico. 'You are both very welcome.' Wiping his hands on his apron, he retreated into the café.

They sat quietly under the shade of a large tamarisk tree, feeling this was the closest they would get to heaven. The cicadas were just as noisy as at night-time, and the aroma of the coffee and the scent from the tree made them feel quite heady.

When they had finished their coffees, Tom went inside to pay, but Nico would not take the money. 'Just say goodbye to my grandfather on your way out. As we are out of the way here, we do not get many tourists and he will have been very pleased to see you both today. He is over ninety now and he has a big respect for the English people.'

As they said their goodbyes, the old warrior stood up to shake Tom's hand and kiss Charlie on the cheeks in farewell.

On reaching the car, Tom realised that a fleeting visit to the caves was all they would have time for if they wanted to explore Knossos properly. Stupidly, they had not left the car in the shade, and it was boiling inside.

'Let's get moving quickly,' he said. 'Open all the windows and the sunroof, although it won't be long until we reach the cave. At least it'll be cooler in there.'

After a short but pleasant drive, still baking hot even with all the windows open, they arrived at Sfendoni. The cave was a photographer's dream and Charlie was in her element. It was a serious hobby of hers and she thought that one day she might like to do it professionally. The rock formations and the colours were breathtaking, and she felt such waves of emotion welling up that she gave Tom a passionate kiss and thanked him once again for taking her away with him.

'My pleasure,' he said. 'We seem to have much more in common than I thought.'

She skipped along happily, putting her arm through his. Having remembered this time to park in the shade of a cypress tree, they set off in a slightly cooler car and headed north towards Heraklion.

CHAPTER 8

Southern Crete, 1941

'Come on, move yourselves!' shouted Bob Neame. 'We've got half the German army on our tails and we've got to get over the mountains to the south coast by the day after tomorrow at the latest. Come on, the pleasure steamers will be waiting to take us on our summer holiday.'

His humour was well received by a few, but many, like Neame himself, had been fighting with their backs to the wall for months now and the novelty was wearing thin.

After a couple of hours in temperatures in the upper 70s, they reached the Askifou plain, which was a pretty sight with meadows full of colourful wild flowers, orchards and streams. It was the perfect place to rest up for a breather, except for the mosquitos, which were so bad they reminded Neame of holidays in Scotland. The midges there were a nightmare, and these were bigger and even more aggressive.

The ice-cold water which had run down from the mountain was very welcome. Corporal Weeks handed round Players' cigarettes, tins of which had been dropped off by the supply truck at Valphe just before they had struck off the coast road heading up to the mountains.

'Thirty minutes rest, that's all,' said Neame.

'Give us a break Sarge,' said Private Stokes. 'We need a bit more than that if we are going mountaineering. I think I'd rather give up now.'

With a deadly serious look upon his face, Neame turned to him and said, 'Now listen here, Stokes. There are thousands of blokes here who probably feel the same way as you, but they're not whinging and moaning. We're a bloody good bunch of guys who have put up a good show. If it hadn't been for the RAF being nowhere to be found and our senior officers making some barmy decisions, we could probably have seen Jerry off. So stop bloody moaning before I kick you up the arse. Got it?'

'Sergeant Neame,' shouted Turner a few minutes later, 'get your men on the move. The Third Hussars are covering our bums and the New Zealanders are manning the pass. We're heading towards the Imbros Gorge where we will be joining up with the Aussies, who are forming a rear guard. Impress on the men that speed is of the essence.'

'Yessir.' What was worrying Neame was the phrase 'rear guard'. He hoped the men hadn't picked that up, because it probably meant that they would be expected to hold up Jerry until the others had got away. Greece all over again.

Henry Weeks, Neame's best buddy in the platoon, had heard the comment. He said quietly to him, 'I wonder what our chances of getting away are?'

'We won't know Corp until we get there. All I know is that everyone is heading for a fishing village called Chora Sfakion, where the Royal Navy is coming to pick us up. It will be a night-time lift so that the Stukas can't have another go at us.'

Corporal Weeks had been a brick over the past few days. He had supported Bob to the hilt with some very unpleasant decisions. It wasn't just that they were good mates – he was a professional soldier with many years' experience, and it showed.

There were about eighty left in Captain Turner's group, some from his own Rangers unit, but there was also a mixed bag of others who had become separated and had fought side by side with them. They had had to leave some of their wounded behind at Maleme, mainly because the speed of their retreat would have put them all in peril. Whilst those left behind said they understood, Turner's men could see the disappointment in their eyes. Leaving them in the bomb craters around the perimeter of the airfield with a white flag was upsetting, but there was no way they would be able to climb a mountain path. It was a thirty-mile walk from Maleme to the port on the south coast, and it included a long trek up the mountains and then down the other side until they came to the gorge. In the heat, it was going to take the best part of a couple of days, but as they passed through villages like Laki, the local people came out with food and water and wished them well with tears in their eyes.

Stokes, ever the comedian and in a better frame of mind since his earlier comments, said to a lady on the roadside, 'Echete domatia?' Roughly translated, he was asking if she had any rooms to rent.

'I see you haven't lost your sense of humour Stokes,' said Neame, who had learnt a few words of Greek when he had lived in North London.

'Well, I thought it was worth a try. My feet are bloody killing me,' Stokes said.

Neame had realised in the last hour just how many men were on the mountainside – Brits, Aussies, Kiwis, Greeks. And they could hear the small arms fire behind them, indicating that the Germans were not that far away. All they needed was for the Stukas to come back and give them a pasting. That thought made him push the men even harder. But it was a challenge for the walking wounded, as the path was rough with many small boulders where it was easy to turn or break an ankle.

CHAPTER 9

Knossos, 2016

As Charlie was studying the history of the Minoan people, it was only right that she and Tom should visit Knossos, the legendary palace and seat of King Minos. Discovered only in the past hundred years by Sir Arthur Evans, the British archaeologist who had bought the site, no one, not even Evans, could have realised at the time the extent and importance of this find. Legend had it that under the palace, the bull-headed Minotaur used to hunt its victims in the labyrinth. After decades of archaeological exploration, it had been proven that Knossos was the hub of the Bronze Age civilisation which had ruled this part of the Aegean over 4000 years before.

'In some respects,' said Tom, 'it was good to get here a bit later in the day because most tourist groups arrive early to beat the crowds and the heat. It's still hot, but it's a bit more bearable and not quite so busy. Did you have anything particular you wanted to see?'

As they walked uphill from the car park, which was full of coaches and still extremely busy, they could see the wonders ahead of them. It was hard to believe that these ruins were thousands of years old.

At the start of the walkway which went around the site, they came across a statue in bronze of Sir Arthur Evans. Whilst he had been instrumental in bringing the ruins to life, it seemed strange to see a twentieth-century statue in the ancient palace.

As they stopped to read the inscription, high above the site birds of prey were very visible picking up the thermal lifts. Even though it was the middle of the afternoon, it was still hot, and they were grateful for the odd patches of shade from the olive trees which surrounded the site. There were tourists from every part of the globe – many of them Japanese who were taking five hundred photographs a minute. Tom wondered what they did with them all.

When paying their entrance fee, they decided to take a guided tour in order to fully understand what Knossos was all about. The guide was excellent, and brought the whole Minoan story to life. Her name was Kyria, and her English was near perfect. They strolled round following her, taking in the sights and listening to her talk. Charlie was mesmerised by the dolphin frescos in the Queen's rooms, where the colours looked almost as vibrant as they would have done the day they were painted.

'Did you see that there was even a bath and a flush lavatory,' said Charlie. 'Four thousand years ago. How advanced was that!'

It took the best part of two and a half hours to cover the whole excavation, and the mosaics took their breath away. They would have liked to stay much longer, but the 5 pm closing time was fast approaching.

On their way out of the site, they saw a life-size statue of Queen Europa, the first Queen of Crete, presumably not the original. Tom said to Charlie, 'You now, she's the spitting image of you. The nose, the hair – she's even got your figure.' He grinned. 'Stand in front of her and I'll take your photo.'

As Charlie mimicked the statue, Kyria, their tour guide, was standing close by, and she too recognised the similarity. Talking to Tom, she said, 'You are English, yes? Please let me take the photo for you. Your young lady is very attractive, just like Europa. Do you know how important this lady was in Greek mythology? The continent of Europe is named after her and she appears on euro coins. She is on many Greek mosaics with the Cretan Bull. The likeness to your lady friend is surreal.'

While she was concentrating on using Tom's camera, a pair of young Germans tried to ask her a question. 'Can't you see that I am busy?' she told them. Turning back to Tom and Charlie, she smiled and asked if they would allow the photo to appear in their marketing. Addressing Tom, she said, 'You sir are so big and handsome, you could be Hercules!' Tom and Charlie thought this was hilarious.

One of the Germans said to the other in his own language, 'Have you noticed how these bloody Greeks seem to love the British but hate us? Let's get the hell out of here and go and find a drink.'

The Germans had parked their car nearby. As Tom and Charlie were about to get in their car, one of them said to Tom, 'The guide seemed to like taking your photograph. Was it because Knossos was discovered by an Englishman?'

Not wishing to get into a lengthy conversation, and sensing a little angst, Tom replied, 'We're here because we're both studying Minoan culture at university.'

'So are we,' he said. 'At Heidelberg University. Are you staying nearby?'

'We are in Chania,' said Tom.

'We are too,' he replied. 'Might see you around.'

CHAPTER 10

Manolas Village, Crete, 1941

Katina and Ioannis Papadakis lived a quiet, untroubled existence in the village of Manolas, situated in the beautiful White Mountains in western Crete. Ioannis's family had lived there for generations and managed their olive groves, cultivating their vines and caring for their flocks of goats and sheep. Ioannis had met Katina, who was from the neighbouring village of Leivada, at a friend's wedding in 1919. Shortly afterwards, they were married. Both families were delighted at the union. It wasn't long before a little Papadakis arrived, swiftly followed by another. A perfect family.

But twenty-two years after they were married, dark clouds appeared. It was April 1941, and the news of the war on the Greek mainland was not good. If the Germans succeeded in driving the Allies out, it was certain that they would come to Crete. For centuries, the island had been in a strategic position in the eastern Mediterranean and if war came, the peace and tranquillity they so enjoyed was likely to be shattered.

Ioannis was fiercely patriotic, and no matter how much Katina pleaded with him, he knew that when the time came, he would never be able to live with himself if he did not do something to help protect his homeland. In the village, the mayor had visited all the houses, preparing the menfolk to be ready to take up arms, but he was surprised to hear that the women wanted to do something as well. He put up notices in the village with the message: 'IMPORTANT MEETING – CAFÉ after Mass, Friday, April 17. Everyone must attend.'

The café owner rubbed his hands with glee, as the takings would be very welcome. But he knew that an uncertain future lay ahead.

The village had been built on the side of a hill centuries before with the houses following the narrow, cobbled road up to the mountain top. The square, which had a memorial to those lost in previous conflicts, stood at the bottom of the village. Benches waited for the elderly men to sit and put the world to rights whilst the ladies knitted or crocheted in the doorways of their homes. The café faced the square, with chairs placed outside under an awning. When the menfolk needed some respite from the sun, they would wander over to the café for some refreshment. The church was next to the café and was always open, providing a haven of cool and solitude for prayer.

When the meeting began you could hardly see across the room for tobacco smoke, and there was a buzz of anticipation in the air, with plenty of raki, tsikoudia and retsina being consumed. Costas, the mayor, stood on a chair and requested a bit of quiet. '*Parakalo!*' he called out with a serious look on his face. 'People of Manolas, there are troubled times ahead and we need to make some decisions about what we should do in case the worst comes to the worst and the Germans or Italians arrive. Ioannis, you were in the Greek army territorials for a while – can you offer us some advice?'

This took Ioannis by surprise, as Costas had made no mention before of asking him for help. He stood with his back to the bar, thinking about what might lie ahead.

'Well, the first thing we must do is to sort out what weapons we have between us,' he said. 'As there are about sixty of us here tonight, we'll split into three groups. George, you take one group, Aleko the other and I will lead the third. We need to make contact with the Greek garrison, who have a base in Chania, to see what they would like us to do. We'll meet back here on Monday night with a list of our weapons and ammunition, and I'll have spoken to the powers that be in Chania by then. Let us hope it will not happen, but it is best to be prepared. It would also make sense to think about what food we can hide away if anything runs short. There are plenty of caves which are dry, cool and good for storing essentials, so please give it some serious thought. See you all next week.'

The gathering broke up in a quiet, sombre mood and some serious concerns were registering on people's faces.

Eager to get back home, Ioannis walked back up the stony

path through the olive groves to his small white cottage with the beautiful bougainvillea attached to the wall. His mind was full of mixed thoughts. Aegeus, a shepherd from the mountains who had been at the meeting, walked with him. He was a giant of a man, quite unusual for Cretan men, who tended to be on the small side. He sported a magnificent moustache, and like Ioannis he wore the typical black Cretan shirt, with breeches and long leather boots.

They strolled quietly, each deep in thought. For the first time in his life, Ioannis felt under threat, not for him, but for his family. They had brought up their two children here, Theodore, who was now twenty, and Christina, eighteen. Theodore had come to the meeting but had decided to stay on drinking with his friends. They had a lot to talk about. He was every bit a Cretan, like his father, and Ioannis knew that the excitement ahead could lead to basic mistakes. He would need to talk to Theodore quietly, but firmly. But that could wait until tomorrow.

When he reached the cottage, he said goodbye to Aegeus, who had a lot further to go as he lived an isolated existence high up in the White Mountains. Ioannis was surprised that Aegeus had not only found out about the gathering but had come all the way down to see what he could do to help. He didn't really need to contribute much verbally; his mere presence was enough.

By the time of the next gathering, the news had taken a turn for the worse, and the mood in the café was sombre. 'I was told this morning that the British, Australian and New

Zealand troops, as well as some of our army, are being taken off the Greek beaches and are heading here or to Egypt,' said Costas. 'So our meeting tonight has a much greater significance.'

Aegeus, who had walked all the way back down again for the meeting, stood up, and at two metres tall with a massive chest, he was not someone to be ignored. He raised his giant arm in the air, brandishing an antiquated rifle of indeterminate vintage.

'Any German setting foot in this village will regret ever coming here. We will be ready!' he roared. With that, the entire room, men and women stood and raised whatever weapon they had in the air, shouting, 'We will be ready!'

Then the serious drinking started.

CHAPTER 11

From the mountains to the beaches: 1941

As the weeks passed, the war from the air intensified. German aircraft were giving the retreating Allied troops a rough time. Cover was very limited, with just the odd dry stone wall, abandoned buildings and olive trees, and with the ground being rocky, pieces were flying everywhere, causing more wounds than the bullets and bombs. Bob Neame himself was hit in the left arm, just below the elbow. Bandaged up, it didn't give him too many problems, but resting his arm on a hard surface to fire his rifle at the diving planes was really painful.

'Corp!' he shouted. 'We must get some holding positions sorted out in case Jerry comes over the crest and down the gorge. The ground's too hard to dig in, so we need to build some protection. We need to find any old trees or boulders, anything we can take cover behind. There are still going to be many men passing through here. We just have to do what we can to hold Jerry up.'

Looking out to sea, Neame experienced a sudden flashback to his days in school when they had been studying Greek mythology, and he remembered the story of Icarus, the son of Daedalus, a master craftsman. Icarus wanted to escape from Crete, so his father made him a set of wings made out of feathers and wax, but as he flew away the sun melted the wax and he plunged into the sea. Don't think I'll give that a try, thought Neame.

Lines of tired and hungry men started passing through, some of them New Zealanders who had come from the Chania area and Aussies and Greeks from Rethymnon and Heraklion. They had come a long way, some by transport, mostly on foot. A battalion of Aussies was ordered to cover the retreat alongside Neame's unit, in addition to the New Zealand battalion Neame had been fighting with since the invasion. They were hardy fighters, many of them Maoris, and it had been an honour for Neame and his platoon to fight the enemy with them. Now they had to do it again – alongside their southern hemisphere cousins, the Aussies.

The walk over the mountains towards Imbros gorge, which led towards the beach next to the little harbour of Chora Sfakion, was steep and rough going. The hillsides were covered in loose rocks and small trees. There were very few places on Crete's rocky southern coast where a mass evacuation could sensibly take place, but the gorges of Imbros and Samaria down to the sea proved invaluable, and German intelligence had not yet realised their importance. The Royal Navy could anchor offshore with landing craft ferrying troops from the beaches. Because the gorge was narrow, the Stukas found it difficult to score direct hits, but their mere presence and the scream from their dives were enough to put the fear of God into anyone. The long shuffling line of soldiers heading down for evacuation was getting more desperate by the minute, some trying to push others out of the way, others smashing their rifles on the ground in frustration.

Back up at the top of the mountain pass, a serious firefight was taking place as a German mountain regiment had managed to infiltrate around the left flank of the Maoris' position. Fortunately, an air attack by Stukas managed to kill many of the Germans' own men and Neame's platoon with the New Zealanders soon saw them off. But it was getting increasingly desperate.

Neame had not seen Captain Turner for a few hours. He had said he was going to talk to the commander of the New Zealand Battalion, but he had not returned. Neame called his NCOS together to assess the state of their ammunition, food and water.

'We need to hold a roll call,' he said. 'Lance Corporal Johnson, get that organised while we see where we are with ammo and grub.'

On the way up the mountain, they had secreted some .303 ammunition in a small and very old Byzantine church, as it had become too heavy to carry. Some Cretan villagers had offered a mule to help, but a bunch of Aussies had killed it and were cooking it in a nearby vineyard. The smell was mouth-watering.

'Corporal Regan, remember the church?' said Neame. 'Take two men with you and bring back as much of the ammo as you can. Leave the mortars behind. But watch out for Jerry, he is getting very close.' He turned to his men. 'Right, we have the 2/7th Aussies on our left and the 22nd New Zealanders on the right, and we are the piggies in the middle. Corp, send a runner to each to acquaint them of our numbers and tell them that God willing we have enough ammo to last for twenty-four hours, but we're getting very low. And Johnson, when you get to the Kiwis, find out where Captain Turner has got to.'

Neame took Corporal Weeks aside and said. 'Corp, we've both had some practice at being evacuated, but many of the men haven't. Keep an eye on them, because they might get itchy feet and feel like they want to join the column making its way down to the beach. We've still got a job to do right here.'

After an hour or so Johnson returned gasping for breath and covered in sweat, even though it had got very chilly. 'Sorry, Sarge,' he said. 'Keeping out of sight of Jerry wasn't easy, but the Kiwis are holding firm and they'd welcome some of our ammo if we have any to spare. I'm afraid Captain Turner copped it during an artillery bombardment. The Kiwi Commander said you were to take charge until the order's given to evacuate or surrender. He did say that the latter is a definite possibility.'

'Thanks Corporal,' said Neame quietly, 'but just keep that from the men. We don't want them getting wobbly.'

He was shaken by the news of Turner's death. Brian Turner had been one of the best, and a true professional. Neame would have to go and see his wife, if they ever got out of there.

The lines of soldiers heading for the gorge and the beach were a sorry sight. They looked beaten, heads hung low; military order and discipline had gone out of the window. But slowly – too slowly, the senior officers thought – thousands of men were being taken off the beach to head for Egypt. As the hours passed, the line of men heading south was falling to a trickle.

'Corp,' said Neame, 'go and see the Kiwi commander again and find out what he says about leaving our positions and following the troops down. Our job here is just about done.'

'Yes, Sarge. I'm on my way.'

Darkness deepened and about twenty minutes later, they heard Weeks approaching.

'Sarge, they've gone!' he panted, badly out of breath.

'What do you mean, gone?' Neame demanded. 'They can't have gone!' Trying to hide his despair, he questioned Weeks. 'Did you look in the right place?'

'Yes, Sarge. You could tell where they'd been. There were empty fag packets and spent cartridge cases all over the place. It was definitely where they were holding the line.'

'That is bloody outrageous, dropping us in the shit like that!' He thought for a moment and then said, 'Corp, get the men fell in sharpish – we've got a boat to catch. And if I catch that Maori commander, I'll do more than rub noses with him!'

The walk down the gorge was tough going. The path was rocky and steep and in the fading light it was difficult to see where to step. They passed others who were aimlessly drifting down, having almost given up, by the look of them. Neame had a few lightly-wounded men with him. They had had to leave the more serious casualties at the top covered in greatcoats because of the cold night air, in the hope that the Germans would look after them.

They passed an old shepherd's hut which was being used as a first-aid post. A large red cross was painted on the roof in the hope that the Stukas wouldn't attempt to bomb it. The platoon was down to about fifty now and they were taking it in turns to help those in need and to carry their rifles and back-packs. Neame's squad were not prepared to give up their weapons yet.

The queue for the landing craft on the beach went back as far as the village of Komithades. 'How long have we got to stay here, Sarge?' asked Weeks.

'We just have to wait for orders, Corp. The beachmaster will decide. I just hope he doesn't leave it too late. It will be getting very dangerous for the Navy offshore. It's they who will decide when enough is enough.'

Just then, an Aussie ran up from the beach and shouted,

'They've gone! The last boat has gone. You're too late. The last one left half an hour ago. All the bloody officers have gone and left us in the shit.'

This was devastating news, and it took a while to take it in.

'What do we do now, Sarge?' Weeks asked.

Neame thought for a moment. 'Looks like we have three options. We fight it out, but we have very little ammo. We wait till Jerry gets here and we wave a white flag, or we disappear up into the mountains and carry on the fight with the Cretans. But I for one don't want to spend the rest of the war in a prison camp.' He pulled Corporal Weeks aside and said, 'I am not giving orders here, Corp. It is for every man's conscience to decide what to do. I was saved by the Navy at Dunkirk and again in Greece, but it's third time unlucky for me. I'm staying put.'

'We've been through a lot together, and I think I'll stay as well,' said Weeks. 'But think of your family, sir. For me it's a no-brainer. I have no one waiting for me.'

Neame's family had more than crossed his mind, but something was telling him that staying was the right thing to do. He had seen how bravely and passionately both Cretan men and women, and some children, had fought the invaders and he felt it was his duty. They had been sent to the island to help them. He couldn't ask Captain Turner now; this was his decision alone.

'Let's tell the chaps, and if anyone wants to join us, we need to get away from the beach area pronto,' he said. 'We must tell them that if they decide to join us and they get caught, they could get shot, whether they're wearing a uniform or not. It's as simple as that.'

CHAPTER 12

Aegeus, the mighty shepherd: 1941

Full of admiration for the way Aegeus had stirred the crowd in the café the night before, Costas decided to walk with Ioannis up from their village, to learn a little more about the man. He had looked after his flock of sheep and goats in the mountains all his life, yet nNo one seemed to know much about him. How did he sell his livestock? No one could ever remember seeing him at market, just the occasional visit to one of the villages in the area to buy a few essentials.

They headed in the direction of Omalos, where Aegeus had his hut and lived a very simple life with his family. After walking for an hour, they could hear bells from some goats over to their left. Going off the track, they breasted a hill and saw a spiral of smoke coming from the chimney of a hut, semi-hidden behind a cluster of olive trees. As they passed over a small stream of pure water running down from the mountainside, Ioannis shouted, 'Aegeus, are you there?'

There was no reply. The only sounds were the bleating of the sheep and goats and the running water falling down the hillside.

'Hello, anyone there?'

Again, nothing. They walked up to the partly-open door and Ioannis repeated his call, but it was obvious there was no one there, even though they could see a fire burning in the grate. They peered inside and in the semi-darkness they were taken aback by the sight that greeted them. In this most basic of rooms was a huge bust of what they assumed was Hercules, the mythological Greek God, with a ring of laurel leaves round his head. It was bigger than life-size and completely dominated the room.

As they stood there wondering what it meant, they felt the presence of someone close by, and turned to see the huge figure of Aegeus standing head and shoulders above them.

CHAPTER 13

Chania, 2016

After a long day visiting Knossos, Tom and Charlie arrived back at the house exhausted just before midnight, having stopped en route for some very welcome souvlaki and chips, washed down with a cold beer. It had been obvious on leaving Knossos that they would not be back early enough to cook a meal as they had planned. Charlie didn't get her swim either, so it would have to wait until the following day. They threw their bags down in the hall and collapsed, tired but happy, on the settee.

'Well, we can cross a visit to Knossos off the list,' Tom said, 'but the museum in Heraklion is so highly recommended that we should go there, perhaps on the way back to the airport at the end of the holiday. Are you ready to hit the hay?'

'You bet.' Charlie gave him a kiss on the cheek. 'Thanks for a great day, Tom. Can we chill tomorrow and grab some sun and a swim? It will be nice just to lie and soak up the rays. That's what holidays are all about, isn't it?'

'You bet, Queen Europa!' Tom said with a cheeky grin. 'I'll wake you at ten. I'll leave a note asking Maria not to wake you in case I sleep in as well. She'll be here at nine.'

'Behave yourself if I'm still asleep, Tom,' she said teasingly. 'You know what she thinks about you.'

Smiling, he wished her goodnight.

The alarm on Tom's phone went off at 8.50 am. Not a welcome sound, but he knew Maria would arrive any minute. She had told them the day before that she would be there at nine.

Maria had let herself in and was going quietly about her chores, but she was not singing in her usual cheerful manner. Tom staggered down the stairs, not quite with it yet. 'Oh hi, Maria. You OK?'

She looked up at him, a serious expression on her face. 'Good morning Tom. Would you like some coffee? You look as though you need it.'

'That would be good. It was a long day yesterday, so I'm a bit sleepy still this morning. Are you OK? You don't look too cheerful.'

'Well I'm OK, but there was a nasty killing in Chania last night. A young German tourist was attacked in the town and he died. Seems his throat had been cut.' She was pleased not to have mentioned to Tom and Charlie yesterday her night out with the two Germans she had met at the protest, or there might have been some difficult questions to answer. When she had first heard about the murder, she worried that it might have been one of them who had been killed. A text had put her mind at ease. It didn't stop her feeling uneasy all the same.

'Gosh, that's awful,' Tom said. 'What a horrible way to die. Was it some sort of a drunken argument?'

'They're not sure, but there's a rumour that whoever did it was shouting anti-German comments as the victim fell to the ground. The papers this morning are full of it. They're also talking about the anger coming out of Germany and the impact it may have on the holiday trade.'

'Do you think it has anything to do with the protest march? From what you said, there was a lot of anti-German feeling about,' said Tom.

Before she could answer, Charlie came down, having heard the conversation. 'Hello Maria. Is anything wrong?'

Tom turned to her and told her what had happened. She put her hand to her face. 'How dreadful! We drove back through the town around midnight and didn't see anything unusual going on.'

'There are police everywhere this morning,' said Maria. 'According to the news politically there is uproar here, in Athens and in Berlin. I'm feeling bad because we were all protesting about what we really think about the German government, but no one could condone the killing of an innocent person.'

'Sit down Maria. You look really shaken. Let me get you some coffee,' said Charlie. But she burst into tears.

Almost simultaneously, Tom's mobile rang and he picked it up.

'Hello?'

'Hi Tom, it's Dad. Have you heard the news?'

'Yes. Maria was just telling us all about it. It's awful.'

'There is another dimension to this, Tom. Whilst this appears to be an issue between Greece and Germany, we are EU partners and there will be advice flying around about how tourists should behave. And as the son of a diplomat based in Athens, you will be put under police escort until they decide where the responsibility for this atrocity lies. I'm sorry if this upsets your holiday, but there's nothing I can do. It's advice from the Foreign Office in London. If it concerns you that much you could fly home, but speak to Charlie and see what you both think. The decision, as far as I'm concerned, is yours. I don't think there's any risk, but please let me know. I'll call you later, but you should expect a knock on the door from the local police any minute. And say hi to Maria.'

Tom took the opportunity whilst within earshot of Maria to tell Charlie what the situation was as far as his father was concerned and to ask her what she thought. 'Of course it is a bit concerning,' she said, 'but we can't let it spoil our holiday. I've fallen in love with this island Tom and I'm prepared to take a chance, if that's what it is, as long as you are.'

Exactly as Tom's father had predicted, fifteen minutes later a police car pulled up and two policemen with sidearms knocked on the door.

'Good morning, sir. Are you Mr Thomas Richardson?'

'Yes, I am.'

'We have been instructed to safeguard your stay on the island following the problem which occurred last night.'

'My father in Athens said that you might be calling,' said Tom with a wry smile. 'What do we do now?'

Maria came to the door. 'Ah, Roussos. I haven't seen you for so long. How are you?'

'Very well thank you, Maria.' Slightly puzzled, he asked, ' What are you doing here?'

'I work for the Richardson family, who own this house,' she replied. 'Is this to do with last night?'

'Yes, it is. Mr Richardson, you will please tell us what your movements are today. Our job is to make sure that you are under observation and stay safe.'

'Wait a moment please,' said Tom. He led Charlie into the kitchen. 'What do you think?' he murmured. 'Stay or leave?'

'I don't want to go back. I love it here,' said Charlie. 'Anyway, we have people to look after us, there is something quite nice about that. Makes me feel important!'

Feeling a little better now that the police had arrived, Maria came up to Tom. 'Would you like me to prepare a picnic lunch for you both?'

'Thank you, Maria. That is very kind, but we are just going to the beach at Georgioupoli. We'll spend a few hours there with our guards and come home for a late lunch, and maybe a nap.'

' 'We Cretans enjoy a nap in the afternoon – in Spain it is

called a siesta, in England it is a nap, here it is called a mikro ypnos after the Greek God of sleep,' she said. 'It is one of the nicer parts of the day, especially if you have someone to share it with.' .

'I don't know what you're thinking but a nap is a little sleep. Go about your work,' he said smiling at her. Charlie looked on, giving him a stern look. Maria flounced off, looking over her shoulder with a wicked little grin. She still had a chance here, she thought.

Tom went back to Roussos and his colleague, who were waiting by the door. 'We are going to the beach today at Georgioupolis if that is OK with you?'

'Yes, of course,' he replied. 'You must just carry on doing what you wish. Please just tell us where you are going, and we will follow you discreetly. You must please tell us if you change your mind. We have a job to do and you are an important guest on our island.'

'Thank you. We will be leaving shortly.'

Charlie had gone upstairs to get her clothes. She shouted down, 'Tom, have you got beach towels down there?'

'Yes, plenty. I'll put them in the car.'

They set off with the police Renault following behind, their car making some strange noises. His father had bought it a few years before and it hadn't been new then, but that was hardly surprising as it didn't get much use. Charlie was plainly very excited about getting into the sea and sunbathing. Tom also thought she was excited about the police escort.

'I've never had such attention, Tom. All these men taking care of me. I rather like it!'

As they drove through Chania town and passed Splantzia, the former Muslim quarter, they came to the place where the murder had taken place. The area was still cordoned off and there was a huge police presence in the town. 'This is a really interesting part, very Bohemian, where the Greeks, migrants and travellers live,' he told Charlie. 'It won't be easy for the police to find who carried out the murder.' The thought of someone having their throat cut made Charlie shudder.

As they headed east, it wasn't long before they saw the naval base at Suda Bay in the distance to their left, still in use as an important NATO facility. Military planes were passing overhead, heading toward Chania Airport on the other side of the inlet.

The beach was only half an hour from Chania and they were soon parked up in a café-lined square shaded by plane trees and heading for a bit of rest and relaxation. They saw the police car pull up a short distance behind. A beautiful blue sea beckoned, and Charlie ran full speed onto the sandy beach,.

'Come on Tom, this is what we've been waiting for!' she shouted. She kicked off her flip-flops as she ran and stopped for only a moment to take off her T-shirt and shorts at the same time before dashing into the water. It was only then that Tom realised she was topless. She dived into the water, turning and waving to him. He looked back at the police officers, who were keeping an eye on them with binoculars. They were having the best posting of their lives.

After a few minutes Charlie came out of the sea and strode confidently up the beach. Tom held a towel out for her.

'Did you like the view?' she said cheekily.

'I certainly did,' he said struggling to keep himself from staring at her breasts. 'And I'm sure the local constabulary did as well!'

'If you've got it, flaunt it!' she said with a laugh. He grinned. She had certainly got it.

She stretched out on the towel, feeling the warmth on her back. 'Tom, can you please put some cream on my back and the backs of my legs?'

'Sure,' he said. He had to admit that it made him feel quite horny to kneading the sun cream into her body. He had a feeling that that was her intention.

They sat for an hour or so in silence, and he read a few chapters of his holiday thriller. Then he said to Charlie, 'You'd better have something to drink. Can I get you anything?' He realised that she had fallen asleep, so he gave her a little prod and said, 'Drink?'

'Ooh, yes please,' she said sleepily.

Maria had given him a cool bag with bottles of water. He took one out and put it on her back.

'Aargh! You rotter, that's freezing!' Taking a long drink, she said, 'I'm going back in to cool down. Are you coming?'

'You bet!'

In the *Frankfurter Allgemeine Zeitung* the next day, it was reported that the murder in Chania had been perpetrated by Cretan youths who had taken exception to comments made by the Germans on holiday in the town about Greeks just wanting to take and not give. They had accused them of being lazy, not paying taxes and wanting huge lifetime pensions. Such talk was guaranteed to inflame Greek hatred for the Germans. Memories of what had happened seventy-five years before on the island were obviously still very raw. The report was without official confirmation, and it was hotly denied by the Cretan Minister of Communications. But Tom felt there was never smoke without fire.

CHAPTER 14

Decision time: 1941

❧

After the huge disappointment of being let down by their officers and left behind, Neame gathered his men around him to address them. While he spoke, other soldiers were still drifting past towards the shore.

'Some of you have come a long way together since landing in Greece, some have just joined us,' he said. 'We've lost our captain and now we have a decision to make.' Looking at their faces, he could see their acute concern about their future. 'The last boat has left, and we have to decide whether to give up and surrender to the Germans or continue to fight with other Allies staying behind to help the Cretan people. From what we saw when the Germans landed, I have no doubt that they will not take the enemy to their bosoms. They are a proud and brave nation – as we saw when the paratroopers arrived. The decision as to whether to wait for the Germans and show the white flag or go back up into the mountains is yours and yours alone. There is no order. I will put it on record that this is what Corporal Weeks and I think is the right way to handle this situation.

'Corporal Weeks and I will be staying, but you must not let this sway your decision one way or the other. It is entirely up to your conscience. We're going to walk away now and wait for half an hour at the bottom of the footpath for those of you who decide to join us. Whichever you choose, good luck to you all. We can walk away from this with our heads held high and in the eyes of the authorities there will be no question of desertion.'

With that Neame and Weeks turned their backs on the men and walked away, leaving them to think it over. Finding a rock to sit on, they lit up cigarettes.

'They had had a rough time, Sarge,' said Weeks. 'We all have, so I'm really surprised at your decision. You have a wife and young kids at home waiting for you.'

'I know Alan, and I'm well aware of it. But if I go in the can, I'll be there for the duration, which could be a year, or a hell of a lot longer. This way, there's a chance that I can do something worthwhile, and who knows, we may be able to get away to Egypt or Libya some time soon.'

Knowing that the Germans were not far behind, Neame kept looking at his watch. Six men had joined them so far, but there were only five minutes to go. There was a firefight going on at the top of the gorge, so Neame was getting very anxious.

'That's it, Corp. Let's get going,' he said. I don't think we're going to have any more joining us. Better grab what spare ammo we can from the other chaps, plus any spare grub. We're going to need it.' He turned to the assembled group. 'Stevens, Fletcher, Simms, Lance Corporal Johnson, Gordon and Fraser, we appreciate your decision to join us. Grab whatever you can carry. Simms, delighted to have you with us a wireless operator, because we will need you to help communicate with our troops in Egypt or Libya and on the rest of the island.'

What Neame did not know was that Simms had been with the Inter Services Liaison wireless station just outside Chania and had managed to grab a B2 wireless set before they were evacuated. The set had a range of a thousand miles. This station had housed the secret Ultra radio operation which had forewarned the British of the impending German invasion. Most of the equipment had had to be destroyed in case it fell into enemy hands.

'Any spares you can beg, borrow or steal for the radio must come with us, including the batteries,' said Neame. 'They're heavy, so no moaning. The radio could save us. Good luck, all of you. Who knows what lies ahead of us?'

As they walked back up the steep gorge heading for an uncertain future, there were still several dishevelled soldiers walking down, beaten, lost and thoroughly dispirited.

Neame spoke to Corporal Weeks. 'Corp, remember that little church where we stocked that .303 ammo? Do you think we can find it? Some of it's been taken, but we had to leave a fair bit so we may be lucky. It would also make a good shelter until we've sorted out how the land lies.'

'Yes, Sarge,' said Weeks. 'It was near the Askifou Plain. It's a fair walk, but I can find it. There's also a good chance that we can meet with some villagers up there. One thing we desperately need is some local maps.'

CHAPTER 15

Manolas, late May 1941

On a Friday the village was always a busy and noisy place with produce being sold in the square and everyone catching up on the latest gossip. But now the atmosphere in Manolas was subdued. Men and women huddled round tables in the café, talking in whispers. Germans were about to enter the village. A Bavarian Mountain Regiment had been seen a few miles down the valley towards the coast, their job to chase the Allies out of Crete almost over. There were just a few stragglers to round up. Now it was a question of maintaining law and order and taking prisoner the beaten troops left behind.

It was obvious that the Germans would not be welcomed in the towns and villages across the island. For the first time since the war had begun, a civilian population had risen up against an invader and had demonstrated how brave they could be, taking on the might of the Wehrmacht almost with their bare hands, attacking them with knives, axes, scythes and the most ancient of rifles. They had killed soldiers in considerable numbers and the German High Command, who were now on the island, took a very dim view of this.

Banging his fist on the table, Costas, the Mayor, stood up and asked for quiet. The room suddenly was very silent.

'My friends, I shall from now on address you as *andartes*,' he said. The word meant guerrilla warriors. 'That's what we are and why we are here, and we urge you to help us to make life as unpleasant as possible for the invader. These scum who have landed without a welcome on our island must be dealt with. Go from here quickly and hide your valuables and put your weapons where they will not be found. The advice from Ioannis after he talked to people in Chania is to hide everything, and when the time comes to rise up against the enemy. We will be ready. Look after your families, for we are all at risk, as the Germans have already demonstrated.

'There will be Allied soldiers in the mountains who did not get away. We need these men to help us and we must do all we can for them. Go now, for the Germans will be here soon. We will meet again at nine in the evening in two days' time, unless a curfew is imposed before then. If that happens, we will get messages to you. The Germans will not want to go out at night. They will be scared. We will then decide how we are going to act against them. I will try and contact our neighbours so we can work together to make the Germans wish they had never come to our beloved island. Ioannis and

I will make preparations. Keep an eye on what's going on and let either of us know anything of importance that you hear. We must share our intelligence with our neighbours. Go!'

Costas and Ioannis walked up the hillside to find the place where Aegeus lived. He had not attended the meeting in the café, and they both knew how important he could be in the coming months. A wisp of smoke led them to a wooden hut tucked protectively behind a small hillock. Ioannis realised that you would never find it unless you knew exactly where to go, which was of course the idea. He was an intensely private man, despite his size.

They shouted his name on approaching, but got no response. Opening the door, they again shouted for him. All was quiet. Looking into the dim atmosphere of the main room, they saw again the marble bust of Hercules sitting on the table. Both deep in thought, they did not hear Aegeus enter the room.

'He is my god,' said Aegeus in a quiet but forceful voice. 'It was Hercules who made Crete great. He is the god who represents the strength, physical and mental attitude of the people. He was sent to the mountains by his foster-father Amphitryon to tend sheep and cattle, just as I was, and offered two life choices – an easy, pleasant life or a severe, glorious life. He chose the latter, and so shall I. I have already spoken with my God; we are as one.'

Costas was no student of Greek mythology, but he could see in Aegeus the build of the man who was replicated in the bust. He was the very reincarnation of his hero.

'The Germans have decided to invade our land and they will pay dearly for that,' Costas said.

Ioannis said to Aegeus, 'Because you are so well hidden up here, we may need to use your land to store weapons and supplies. Keep a look out for any Allied soldiers who may need assistance, and find somewhere where they can be safe until we can meet again.'

'Don't worry. I am pleased to help. I hate the Germans. Hercules will know what to do.'

Costas and Ioannis walked back down to Manolas in the dark, chilled to the bone, and not just from the outside temperature. Aegeus's comment about Hercules had made them worry that he was not quite right in the head. That could spell trouble for the whole village.

CHAPTER 16

Chania, 2016

After a few hours on the beach, Tom and Charlie were beginning to fry. 'I think I've had enough of the sun for one day,' said Tom. 'Shall we get packed up and head back?'

'OK, good plan,' said Charlie.

They headed back to the car, telling the police officers that they were returning to Chania before going out to a club in the evening.

'We will need to talk about that later, sir,' Roussos said. 'I do not think visiting clubs is a good idea for you now. I must speak to my superintendent for advice.'

The car was baking hot, and Tom wished they had air-conditioning. They opened all the windows to let as much breeze as possible into the vehicle.

'That was a beautiful beach Tom, and it was so nice to be able to swim in the sea almost without anyone else there,' said Charlie.

'Talking of treats, you certainly gave our escorts an eyeful when you took your top off', said Tom.

'I hope it brightened up their day!' she replied cheekily.

They pulled up just around the corner from the house and Tom emptied the car, giving the police a polite wave. The house was cool, being protected on three sides from the sun.

'You've got burnt on your shoulders, Charlie,' Tom said. 'Have you got some after-sun?'

'I'll just pop up and get it,' she said. After a few minutes, she shouted down, 'Tom, can you give me a hand?'

He went upstairs and found her lying face-down on the bed. She was completely naked.

'There. Now you have seen all of me. Do you like me?' She looked longingly over her shoulder.

Some two hours later, as they lay together on the bed, she said, 'I have a confession to make.'

'I don't want any bad news now, that was just the most exciting sex I have ever had,' Tom said.

'No, it's not bad news at all. I've pretended for months that you did nothing for me, and I know many of my friends wanted to get into your trousers, but I have had the hots for you since I first laid eyes on you at uni. But I'm not a girl to go doing the chasing. That's your job. Then I saw when I asked you to cream my back and legs on the beach the effect it had on you, and that's good enough for me. And by the way, it was wonderful for me too – as I'm sure you noticed!'

She cuddled up to him and promptly went to sleep. A few minutes later, Tom's phone rang, waking them both up.

'Hi Tom, it's Dad, you OK?'

'Yes fine. What's happening with you?'

'Fine thanks. There has been a bit of a backlash in Germany over the murder, but I hope you two are having a good time. I assume you've decided to stay?'

Charlie had put her arms around Tom, and he tried to push her away gently so that he could talk to his father.

'Yes, we have. We have two very able policemen looking after us and everyone here is so nice. I think there is embarrassment and anger over the murder, but there was a protest march here the day we arrived and Maria took part. Apparently, there's a real problem here over Germany's actions regarding the bail-out, and the media are stoking the fire.'

'Those of us who have dealings with the Greek people and the government are very aware of these feelings, but of course Germany's the driving force in the EU and as far as the Greek people are concerned, that just makes the situation worse. Anyway, keep in touch, but enjoy your stay.'

After saying goodbye to his father, Tom said to Charlie, 'I won't be able to sleep now, I'm too awake. Funny how Maria thought a nap was something a bit more active. She was right!'

Smiling to himself, he went downstairs to get a drink. He shouted up to Charlie asking if she wanted one, but there was no reply. She had gone back to sleep. Looking at her naked body, he had to admit that she was beautiful, very appropriate for the 'island of goddesses'.

He tiptoed out and went down to ask the police whether their superintendent thought it was OK to go clubbing, but was told that on no account should they go. That meant a restaurant was the only answer, but maybe after the new turn in their relationship, that was no bad thing. They would still have to have police protection, but hopefully at such a distance as not to be intrusive.

Oddly, while walking to the restaurant they saw the two Germans from earlier at Knossos, drinking large beers outside a bar.

'Don't look now,' said Tom, 'but those guys who talked to us at the museum are sitting at the bar over there.'

Tom smiled in recognition and kept walking. Looking at them had reminded him of two characters in one of his favourite films, The Odessa File. The film was about SS officers after WW2 who still thought that they deserved to rule the world. These were young, arrogant men, one blond, one with a very short crew-cut. One was over six foot and slim, the other shorter and stockier. The blond one nudged the other, nodding towards Charlie's rear, and they exchanged lustful sniggers.

As it happened, a quiet evening eating out was every bit as good as dancing the night away at a club. There was a famous street in Chania called the 'Street of the Knives', which despite its name was full of cafés and restaurants selling local dishes in a relaxed and romantic atmosphere. Its name came from the knife workshops which had stood there at one time.

The wine and the superb food promised to serve as the ideal precursor to an active evening in the bedroom.

As they walked back through the busy streets slightly worse for wear, they came upon a major altercation between a taxi driver and a woman passenger, who was apparently arguing about the fare. From her accent, she was clearly German. She was saying that as Berlin was handing over billions to keep the Greek economy afloat, she should not have to pay the full amount. He was getting increasingly angry, and several other taxi drivers got involved.

'Greece already owes us a lot of money and you should not be taking German tourists for a ride!' she shouted.

That was enough for the drivers, one of whom began calling the police on his mobile. Tom said to Charlie, 'Come on, let's leave them to it. We need to save some energy for our walk tomorrow. So please ma'am, be gentle with me tonight!'

As soon as Tom had closed the front door behind them, she seized his hand and pulled him up the stairs.

CHAPTER 17

Athens, June 2016

The telephone rang, disturbing Neville Richardson in a moment of quiet contemplation.

'Sir,' said Holly, 'the German Ambassador would like to pay you a visit some time today. The only free time you have is at the end of the day. Is it OK to ask him to call in at 6 pm?'

Neville felt a bit uncomfortable. He well knew what it was about. The German nation was against pumping more hard-earned euros into the Greek economy, and Britain was not exactly flavour of the month for not contributing to the bail-out fund. And there was the killing in Crete. Whilst Britain was not directly involved, the rhetoric flying around appeared to suggest that the death of a German subject was down to anti-German sentiment, whilst Britain was known to be favoured on the island.

'Yes Holly,' he said with a wry smile. 'I'll see him in my office. Can you stay until he arrives?'

She grimaced, as she had a first date with a handsome young Greek soldier, but she had huge respect for her boss, the best she had ever worked for, so she did not hesitate to oblige. 'Of course, sir, I'll bring him up when he arrives. I'll alert security.'

Promptly at six o'clock, Kurt Schreiber walked into Neville's office.

'Hello, my good friend,' he said, his giant frame striding across the office floor offering a firm handshake.

'Good to see you, Kurt. Will you join me in a twenty-year old malt? I can assure you that it will help reduce all the day's stresses.'

The Ambassador smiled. 'That's the best offer I've had today. Tell me, is it called Scotch and the people are Scots or the other way round? I get them always muddled up.'

Passing him a glass with a generous measure in it, Neville said, 'you're right on both counts, and don't worry, even many of us still get it wrong! Cheers.'

Taking a seat in a very comfortable leather chair away from Neville's desk, Schreiber gave a big sigh, saying, 'Thank you for agreeing to see me at such short notice, and may I firstly apologise for leaving the talk the other day. Whilst that man was speaking the truth, he seemed to be making too big a point about it to me. Still, it was childish to, as you English say, take up my sticks and walk out. Now, I need to talk through the events concerning these comments in the media, just to reassure all parties that we are as one in dealing with issues arising from this situation. And of course, the unpleasant death in Crete.'

'You sound just like a politician,' said Neville. 'Have another dram.'

The big German let out a booming laugh. 'We have known each other a long time, Neville, so it is easy for us to talk about little difficulties,' he said. 'We are both, how you say, singing from the same hymn book when it comes to what we think about the continuing bail-out issue. Your Government cannot directly contribute because you are not in the euro. I understand that my friend, but there are factions in Germany who are using this to stir up anti-UK feeling and we need to pour oil on troubled waters, maybe olive oil from Greece,' he said with a broad smile.

'Do you believe that that is the only reason these extremists are mouthing off, or is there something else behind it?' asked Neville.

'It is difficult to say. Your economy is doing well with continuing low unemployment, so there may be a little envy from other countries in Europe who are struggling, including ours at present, saying that you should contribute because you can afford to do so. We are also having to deal with the rising right-wing elements – particularly those getting exercised about the immigrant attacks on German women. There is trouble around the corner wherever you look these days. But maybe a gesture from your government to help smooth things along somehow?' he asked with an inquiring look.

Neville got up from his chair. 'That's a big ask, Kurt. The Government manifesto has always been to protect the British taxpayer over this bail-out and I can't see any movement there. But as you say, maybe something can be dressed up to smooth troubled waters. Leave it with me for a while.' He stopped to look out of the window at the groups of youths gathering in the streets again. 'You haven't mentioned the business in Crete, which I was very sad to hear about. I know this is an issue between you and the Crete authorities, but my son is on holiday there and he's been given police protection, just in case. I hope they find the perpetrator soon. I have been to Crete several times and love the island, but sadly there are communities there who find it hard to forgive and forget the past. Fancy one more for the road?' he asked, bringing over the bottle.

CHAPTER 18

Chania, 2016

Tom was up bright and early, if a little jaded, and when he brought the car round he noticed that their police guard had been replaced by new officers. Maria arrived just as they were about to leave, also looking jaded.

'Hello, you look as though you had a late night.'

'Yes. I went clubbing with a friend and met a group of holiday-makers and got a little drunk.' Tom and Charlie looked at one another, wondering. 'My parents would not be pleased about me drinking with German boys,' she went on. 'The war, you know. So please don't tell them, I'd never hear the last of it.'

It was obvious to Maria that something had happened between Tom and Charlie. They had that particular look on their faces. 'You are looking a little tired, Tom,' she said. 'You have obviously had a busy time last night, you lucky man!'

Her thoughts were a trifle muddled, but she was still very envious of Charlie.

He smiled at her, looking for a way of changing the subject quickly. 'I believe your family come from Manolas up in the mountains, is that right?'

'Why are you asking?'

'Because my father suggested we should go there, as he has been there with your parents,' Tom replied. 'He was keen that we should understand modern history as well as the ancients. And I believe it's the seventy-fifth anniversary later this week of what happened in the war, particularly in the village.'

'My parents will be very pleased that your father suggested that,' said Maria, distracted from her earlier thoughts. ''ll find out what is planned from my father and grandfather, and my great-grandfather Theodore, who is ninety-five years old. He was active with the resistance. They are bound to be involved. May I suggest that you do the Samaria Gorge walk today as it is a little cooler, and if it interests you, my mother and father could come round one evening and tell you all about my family and the war before you go there.'

'That sounds like a plan, and I'm sure our security would support that,' said Tom. 'Except they'll have to walk down the gorge with us. Not sure they will be happy with that!'

Maria remembered some important advice regarding the walk, which was how to get back. 'Tom, when you get to the bottom by the sea, you have to either catch a boat round to Chora Sfakion or walk all the way back up. So think about how you get there, and how you get back. My cousin could take you to the top in his car and collect you and the police from Chora harbour and bring you back to Chania. He is very cheap.'

'What do you call cheap, Maria?' He asked with a wry smile. 'Usually when people recommend their cousins it turns out to be very expensive.'

'He has a very nice car – it's only twenty years old! I'll give him a call.'

While waiting for Maria's cousin to arrive, Tom and Charlie walked around the corner to the small supermarket to get a few essential supplies. One of the policemen followed discreetly. Maria began the job of tidying the house and changing the linen. She could not help wondering if they had made love there last night. She went to the drawer where Tom kept his boxer shorts, then to Charlie's suitcase, where her very seductive underwear was tidily packed away. Suddenly a feeling of guilt came over her, and she slammed the case shut.

CHAPTER 19

Cretan mountains, 1941

For Neame and the others, it was a weird feeling. Here they were, intruders in a different land, walking for what seemed like forever across mountains, hills and plains, keeping low so as not to be seen by the Germans. The group who had decided to stay had reached the remote church where they had stored their spare ammunition. The number of small churches dotted all over the countryside came as a huge surprise during their walk. Many were in the middle of nowhere, and some dated back to the Byzantine period. It was remarkable that the group had remembered exactly where their church was among the many others. Detailed maps were non-existent.

En route they had picked up three more soldiers who had been left behind. One was a stretcher bearer from the RAMC. Wearing their thick infantry uniforms, tin helmets, ammunition pouches, front and back packs and groundsheet rolls was not very sensible in the heat of the day. They also had weapons to carry, but Neame had told them that when they reached their destination, he would tell them what they could leave behind. In the meantime, it was important to keep a full British uniform on in case they were captured.

Entering the church was a huge relief as it was at least twenty degrees cooler inside. Neame took up position on a large rock outside and surveyed the area with his binoculars. He could see nothing of concern. It was hot and although fresh water was not a problem, their supplies of food were not going to last for many more days.

He turned to Weeks. 'We need to contact some villagers, but they may not be pleased to see us. Fraternising with the enemy would be a capital offence to the Germans.'

They went back inside the tiny church and Neame posted Fraser as look-out while they settled down for a bit of a rest, out of the midday sun. Apart from the occasional spotter plane and sporadic gunfire from some distance away, it was a peaceful scene. Neame lay on the floor to cool down, thinking of his family back home and wondering whether he had been reported as missing. He looked at the hieroglyphics around the church walls, wondering what they all meant. He presumed that this was a Greek Orthodox church, but one thing for sure, it was very old. But then so was Cretan civilisation.

The floor was hard, so after he had cooled down for a while Neame settled on one of the rough pews. He had just nodded off when Fraser shook his shoulder, saying, 'Sarge, there's a shepherd with a flock of sheep and goats coming up the hill.'

Neame went outside, ducked behind a boulder and took a long look at the man through his binoculars. He was the biggest man Neame had ever seen. He was whistling to his dogs to bring the animals under control. Neame wasn't sure how he was going to communicate with him, or any other Cretan as it happened, as he only knew a smattering of Greek from a family he knew in North London before the war. He walked towards him, not holding his rifle but retaining his sidearm. He raised his hand in greeting.

'*Milate Anglika*,' Neame said.

The man looked at him with a total lack of expression, and replied, '*Den katalavaino*.'

Weeks had come alongside Neame. 'What did he say?'

'I asked him if he spoke any English and he indicated that he didn't understand. All I can do is point to my uniform and demonstrate that we are hungry and see what happens.'

The shepherd went into the church, and on seeing the other men, he signalled to them to follow him. Shouldering their weapons, they went down the hillside for around half an hour, until he stopped and pointed to a hollow off the beaten track, where he indicated that they should stay in. Then he left them, putting his finger to his lips, presumably telling them to be quiet.

They lay low for the best part of an hour before he reappeared. Accompanying him was a smaller man, but obviously a Cretan andarte. It was he who went up to Neame with his hand outstretched and said in poor but understandable English, 'Me Ioannis Papadakis. You?'

'I am Sergeant Bob Neame, I'm a British soldier. Can you help us? We will help you to fight the Germans, but we need food and somewhere to hide.'

There was a pause while Ioannis tried to understand what Neame had said. He then pointed to the shepherd, 'Him Aegeus, you go him up.'

CHAPTER 20

Samaria Gorge, Crete, 2016

❧

Maria's cousin Yanni knocked on the door at the promised time. He was short in stature and muscular with a well-groomed moustache which, Tom imagined, was the envy of many. He had parked his old Mercedes around the corner under the watchful eye of the police escort.

'Hello Tom, I am Yanni. Maria has told me much about you and it is pleasure to meet you. I have driven your father two times when he has visited the island. Very nice man. I will drive you to the top of the gorge where you can get something from the café before you set off, then I will collect you from the harbour along the coast. Maria tells me that I must follow the two policemen who she knows, George and Stathi. That will be a first thing for me. Normally, they are driving me! That is joke, me, I respect the law.' He grinned. 'I then drive you all back to the top of the gorge so that the police can collect vehicle for drive back to Chania.'

Maria had warned them before they set off about the uneven footpaths on the descent, so trainers were the order of the day, along with high factor sunblock and lots of drinking water. The spectacular gorge began four thousand feet up in the White Mountains on the Omalos Plateau and ended seventeen kilometres and seven hours later, at Agia Roumeli beach on the Mediterranean Sea. Tom and Charlie had heard wonderful things about the gorge and were hoping not to be disappointed.

Yanni was forced to drive with care due tof the fact that a police car was in front of him, and when the old Mercedes came to a stop in a cloud of smoke outside the café at the top, they felt some relief that they had made it, as the car was making some strange noises from under the bonnet, and there was no air-conditioning.

The police driver gave Yanni a filthy look. 'Get something done about this car Yanni, it shouldn't be on the road,' he said in Greek.

Tom wasn't quite sure what Yanni's response was, but he could guess from his gesture of dismissal.

'Do you need to visit the loo before we set off?' he asked Charlie.

'Better had,' she said. 'Don't want to be caught with my trousers down!'

Tom asked the police if they needed anything before going into the café to buy a coffee and some water. Then, full of anticipation, they set off hand in hand, smiling and feeling very comfortable in each other's company. Tom was wearing a cap to protect his head from the sun, which made him look very different.

'I haven't seen you wear a hat before,' Charlie said. 'I kind of like it.'

After a few minutes' walking, she said, 'Isn't this spectacular? I have never seen anything like it. Such tall peaks reaching up on both sides and the trees are amazing. The aroma is quite intoxicating.'

The first mile was very steep as they dropped almost a thousand metres, and occasionally they slipped on the loose stones. Charlie was grateful that Tom was holding on to her. Looking across to her left, she said, 'Can you see that old building? I wonder how long it's been like that.'

Tom replied, 'I think it's an old chapel. Look, you can see the cross on the roof. I read somewhere that there are quite a few old buildings on the slopes. They were used by shepherds, but they left them fifty years ago. It seems such a shame, but apart from shepherding, what on earth would you do here? Maybe sell cold drinks to the tourists! The King of Greece walked this gorge in 1941 apparently. He had left the mainland when the Germans invaded and a Royal Navy ship brought him to Chania where he set up a temporary government. Then it was decided that he should leave and he was evacuated again by the Royal Navy and headed off to Egypt.'

They had been walking for about an hour when they passed a donkey with a Red Cross blanket under the saddle going back up. It was carrying a woman who had hurt her ankle.

'Did you see the shoes she was wearing?' Charlie asked. 'They were high heels! How ludicrous!'

They stopped a few times to rest awhile, and to give the police time to catch up. The officers were obviously not very fit. Their shirts were wringing wet with sweat and they were breathing heavily.

'This is pretty special isn't it?' Charlie said. 'It's hard going, but I'm enjoying every minute. Especially with you, Tom.' She kissed him gently on the lips. Her shirt was sticking to her body, emphasising her curves. She was exciting Tom to the point where he had to turn away.

'Yes, it's spectacular. Having said that, I can't wait to get into the sea for a swim.'

It was a long walk in the heat, but as they approached the bottom of the gorge, they saw with huge relief that the end was in sight. With their legs by now really aching, the sides of the gorge closed in and then opened out to form a majestic vista with the deep blue sea beyond welcoming them. The last few hundred metres seemed to take forever, but at the thought of getting into the Mediterranean sent them both running towards the water, Tom tearing off his T-shirt and Charlie overtaking him and doing the same. The pebbles on the beach were blisteringly hot, making them run even faster. For the second time in as many days, Charlie was exposing her breasts to the world at large. This time, the police were so far behind that they missed out.

As they swam together, Tom came up behind her and cupped her breasts in his hands. She turned to kiss him.

'You'll have to wait till later,' she said.

'I'm not sure I can,' he replied.

They emerged from the water and collapsed in a heap.

'I couldn't do that again if you paid me a million dollars,' Tom said. 'I'm obviously not as fit as I thought.'

The police officers arrived looking exhausted, desperate to sit in the shade and cool off.

Charlie said to Tom with a smile, 'You seem to be doing all right so far. You had plenty of energy last night!'

They dried off and ambled over to the beach café, ordering a Greek feta salad with tuna and a couple of cold beers. Halfway through their meal they began to rush, realising that the transfer boat which would take them to Chora Sfakion was about to arrive. The policemen looked thoroughly fed up. They were not allowed to drink anything other than water, and they had not been quick enough to get something to eat, so they could hardly wait to get back to their car.

It had been a long day for Tom and Charlie, but a hugely enjoyable one. Riding the waves in the boat was extremely relaxing and invigorating, but it was not long before the small harbour came into view. Yanni was standing on the quayside smoking a cigarette. The thought of a long journey in a hot smelly car up the mountainous roads with two moody policemen did not fill them with joy.

When Tom and Charlie arrived back at the house, they were hot and tired. The first thing they noticed was that the front door was ajar. They opened it apprehensively to find Maria and her parents waiting for them. All Tom and Charlie wanted was to have a shower and be on their own, But Maria had obviously thought that this would be a perfect evening to meet up and hear about her family.

CHAPTER 21

Cave dwellers, 1941

It was approaching midnight, and the soldiers were tired out. Aegeus had escorted them back up to the church and indicated to them with sign language that they should sleep there. Neame posted Fraser and Lance Corporal Johnson outside to keep watch in the pitch black night. He would take over with Stevens at three in the morning and then Henry Weeks, with Fletcher, would do the last stint. It got cold at night up in the mountains in May, even though the temperatures during the day were well above 25 degrees. Aegeus indicated that when the sun rose, he would return. Neame wondered how much he had to eat each day to keep his body weight up. He had muscles on him like a leviathan.

It wasn't easy sleeping on a cold floor, or on the church pews come to that, but Aegeus had brought a couple of bales of hay, carrying one under each arm, which made life a bit more comfortable. They lit one of the church candles so they could see what they were doing, making sure that they covered the windows so that their presence would not be detected. They had not had a hot meal for two days, having existed on dry rations which were fast running out. Lighting a fire would be no problem, but there was a real risk of being spotted by the Germans, so for not it would have to wait.

It was a quiet night except for some distant gunfire and the occasional call from a wild animal. Looking up at the sky, the stars were dazzling, and Neame wondered whether they could be seen as brightly in Maidstone. Maybe his wife and children were also looking up at them. Sad thoughts went through his head.

Tired as he was, Neame found it hard to get to sleep. He and his men were miles from home, alone and abandoned, and he felt an acute responsibility for the men under his command in a foreign land. At least he had Henry Weeks with him for support. The most important thing to do was to make contact with Egypt. They would try in the morning to see if their radio was up to the job.

At first light Neame went out to find Weeks sitting quietly, smoking a Woodbine and appearing to be quite content. It was a beautiful if somewhat chilly morning, and high up in the clouds he could see a bird of prey seeking out some breakfast. He told Fletcher, who had been on watch, to go and rest up for a couple of hours.

'What I would give for a cup of tea,' Neame said. 'We need to find somewhere hidden away where we can cook some hot grub for the boys and then make contact with local people who can help us. That chap Ioannis seemed to be keen, and I wonder what they're doing about forming a resistance. With Ioannis and the shepherd, I think we could make some progress.'

During the morning a Luftwaffe reconnaissance plane came over, causing the men to take cover back in the church. When it had disappeared, they emerged from the building and immediately heard the sound of goats' bells and bleating; it was getting closer. They grabbed their weapons, but they relaxed when Aegeus appeared wearing a big smile and whistling away to himself. He signalled to Neame to follow him.

'Keep the lads on their toes Corp, until I get back,' said Neame.

Although Neame was five foot ten, he looked like a dwarf when standing next to Aegeus. The Greek covered the rough ground with enormous strides, Neame having a job to keep up. He was glad that he still had his army boots. As they rounded a bend, they came across a group of typical white-painted Cretan houses, many covered with stunning bougainvillea and vines. They had reached the outskirts of Manolas.

Aegeus knocked on the door and it was opened by Ioannis, who smiled and motioned them to come into his house. It was quite dark inside. Ioannis introduced his wife Katina, his daughter Christina and his elder son Theodore. A handsome family, Neame thought. The children looked as though they were in their teens or early twenties.

'You are very welcome to my house and to our village,

sir,' said Ioannis. 'Our daughter Christina speaks better the English, she will help.'

'Thank you,' said Neame. Addressing Christina, he said, 'Our group of soldiers want to do all we can to help the Cretan people, but we need food and some help with finding a cave up in the mountains where we can operate from away from your village. There are eleven of us in total, including a radio operator. We have enough ammunition for the time being, but we need to contact our unit in Egypt for some help and supplies. Is there someone in your village who is organising some form of resistance?'

Christina listened, then told her father the gist of what Neame had been saying. Katina then brought Neame and Aegeus a cup of coffee from the kitchen. Neame thanked her, and she bowed her head shyly and took her place back with her children.

'This is wonderful,' he said, wrapping his hands around the cup. 'We have had nothing hot to eat or drink for over two days.'

Ioannis and Christina talked to one another; she was obviously explaining again to her father what Neame had said. Neame could see that he was deep in thought.

Christina stepped forward and spoke very quietly. 'My father is not sure about what you say, but I tell him what help you want to be able to help us. He say that it is honour for the Cretan people to help those who have come such a long way to fight the barbarians, and this is something we have been doing for thousands of years. The person organising resistance in the village to help you is Costas, the mayor. It is he we must talk to, but first Aegeus will take you to a cave, which is about two miles from the church where you have been hiding, and it is very well hidden. We will send some food and wine. Water is plentiful up there. My father says that we will also bring cigarettes.'

Neame thanked her, noticing how pretty she was and how much like her mother.

Ioannis turned to Neame. 'Follow please Aegeus to cave. We are very happy you here. Food will come. Christina and Theodore will help, they bring supplies and take messages.'

'Thank you,' said Neame. Talking to both Ioannis and Christina, he said, 'We will get in touch with Egypt to see what help we can get. Can we meet Costas soon?'

On leaving the Papadakis home, Ioannis walked back up the hillside to meet Aegeus and to collect the men on the way. It was a long haul up the mountain to the cave. When Aegeus pointed to their destination, Neame could see no sign of a cave. When he looked more closely, he saw the entrance discreetly hidden behind a large bush.

Neame went in and immediately felt relieved. It was perfect. It had a second entrance or exit, just in case of an emergency; it was dry and big enough to accommodate all of them, plus quite a few others, and it could not be seen from the air or the ground until you were right on top of it. It was like a real British army HQ.

Aegeus explained to Neame in sign language that there were caves such as this all over the island. All they needed now was some food and a fire to heat it, and to be able to communicate with the outside world. As they were now almost six thousand feet above sea level, the short-wave radio might be able to communicate with a passing British naval vessel, contact Egypt or even possibly reach England. For the first time in quite a few days, they felt they could relax. Making contact with the local population had been a major success. They were not alone any more.

CHAPTER 22

Athens, June 2016

In the embassy, the phones were frantic. Relationships with the Greek government and the EU were not good. Accusations of backstabbing were rife; mistrust was everywhere. Neville and his team had their work cut out just carrying out ambassadorial duties, let alone keeping abreast with what was going on with the country's finances.

There was also his son to worry about. The murder of a German tourist had affected Tom and Charlie's holiday, and all the time the killer was at large the police had a considerable duty of care to protect them. He couldn't help thinking about them.

Relationships between Britain, the EU and Germany were not great either. Britain were angered by moves promoted by the European Commission to help fund the Greek bailout by using the European Financial Stabilisation Mechanism as a bridging loan – a fund involving all twenty-eight EU members.

Britain had one billion pounds of taxpayer's money tied up in the fund and the British Government described the move as totally unacceptable and a breach of the agreement between EU leaders. One EU official said in support of the idea that using the fund may prevent Grexit, but it would cause Brexit. The UK was not in the euro, so it had no responsibility to help finance a bailout package, Prime Minister David Cameron reminded them. He also reminded them that the 2015 Conservative manifesto, which the country had voted for, had boasted that they had taken themselves out of the Eurozone bailouts, and that included Greece.

Little did the EU realise – maybe it did not want to – that in the space of seven years the economics of Europe had just about gone down the toilet.

Neville Richardson's office in Kolonaki in the centre of Athens overlooked a beautiful park. He had seen the start of the street protests in recent years, and now they were becoming ever more frequent, angry and aggressive. He could see both sides of the coin. The Greek people had been promised the earth by a succession of socialist and communist regimes under which it was the norm not to pay taxes, or at least to cheat the system to pay as little as possible. And the left-wing parties were re-elected time and time again based on promises of low taxes and full pensions for life. The ordinary man in the street never had a thought as to how it would be funded; that was what someone had promised them, so that was what they demanded. Did they really believe that money grew on olive trees? Maybe so in the days of the drachma, but not the euro. The billions coming out of Brussels just to keep the country afloat were truly mind-boggling. That word 'austerity', so alien to the Greek people, was to become the word on which governments were elected – or thrown out.

The German Government was the main target of the Greek people, old wounds being re-opened with images being shown in the Greek media of Angela Merkel and Gerhard Schäuble wearing Nazi uniforms. These were not sights which Neville liked to see, regardless of what he felt about the current German administration. That very evening he was due at a soirée which all the principle ambassadors would be attending, including his close friend Kurt Schreiber, the German Ambassador. They had met recently to quell some of the media coverage in the German press reporting anti-EU feeling from the extreme left and right-wing political groups.

The ambassadorial meeting had been kept secret in order to avoid street protests, but twenty or so youths wearing face masks and carrying anti-EU messages tried to block their entrance. They were held well back by police while the dignitaries arrived in unmarked cars. Inside, the meeting hall was like a drinking club for members, where everyone knew each other and all were well-rehearsed in how to play the game. The Greek Minister of Justice gave a short talk suggesting that in the current political climate it would be wise for ambassadors and their staff not to go out on the streets unaccompanied whilst there was still some civil unrest. There were elements who were determined, he said, to cause damage to persons and to property and certain ambassadorial buildings might come under threat. The German embassy was one which was sure to be a target, but extra riot police would be posted for protection.

Kurt Schreiber said to Neville, 'We are in strange times, Neville. The Greeks hating us, and you Brits not our best friends.'

'I think it will be OK, Kurt,' said Neville. 'The issue which is exercising Merkel most, the non-contribution by Britain to the euro fund, will fade, and I think there are those in Germany who are a little envious of our economic position. But the wheel will turn and your economy will bounce back. The average German, I understand, is not keen on seeing the continued pouring of hard-earned taxpayers' money into what they see as a failing nation. And that is, off the record, the truth behind the problem, and understandable.'

Kurt gave a little laugh. 'You are right Neville, I think. We understand each other well. I have spoken to Berlin about the angst against the UK about the funding. But they knew well your position and Jean-Claude Juncker is known to stir things up. Your country is doing well, and it is obviously grating a bit with Merkel. But the signs for us are good. We've just got to sort the Greeks out.'

Much as he liked Kurt, Neville thought his comment was typical of the German: 'we've' got to sort them out. It was not a German issue; it was a European one. And this arrogance was one of the things which really wound up the Greeks. When would they learn?

CHAPTER 23

The Papadakis family, 2016

Freshened up after their day walking the gorge, Tom and Charlie, having excused themselves for a quick change, came down to meet Maria's parents, who were obviously delighted to meet Tom again and had been fully briefed by Maria about Charlie.

'It's so good to see you again Tom,' said Nikos, giving him a big hug. To Nikos, Tom was the son he had never had. 'Welcome back to Crete. Maria tells us that you have brought a pretty friend to stay with you.'

Melissa came up to Tom and gave him a huge hug and a kiss on each cheek. 'Maria told me what a handsome young man you have become. She is right!'

Tom smiled, giving her an extra hug as he was very fond of Melissa. He turned and introduced Charlie to them both.

'We are very pleased to meet you, Charlie,' said Melissa. 'Tom grew up with Maria over the years and we thought that one day they might get together on a more permanent basis.'

'Mother, you mustn't say things like that,' said Nikos.

With everyone looking embarrassed, Charlie took the initiative and said, 'Maria is very beautiful and I can see that they would make a lovely couple. Tom is very handsome and with well-off parents and a diplomatic posting in Greece, what more could you ask for!'

They all laughed, including Maria, who had secretly wanted to punch her mother on the nose for her indiscretion.

Charlie played the perfect hostess by offering them drinks before Nikos asked Tom how his parents were.

'Oh, they are fine, thank you,' said Tom. 'They both wish to be remembered to you. My father will almost certainly be coming out here again shortly. Dad has been keeping me in the picture. I understand that your brother Yiannis is in the Greek parliament.'

'Yes, it's a real mess,' said Nikos. 'And I'm not sure what the solution is. We need help from our European partners and there is one country which seems intent in bringing us down. And it's not the British!'

Maria said, 'Now Dad, that's quite enough of that. Neville had told Tom about Manolas, and Tom was wanting to pay it a visit. I thought you ought to tell Tom and Charlie about our family and how our roots are still there today.'

'How much do you know about Manolas, Tom?' Nikos asked.

'Absolutely nothing,' said Tom, 'except I remember Maria telling me once that her grandparents still live there.'

'That is perfectly true, but also her great-grandparents are still with us and still living in the village. They are, as you English say, part of the furniture. Theodore and Lalika are now well into their nineties and their son Stelios and his wife Marianna, my parents, live close by and can keep an eye on them. It was our home until Melissa and I found work in Chania and it made no sense to travel back and forwards every day.' Turning to Melissa, Nikos said, 'It was also your home darling, when you were young.'

'Yes, it seems a long time ago now,' she replied. 'It's a very pretty place high up in the mountains.'

'My parents, Maria's grandparents, Stelios and Marianna, have lived there all their lives,' said Nikos. 'They are still well and active today with a large olive grove and some sheep and goats. They were both born just after the Second World War. And there is an amazing and tragic story to tell. I hope you are managing to keep up with this Tom.' He smiled.

'I'm sort of there,' he replied. 'No doubt it will become clearer as we go on!'

'You need to try and understand what Crete was like in 1941 when the Germans invaded,' said Nikos. 'Firstly, we did not greet the Germans with open arms. Everyone, men, women and children, fought them with anything they could lay their hands on. This was the first time in World War Two that a civilian population had taken up arms against the Germans – we have had many centuries of experience repelling the invader. Paratroopers were shot as they fell from the sky and killed as they landed on the ground. Some

German units lost eighty to ninety per cent of their men. The senior commanders were taken by surprise at the tenacity of the brave people of Crete in protecting their homeland.'

Charlie asked him if he wanted a top-up to his drink.

'Yes, that would be nice, thank you.' He carried on with his story. 'This was probably why the Germans committed some terrible atrocities against the Cretan people.'

'But surely all they were doing was protecting themselves and their families?'

'Of course, but they thought they were the master race. In fact they still believe that, I'm afraid to say.'

'I'm trying to think back seventy-five years as to what life would have been like then, up in the mountains where life was probably quite tough,' said Charlie.

'It will help you to look at these old family photographs. This one shows my great-grandparents, Maria's great-great-grandparents, Ioannis and Katina Papadakis, outside their house. They had two children, Theodore and Christina, who were quite young when the Germans invaded. Doesn't Christina look like Maria? So pretty.'

Maria turned her head away, looking slightly embarrassed.

'As we have said, they lived in Manolas up in the White Mountains. When the British and their Allies were being evacuated, some got left behind. A group of them came to the village to seek help. They were young men, a long way from their homes. And here they were, fighting the soldiers who had invaded our country. What else could we do other than to take them to our villages and do all we could to help them, as they were risking their lives for us?'

'Why did they go to your village?' asked Tom.

'We don't know, except that they had tried to get away with their comrades through the Imbros gorge and missed the last boat. They had left some supplies which were too heavy to carry at a mountain church which was not a huge distance from our village. We can only assume they came to collect the ammunition and use it as a place of refuge until they worked out what they were going to do. It was then that they met a shepherd called Aegeus, a giant of a man. He introduced them to my great-grandfather Ioannis. Not long after that the Germans arrived in Manolas.'

Maria took herself off to the kitchen. All this talk was unsettling her, and she needed a period of quiet reflection away from her parents, who had a different attitude to her about Germany, and the German people. It was obvious that they still had no time for the 'master race', as they had called themselves.

CHAPTER 24

Chania, 2016

❦

Tom's phone rang while he was in the shower. 'Tom,' shouted Charlie from the kitchen, 'phone!'

He pulled a towel around himself and grabbed the phone out of her hand.

'Hello, hello... blast, missed it,' he said. He went to 'contacts' and called his father back. 'Hi Dad, sorry I missed your call. You OK?'

'Hello. Fine thanks Tom. But this killing in Chania with apparently no suspects anywhere in sight is causing real strain between Berlin and Athens. Whilst no one wants to see anyone killed at any time, this has come at a very sensitive time and the German press are having a field day. The German authorities want to send in their own investigators whilst Greece are saying it's out of the question for them to interfere in internal affairs. All getting rather unpleasant. I know this has nothing really to do with you, but please do what the police ask and don't take any risks.'

'Yes, of course Dad. That goes without saying. We have been advised not to go clubbing so we're restricting ourselves to low-key entertainment. Are they saying in Athens who they think is behind it?'

'On the QT, they think that it was just a drunken moment, not premeditated. When the German and some of his friends just opened their mouths a bit too wide, a Cretan or Cretans took exception to it. Even after all this time, the wounds from the war are still hard to heal. And the bail-out issue hasn't helped. German tourists are being told to respect the Cretan people and not get involved. Tourism is extremely important to the economy of Greece, which includes Crete, so governments are playing down the possibility of any further attacks. Anyway, keep that to yourself, but keep alert.'

Tom told his father what had happened with the taxi passenger who had not wanted to pay her fare.

When the conversation was over Tom sat down with Charlie, still just wearing a towel. Whilst not telling her everything his father had said, he outlined the need to take care, and to be aware.

'I think a day on the beach with maybe a walk around the town after would be in order. You OK with that?' he asked.

'That's cool. I'd quite like to find somewhere with some water sports. I've always wanted to try paragliding.'

Tom picked up his tablet. 'We can look on the net. I heard that there was a beach just outside Chania called Oasis which has all kinds of water sports. Let's have some breakfast then we can sit out on the terrace and check it out.'

He looked out of the window, just to make sure that the police officers were in place. Seeing George and Stathi standing by their car, wearing dark sunglasses he was reassured. At the same time, a smartly-dressed man walked up to the door and knocked. Tom walked out into the hall and undid the latch.

'Mr Richardson?' asked the man.

'Yes, I'm Tom Richardson. Can I help you?'

The man shook Tom's hand. 'I'm sorry to trouble you but this is just a courtesy call. I am the German Consul in Crete and I have been asked by my ambassador in Athens, Kurt Schreiber, who is a friend of your father I believe, just to make sure that you are OK and whether there is anything I can do to help. The recent troubles have not been what we like to see and are not typical of the rest of the nation.'

'That is very kind, thank you. You needn't have put yourself out, we have the police keeping an eye on us, but I really appreciate your call. May I take your card, just in case?'

'Of course. My name is Markus Rolf and my number is available anytime.' With that, he walked back down the street. How very polite and helpful, Tom thought.

'Who was that?' Charlie asked as she came down the stairs.

'He was the German Consul, just making sure all is OK. My father's friend in Athens had presumably prompted the move. Anyway, that was very nice. I must remember to thank my dad.'

Having packed the car with a few essentials, they set off to the beach near Galatas, discreetly followed by their uniformed escort. It had looked enticing on the web and before they had even arrived, Charlie could see paragliders taking to the sky.

'That's for me,' she said.

'Well', he said jokingly,' don't expect our police friends to follow,and keep your top on!'

Tom had brought a new thriller with him, the Kindle version of the latest Kate Atkinson novel, and he was keen to get some light reading done. Nothing too heavy, after all he was on holiday. When Charlie had gone off to get fitted out with her harness by some Greek Adonis, Tom lay on a sun bed and started his book, keeping one eye on Charlie, just to be sure she kept decent. He watched her fly past a couple of times, waving frantically at Tom, until finally she landed very demurely in the shallow water. She walked back to where he was lying on the beach

'That was just great!' she said. 'It's amazing how much more you can see from up there.' She took off her harness. 'I'm just going for a swim.'

Tom watched her for a while, then dozed off. He was awoken by the shock of cold water on his body, and opened his eyes to see Charlie shaking her wet hair all over him.

'I'll get you for that!' he said playfully.

After a couple of hours on the beach, they had lunch in a beachside café before going back into Chania town. They parked outside the restaurants on the waterfront just along from the Ottoman mosque down on the harbour-side, and the view it took Charlie's breath away.

'It is lovely here Tom,' she said, putting her arm through his. 'Everywhere you look there's something of interest – the harbour, the lighthouse, the mosque. And it's because Crete has been occupied so many times by so many different nationalities. History just oozes out of every corner.'

Noticing that the mosque was open for an art exhibition, Tom suggested that they go in and look. 'If it's modern art,' she said, 'I'm not into that. Give me an old building to look round anytime.'

'The mosque dates from the seventeenth century and it's the oldest Ottoman building on the island,' he said. 'It was built around 1650 I believe. As you can see, it's surrounded by Venetian buildings and fortifications. There are also some Turkish buildings as a reminder of their 250-year rule. Everyone has been here at some time or other – Minoans, Venetians, Turks, the Germans. And of course, it is the prettiest town on the island. But I would say that, wouldn't I!'

'It is so attractive Tom,' she said. 'I can quite understand why your parents wanted to buy a home here. I love it!'

'Come on, I've got lots more to show you. But first, a large ice cream and a cappuccino. We'll do a couple of museums just to get out of the afternoon heat. We can also do the shops – they are the best, but they're pricey.'

'Don't tempt me with that Tom,' she said, 'I'm not loaded.'

They wandered round the Venetian Quarter, where there were some fine sixteenth and seventeenth century mansions, retaining the Venetian architectural style. They also visited the naval museum in the Firkas Fort by the harbour, where the Byzantine collection of coins, jewels, mosaics and icons appealed hugely to Charlie.

'This is what Greece means to me,' she said. 'All I want to see now is some more statues like the superb ones we saw at Knossos.'

'Will I do?' he suggested, tongue in cheek, striking a pose.

'Maybe, but they all had tiny penises. I want a bit more than that!'

With that, she walked ahead. 'I'm falling head over heels for this girl,' he murmured to himself. Or was it just a holiday romance? Only time would tell.

CHAPTER 25

Manolas, 1941

❧

The deep throb of engines approaching could be heard all the way down the valley, disturbing a beautiful day. Smoke from the aircraft exhausts was clearly visible from the front of the café. The reality was that the villagers knew this was the moment they had been dreading since the paratroopers had dropped out of the sky. For the moment there was nothing they could do except wait for the inevitable. Men and women gathered in the square, smoking but not saying a word, just deep in thought.

A short while later, a motorbike with sidecar raced ahead of the convoy and stopped in the middle of the village square. A sergeant alighted and entered the café, demanding to see the mayor. Costas raised himself from his chair and stood proudly.

'I am Costas Pavlopoulos and I represent the community of Mandalos. And who pray are you?' he said in Greek.

Realising that any conversation was going to be difficult, the officer passed a piece of paper to Costas demanding that he should find an interpreter so that his commanding officer could address the villagers. Costas thought the best person was Christina; although she was young, her English and German were passable. He set off up to her house, indicating to the sergeant that he would return in fifteen minutes.

It took slightly more than that, with Costas and Christina running down the hill and her parents following. Pushing her forward, the officer appeared and asked Christina if she could translate. She just nodded, looking terrified. He banged his stick on the side of a truck to get their attention.

'I am Oberleutnant Mueller from the 15th Bavarian Mountain Regiment and you are now under our jurisdiction,' he barked. Turning to Costas, with Christina translating, he continued, 'You will gather all villagers into the square, where I will address the people and your girl here will translate into Greek. You have one hour to arrange this or someone will be shot. He looked at Costas. 'it could be you!' He clicked his heels, did a smart about turn and was reunited with the sergeant and his motorcycle, who were waiting for the rest of his unit to appear.

Costas followed him with Christina and explained that the village was spread over an area of a few miles, so it would not be possible to get everyone there in an hour, but they would spread the word immediately and anyone not getting there would be contacted with whatever message they had for the village. Whist this was not what the officer wanted to hear, he knew very well that there was no option but to accept.

So as not to antagonise the Germans unnecessarily, Costas gave his orders within earshot of the German officer. For a moment or two he considered whether to tell Aegeus. In the end he thought that he should but even if someone left straightaway to go to his house, they would not be back in an hour. But they would have made the effort. The village must show strength at times like this and Aegeus would be the man to do it, if he could keep his temper in place.

An hour later the square was full of people of all ages, some standing proud, some forlorn, some indifferent. In the centre was the Oberleutnant, standing on the seat of the sidecar. Christina was ordered to translate again.

'People of Manolas. We are here to tell you what we expect of you and providing you carry out our orders, we will get along. If not, you will feel the wrath of the German army.' He looked round to make sure he had their attention, firing his Luger pistol in the air, which caused some to duck, others to shake with fear. He continued, 'To start with, anyone who has weapons must hand them in within seventy-two hours. Anyone found in possession of any weapon after then will be shot. We need every able-bodied man to work on the island's defences. You will give your names to the mayor and we will collect this in three days.

'Anyone between the ages of seventeen and sixty must sign up. Anyone found not complying will be imprisoned. Any member of this community who in any way conspires against the occupier will be shot and their possessions confiscated. We require all your excess food, including animals, and we will decide what is excess.' He smiled. 'There will be a small unit billeted here and we will confiscate the property we require and the owners will have to move out. There will be no compensation. There will be a curfew from six in the evening until seven in the morning. Anyone found outside during these times will be shot on sight. Anyone communicating with, or being part of, any political or resistance organisation will be executed by firing squad with their entire family. There will be no appeal. Follow these rules and we will get along. If not...' he indicated the consequence by running his finger across his throat.

'We will return in three days to collect the list of men and lorries will be here ready to take the men to the coast. We will also occupy the houses we need. In the meantime, respect the German forces and do not attempt to hide your valuables and food away because if we find it, you will be shot and your house burned to the ground. Everyone will have an identity card which will be distributed by the Mayor with the help of the sergeant who will be billeted here. If you are found without one, you will be arrested. There will be no listening to the BBC or to Athens on the radio. Anyone listening to any broadcast will be imprisoned. Understood?'

No one moved or said anything. Even the birds had stopped singing, as if they knew that they too would be shot if they did not keep silent.

Christina stepped away, terrified after her ordeal, her

hands shaking after the stress of translating what the officer had said. She felt physically sick. At the back of the crowd, head and shoulders above everyone else, she saw Aegeus, with the strangest look on his face. He had raised his face to look up at the heavens as if asking for divine guidance and supreme strength for what lay ahead. Hercules had fought many battles in his lifetime. Perhaps he was thinking that he would guide Aegeus in the challenges ahead.

CHAPTER 26

Cretan Mountains, June 1941

After a couple of days in their cave hideaway, life had become relatively comfortable for the soldiers. It was all rather surreal. There were those who wondered what on earth they were doing there and missing England and their families, and there were those who were excited by the prospect of fighting a secret war up in the mountains against the Germans.

The first night was very unsettling, even though lookouts had been posted, and every noise was magnified many times over through fear of the unknown. On the second day, Aegeus appeared with a goat slung over his shoulders, its throat recently cut, along with extra hay for bedding and firewood. On his back was a bag with olive oil, bread, hard-boiled eggs and lentils. The men could not believe their luck. He looked magnificent, every part the Cretan warrior. Over six feet six tall, he was wearing long black leather riding boots, baggy trousers, a red cummerbund, a black bolero and a tight-fitting woollen hat. He also had a magnificent curled moustache.

Taking out an exceptionally sharp knife which had been in a scabbard hanging from his waist, Aegeus set about butchering the goat. Not having a saw, he simple broke the bones with his bare hands. Neame wondered what he might do to a German if he met one. When he had finished, he explained using sign language that it needed cooking over an open fire and what was left after a meal should be wrapped in straw and placed in the coolest part of the cave. They could now look forward to their first hot meal in what seemed like forever.

While this was going on, Simms, Neame's radio operator, had positioned himself up on the rocks above the cave in order to attempt to make some contact with a Royal Navy ship in the area, or better still forces in Egypt or Libya. Using a short-wave frequency and trying not to run the batteries down, he tried for about ten minutes, without success. He would try again the next day. Unlike the men, who could sleep to recharge their batteries, the radio batteries were not rechargeable, so they had to be used with great care.

Late in the afternoon, Costas and Ioannis approached and gave the agreed signal, one long whistle followed by three short ones. As mayor, Costas had assumed a leading role in discussions about possible resistance, with Ioannis lending some military guidance from his time with the territorials. Several men in the village were active reserve soldiers, but there was every chance that they would be taken as labourers by the Germans.

Costas spoke no English, so Ioannis had to help as best he could. They tried to explain to Neame that the Germans had arrived in Manolas the day before and that the menfolk were being transported to help build defences on the island. But communicating wasn't easy and he hoped that Christina would come so she could explain it properly to him. It seemed that Costas was eager to help build a relationship, but without speaking English it was almost an impossible task. They parted with kisses on the cheeks, smiles and strong handshakes. Neame felt that until some help arrived from Egypt, any way forward was going to be problematical.

The following day, the signal was heard again. This time it was Christina wearing the traditional headscarf, black dress and cardigan and carrying a message from Costas for Neame, which she had translated. In a pack on her back were some provisions, including cigarettes, vegetables and two bottles of local wine, which were very welcome.

Neame went outside the cave to read the message and to write a response. The message said that he and Ioannis might not be around once the Germans returned the next day, and warned them that a small detachment of soldiers was to be based in the village. This would make communicating with them difficult. He dictated a reply to Christina, which she scribbled on a small piece of paper. She concealed it in her clothing, aware that the consequences of being found with it by the Germans would be severe. She shook his hand, and with a smile she said goodbye.

Early the following morning, Simms made another attempt to make contact. The atmospheric conditions were good, and he got through almost immediately.

'This is Crete calling... this is Crete calling,' he sent.

There was a pause before the response came. 'Hello Crete, this is Kimberly receiving you. Kimberly receiving you. Give me your position.'

Simms quoted their location, not having a map reference, and said, 'British soldiers stranded on Crete. Need assistance, need assistance. Please make contact.' He was feeling euphoric at the contact. The response came back: 'Willco. Stand by.' The radio bleeped and a message came back 'Contact will be made at 0900 tomorrow, repeat contact tomorrow at 0900. Over and out.' Simms, elated, rushed back into the cave to tell Neame the good news.

An anxious evening followed. Fraser, something of an amateur cook, prepared a simple meal that tasted wonderful. There was meat and vegetables and a few herbs for seasoning – no gravy, but the men did not care. It was a damn sight better than the Army grub back home, and this was heaven. After they had finished the smell of the stew lingered in the air, making everyone continue to feel very hungry. They lay with glasses of wine by the warm wood fire, smoking rough cigarettes. The only thing missing was home.

The next morning Simms was back at his post with the radio. At 0900 sharp, the welcome 'Ping' came. The light came on and the message was heard.

'Crete, this is Alexandria calling. Alexandria calling. Help coming. Help coming. Will advise when. Will advise when. Over and out.'

Neame called the men together, talking quietly. 'Right, we have to be on our guard. The message we had yesterday from the village said that Germans had arrived in Manalos. The village is a few miles down the hill from here. They are forcing the men away from their homes and villages into labour battalions and taking them away to build fortifications, leaving a small detachment of soldiers in the village. There's a chance that Ioannis and his son Theodore will be taken, so, we have to be alert until more help arrives. Careful with the fire smoke. Keep your voices down. Ioannis's daughter Christina speaks a little English and German I believe, and she will come when she can to bring us messages. And Aegeus almost certainly will not submit to being taken, so he will stay hidden away up here.

'From now on we must assume that there will be enemy patrols up here in the mountains. Hopefully, we may get some help from other Allied soldiers on the island who are in the same boat as us, so together we can make life as difficult as possible for the enemy. Simms has made contact with Egypt, so at least someone knows we are here. We just have to wait it out for now. At least we will be well fed.'

CHAPTER 27

Manolas, June 1941

❧

'Achtung! Achtung!' shouted Oberleutnant Mueller through his megaphone. A dozen soldiers from the Bavarian Regiment were standing behind him with rifles at the ready. The motorbike sidecar, with a heavy machine gun, was stationary in the square, pointing menacingly at the crowd. Christina was standing alongside the officer ready to translate again.

'All men line up over here,' Mueller went on. 'Give your names and stand by the truck. You will be working for the Reich. One day off a week. Rest of the time living in barracks. The village roll shows one hundred and twenty-two men — let's see how many are here.'

Walking forward slowly one by one they gave their names, with their families looking on sombrely. This was a tragic day for Manolas, and the true impact of the loss of their menfolk would be difficult to imagine.

'There is a major problem here, because at least thirty-seven men are not accounted for' said the Oberleutnant. 'Sergeant, go to these houses now and do a thorough search. If the doors are locked, break them down!'

This search took another hour, by which time the people standing out in the square were getting increasingly angry, although they were powerless to do anything. Nine more men were found, some over the age limit, but that still left quite a number missing. The soldiers were helping themselves to everything of value they saw during the search, including jewellery, watches, food and wine.

'Right,' the Sergeant said, 'let's get these men away and we'll hunt for the rest later. And God help any that we find.'

The womenfolk were distraught. They waved desperately as their men looked back through the dust kicked up by the disappearing lorries. They had no idea where they were being taken or if they would ever see them again. Katina and Christina were shattered to see Ioannis and Theodore taken away, and were only mildly comforted by what Ioannis whispered in Katina's ear: 'We won't be long. Be ready.'

Aegeus was standing high up on the hill watching the events unfold. The giant was watching to see which house the German officer would commandeer for him and his men. The mayor's house was the largest, and Costas had been saved from the labour camp because the Germans needed him in the village. But it appeared that this did not stop them, for as far as Aegeus could see, they had marched into his home with Costas just standing outside, his wife wondering what was going to happen. The beautiful house in which they had lovingly brought up their family was going to be desecrated by these terrible people. It was almost too much to bear.

Aegeus had seen enough. He knew they would come looking for him at some stage, and he needed to make sure his wife and family were secure. He also felt a responsibility towards the soldiers in the cave. They needed supplies, and until a network of people was established to push these hated invaders back into the sea, they had to be cunning and bide their time. They had given the Germans a very bloody nose when they had landed. They were going to have to do it again.

CHAPTER 28

Christina the runner, 1941

❧

Reaching the cave high up in the mountain was no easy task. It was a difficult climb on the loose scree, but Christina knew the route backwards. With the Germans in the area however, she had to be doubly careful. The trees afforded some cover on the slopes, and Neame was hopeful that the Germans would not want to risk coming too high up for fear of ambush. They had learnt the hard way what messing with the Cretan people could do.

Christina gave the signal, and Henry Weeks waved to her to approach. Neame left the cave, and when he saw her take the small piece of paper which contained a message from Costas out of her blouse, it became obvious that something was not right. She had translated the message for Neame, but there were tears in her eyes.

Taking her aside, he asked, 'What's happened, Christina? Why the tears?'

She turned her head away, took a deep breath, and spoke in a voice which Neame could hardly hear.

'The Germans came yesterday and took my father and brother along with many men from our village. They are going into forced labour camps, and we know they will be roughly treated. It is terrible.'

Neame did not know what to say to her. He had seen such misery already in this war, in Belgium, France, Greece and now Crete.

He took her hand and gently squeezed it. 'I'm so sorry Christina. That is really tough for you and your mother. Until we get coordination with other soldiers and people like Costas, it's difficult for us to get back at the Germans. But I promise you we'll try.'

She smiled and kissed him on the cheek. 'We're so pleased that you're here to help us. With our men gone, we will feel very much alone, and without you we just don't know what we would do. We hear about resistance groups, run by men like Costas, but some are led by men who are not doing it for Crete but for personal gain and others are starting to fight one another, particularly the communists. That's the last thing we need.'

Neame was full of admiration for this young woman's bravery. Acting as a runner with messages concealed about her would mean certain death if she were caught. He said goodbye to her, wishing her god speed, and as she started her descent from the mountain hideaway, she turned and waved. It made his heart give a little lurch, seeing her on her own taking on such a huge responsibility for running messages and the danger which came with it. He had only met her a few times, but he was starting to feel something for this very special young lady.

The message from Costas was short; it was just to say that Christina would be their runner with the help of her brother Theodore, that they could trust them completely and that six other resistance groups were being formed in western Crete. The distances they would have to travel were great, but they knew the countryside well and were fit and able to run many miles in a day.

A sudden shout from Henry brought him back to his senses. 'Sarge! There are Germans down on the lower slopes. Fortunately they're not in the direction Christina was going. I have extinguished the fire and told the men to arm up and stay very still and quiet.'

Neame could hear engines, and a strong scent of thyme wafted across the hills. It seemed so incongruous; great danger on one hand, and the peaceful smell of mountain herbs on the other. They stayed silent and motionless and eventually the Germans passed them by, heading east at a much lower level.

'Keep the men on alert,' said Neame, 'and post Fraser and Stevens up above the cave so they can keep a lookout.'

He went into the cave to re-read Christina's translation of Costas's message. He was looking worried.

CHAPTER 29

The Papadakis family, 2016

Nikos was getting very emotional as he continued the story of his family. 'A few days after the last British boat had left, leaving many soldiers behind, this group appeared in the hills above Manolas. My great grandparents and many from the village felt they had a duty to help them by giving them somewhere to hide, food and clothing. They had already helped other men who were passing through. There was a shepherd called Aegeus, a giant of a man who lived a remote existence in the mountains with his family, and it was he who first brought the leading soldier to Manolas, a sergeant called Bob Neame. Being a shepherd, Aegeus was able to help them with food, and so did some of the villagers. Ioannis and Katina's daughter, Christina, became a runner. Her job was to take messages to the soldiers in the cave and other isolated cells from the leaders of the resistance in the area, including Costas, who was the mayor of Manolas.'

'That must have been a very dangerous job for a young girl,' Tom said.

'Incredibly dangerous. If she was caught, the Germans would show no mercy.' He took a drink. 'Then the Germans came to the village and my grandfather Ioannis and his son Theodore were taken away with many of the men to work in labour camps, the ones aged between seventeen and sixty. It was a really difficult time. Conditions in the villages got worse quickly . Fear, hunger and poverty set in and the lack of freedom to move around was particularly hard. Food became scarce and money was hugely devalued, so it became useless. Necessities for the Cretan people, like olive oil, wheat, barley and leather, became outrageously expensive, and items like coffee and sugar were all but impossible to find. Bartering was the only way to survive, and it became a way of life. Many of the farm animals were confiscated. The Germans cut off all electrical power and mountains, beaches and harbours were all put out of bounds. Communities like Manolas were almost isolated, and families had to work together just to exist.'

'That sounds terrible. Without the menfolk at home, life must have been really hard,' said Tom.

Charlie asked, 'What happened to your grandfather Ioannis and his son?'

'He had decided that he would escape as soon as he could, but of course he would have to involve Theodore,' said Melissa. 'Katina, his wife and Christina would be at great risk in the village and would be executed if he was found missing from the working party. The men from the labour camps were allowed home one day a week on a Sunday, so they could go to church. Ioannis had arranged with his family to be ready with whatever they could carry from their home to leave for the mountains when they came back, and that's what they did. It was a tough life with Ioannis and Theodore being members of the resistance, as well as Christina who continued to be a runner. Danger around every corner, and not just for the resistance but for the English soldiers as well.'

Tom did not want to ask them to leave, but he had booked a restaurant for dinner. 'Perhaps you'd like to come here for a meal tomorrow and finish the story?' he said. 'We're going down to the harbour for something to eat this evening, so I need to get ready.'

'Oh sorry,' said Nikos. 'We have been talking away and not realised the time. That would be lovely. We'll see you tomorrow. I see the police are keeping an eye on you both.'

Tom turned to Maria. 'Would you like to come with us?'

Looking a little shy, she said, 'I would really like that, if that's all right with you and Charlie?'

'If you hadn't asked her, I would have done it myself!' said Charlie. 'We can't go clubbing because of the trouble, but just a nice meal in a nice restaurant. Perhaps you can recommend some good local dishes.'

Nikos and Melissa were very pleased that Maria had accepted, and wished them a good time as they left.

It proved to be a perfect evening, although Tom embarrassed both women in the restaurant by going on his knees in front of Charlie and saying jokingly, 'I bow to thee, your majesty. I await thy command.' Charlie was mystified for a moment, until she remembered that in Knossos Tom had told her that the guide thought she looked like the depictions of Queen Europa, and she had styled her hair that evening like a Greek Goddess.

'Stop it, Tom. You're making me blush,' she said. Other diners were wondering what was going on. Had he proposed to her?

The only thing that spoiled the evening for Maria was seeing Tom going back to the house with Charlie and not her. Having said goodbye to Maria outside the restaurant, Tom and Charlie walked back with their police escort a few paces behind. As soon as they had entered the house, Tom's phone rang.

'Hi Dad. What's up?' The reception was not good, but Tom could just make out what he was saying. It seemed there had been a development in the investigation into the killing, and a bouncer from a night club had been taken in for questioning regarding the incident. 'Hold on Dad, I'll just go out to get better reception,' he said. He stepped outside. 'Hi, now try that.'

'That's better. It was just to let you know that a bouncer from the night club had told the police that someone called Hercules had committed the murder, but he wouldn't say anything more.'

'OK Dad, thanks for that. Not sure what that really means, but it's progress of sorts I suppose. For all that, we're both having a really good time. Everything good with you?'

'Not bad, Tom. The street protests here are continuing. I can't see an easy answer to the problems. But everyone is trying.'

'Sorry to hear that. Give mum a kiss from me. If I hear anything, I'll let you know.'

Charlie was in the kitchen when he returned.

'Fancy a nightcap?' she asked.

'What did you have in mind?'

'Come with me.'

CHAPTER 30

The Royal Navy arrives, 1941

❧

Christina, making yet another trip up to the cave, gave Neame a message from Costas. It was to say that a British naval officer was due to arrive by submarine in the next few days. The location was being kept secret for now for security reasons. A central intelligence unit had recently been set up in Heraklion by British officers who had been left behind, and working with Cretan resistance leaders, they had picked up a message from Mersa Matruh in North Africa to say that the naval officer was about to arrive. It said that he was to organise the evacuation of those troops still left on the island, as they were urgently needed elsewhere. He was also to liaise with the resistance leaders to start co-ordinating an action plan against the Germans. This second part was good news, because Neame's men were getting restless and bored even, though their resolution to stay was still as strong as ever.

Christina sat in the shade and accepted some refreshment

from Simms, as the journey up the hillside had been hard in the heat, even for someone used to such conditions. Apart from the fact that she was tired, Neame thought she was looking a lot happier than when she had come on her last visit. Seeing her made him forget momentarily about the war. The attraction wasn't just physical; he greatly admired the way she carried out her dangerous missions without a thought for her own safety. He had the impression that she liked him too, and he was right, but the feeling was a new experience for her and she was shy. He was a British officer, and she was a young girl working closely with the resistance. Any distraction could be bad news, for both of them.

On her last visit she had kissed him on the cheek, which had taken him by surprise. She had been very emotional about what was happening to her family. Now it was obvious to him that there was some warmth in their relationship. The original shyness was starting to dissipate, and she seemed really pleased to meet up with Neame and the other men. She had become part of the team. It was good for them to have her around, as she added a bit of life into an otherwise fairly boring existence, for now anyway.

'I'll be back in a minute, Corp,' Neame said to Weeks. They walked up the hill and sat down, still in sight of the men.

'Bob, you must please tell me a little about you,' she said. 'We talk only of the war. Where do you live in England? What kind of house do you have? Do you have brothers and sisters? Are you married?'

He didn't see any point in lying to her. 'Yes, I am, with two young children. I haven't seen them for such a long time. I thought long and hard about them before deciding whether to surrender to the Germans or to stay and do the job we came to do. Obviously I chose to stay.' Looking her in the eyes, he said, 'I'm so glad I did.' He discreetly took her hand, squeezing it gently. He could feel many pairs of eyes watching them from a distance and not wanting to get any grief from his men, he added, 'let's continue this conversation when we can be alone.'

She squeezed his hand in return and stood up. When she had recovered her emotions, she asked him if he knew where she hid her messages in case the Germans stopped her. 'Inside here,' she said, indicating her breast. He had not made love to a woman for almost a year, and suddenly his desire for her became almost unbearable. She saw the look in his eyes and knew what he was thinking.

'Bob, I must tell you that I have not been with any man before,' she said. 'I want my first time to be with you, but I want it to be at the right time and in the right place.' She could sense the depth of his yearning. 'So we must save it for a time when we can relax a bit and be truly on our own.'

When they came back down to the cave, Weeks gave Neame a meaningful look. It was clear that he could see something was brewing between the two of them.

When Christina had left, before Weeks could say anything, Neame said, 'Don't lecture me Alan, nothing of consequence happened. I wanted to, sure. I know it wouldn't have been right, but I'm just a normal bloke like you and all the others. She is just beautiful, exciting and very brave.' After a pause, he said, 'Call the men together. I have something to tell them which may cheer them up a bit. The Royal Navy is due!'

Three days later Christina returned, this time with Costas. Neame could see that she was troubled. Taking her aside, he asked her, 'Are you all right?'

'Oh Bob,' she said taking his hand. 'My father and brother came home yesterday and life in the labour camp is really tough, and it showed. They have lost a lot of weight and look ill. I don't think they will be able to take much more. They are beaten every day and fed on worse food than we give to the animals.'

'Oh my god, that's terrible,' said Neame. 'It must be a real worry for you and your mother. Don't worry, hopefully something good will happen soon.' She saw the look on his face as he said it and knew that hope was all they had.

'The naval officer arrived with the high tide yesterday,' said Costas. 'A dinghy brought him ashore from the submarine. He was met by the resistance leaders from Omalos and Sphakia. I can't tell you their names, just in case you are caught. He was taken to the monastery near Samaria where the priest is a good friend of the resistance. The officer will come to meet you tomorrow to try and persuade you and your men to leave for Egypt or Libya. We would like you to stay and help us of course, but you have to do what you think is right.'

In his heart, Bob knew that this question was going to

come again. It wasn't that long ago that they had decided to stay and fight rather than surrender. Now the question was different. They were being offered a chance to leave with a guaranteed form of transport. They could still stay and fight, and by now they had a much better idea as to what was involved, but now it was not a case of surrender but the opportunity to get back to their units and mates. Neame would talk to them at supper to see if their views had changed.

The next morning warm rain was falling, bringing out the smell of the wild flowers and herbs which covered the hillside. At around ten o'clock, Fletcher, who was on look-out, spotted two men approaching with armed guards walking behind, and gave a warning whistle. The men in the cave were put on alert by Neame. The Cretan resistance leader, Aleko, dressed in full Cretan dress, raised his hand to acknowledge their approach.

Lieutenant John Penrose RN and his escort were at the cave within a few minutes. Neame saluted him and asked him to sit, making sure that there were men on sentry duty outside, just in case. Coincidentally, Aegeus had just arrived with more food and wine, and he wanted to stay even though he could not understand what was being said. Neame did not have the heart to ask him to leave. After all, it was his country, he had been very generous with food for the men and he was known to Aleko.

Penrose said, 'It's good to meet you Sergeant, I expect you know why I'm here?'

'Yes, I believe so sir. We heard on the grapevine that you were here to encourage us all to leave and go back to our units. I have spoken to the men about it.'

'That's the general gist of it, Sergeant. Although you were let down when the Navy carried out the evacuation, word has come through from on high to say that those who decide to stay could be charged as deserters, regardless of what you may have originally been told. I have to tell you in all honesty that I do not believe that, as I know that there are imminent moves afoot to bring SOE operatives to the island who will need the likes of your men here, fully-trained British soldiers to join them as active units with the Cretan resistance. This is of course the second part of my brief. From what Aleko has already told me, you have established a good rapport with the local people. That is to be applauded.'

Neame gathered everyone around him, including the two on sentry duty. 'Right men. You know what this is all about. We had a chat last night, but Lieutenant Penrose has explained to me just now that Special Operations Executive officers may be landing soon to co-ordinate guerrilla activity on the island. However, the army needs us in Egypt and there's a threat that we could be charged as deserters if we don't return in the naval craft they are sending for us and many others on the island. But again, they will need us here if they are to be successful in building up an army of resistance. I am afraid that you, Simms, will be needed here because of your radio skills, that is a special request from HQ. I will stay because these people need us, but for the rest of you, it's your choice.' He saw Weeks give him an old-fashioned look, as if to say, 'I know why you really want to stay'.

'As an officer, I have to advise you that this is officially an order,' said Lieutenant Penrose, 'but I do accept that you have been through a lot, so if some of you decide to stay I'll be advising my superiors that you are doing so in the interests of the people who you were ordered to come and help in the first place. Anyway, good luck to you, whatever you decide to do.'

Gordon and Fletcher were career soldiers, and they felt that an order was an order and they must obey. Fraser and Stevens stood with Neame and Lance Corporal Johnson to indicate their desire to remain. Those who had joined them in dribs and drabs since the main evacuation were ambivalent, and Neame assumed that they would decide when the moment came whether to go or stay. He could tell that Henry Weeks, his number two for so long, was troubled. Whether it was to do with Neame's friendship with Christina or his real concern about being treated as a deserter, Neame wasn't sure.

Penrose turned to leave. 'I can tell you that a Greek-speaking SOE officer is thought to be due in the next few days,' he said. 'I wanted to leave this piece of information until you had made your decision, but it's important for you to know, and of course this must be kept quiet. I'll get a message to Sergeant Neame when the Navy are due to collect those who wish to return. Until then, stay out of sight and await further instructions.'

CHAPTER 31

Rethymno, Crete, 2016

For the first time since Tom and Charlie had arrived in Chania, traffic noise had woken them up. Maria had mentioned that market day was due, hence all the noise and exhaust fumes. The early morning sun was pouring in through the shutters on their bedroom window. Tom turned over, giving Charlie a kiss on her shoulder, and went down to get a glass of water. After the alcoholic intake from the previous night, he needed to cleanse his inner being. Charlie joined him in the kitchen, rubbing the sleepy dust out of her eyes.

'Maria said at dinner last night that there's a wine festival on Rethymno all this week,' said Tom. 'It is a pretty town and well worth a visit, even apart from the free wine. Fancy going?'

'Can we just rest-up for a couple of hours?' she asked. 'I know you are keen to show me the sights but it is also a holiday and I would rather not be chasing around every day. Is that OK?'

Charlie, in something of a dream world, laid her head on Tom's shoulder. 'I just love spending lazy times with you at breakfast,' she said. 'It's a very special time. Waking up next to you and just wandering down to some fresh fruit, courtesy of Maria, and some really fresh yoghurt. Simple things which mean a lot. I never do this at home, so thank you, Tom.' She spoke with real affection.

'It's my pleasure, and I mean that,' he said.

'And in answer to your question, that's a really nice idea. Leave about midday? With a wine festival comes food, so there should be some interesting tastes there too.'

Her eyes were to die for, he thought, and when she looked straight at him, he felt himself melting.

'Come on,' he said. 'If we keep talking like this, we'll end up back in bed.'

'And what's wrong with that?'

'There's a time and place for everything,' he said. She poked her tongue out at him.

Walking out to the car a bit later, Tom could feel a different sort of heat, really intense. 'It's going to be really hot today. Have you put some cream on?' he asked.

George and Stathi acknowledged them and indicated that they would follow. Rethymno was no great distance from Chania, about thirty miles or so, and very old. It was situated on a wide, shallow bay with a beautiful beach. Tom thought Charlie would love it.

After a couple of hours soaking up the sun and a couple of swims, Charlie dried off and got dressed, and they walked arm in arm along the promenade towards the old town and the huge five-hundred-year old Venetian fort.

'I think the time has come to have a bowl of pasta to line the stomach before testing the local wines,' said Tom. 'There are loads of places along all these little streets. Let's go and find somewhere cool.'

They would remember this day for its warmth, simplicity and total relaxation. Lunch was a dream, and afterwards they headed off to find the annual wine celebration. The atmosphere was full of bonhomie, everyone befriending everyone else. They were not particularly impressed with the quality of the wine, but it mattered not. As the afternoon wore on they became somewhat the worse for wear, and all they wanted to do was to find a cool, quiet corner on the beach to sleep it off. The police officers, bored by the whole procedure and keen to get back to Chania, suggested that, because Tom had been drinking, they should take them both back in the police car. They would get colleagues to collect the car and bring it back later.

'Brilliant idea,' said Tom. 'Thank you very much.'

Charlie fell asleep in the back almost before they had left the town. This gave Tom a chance to look at her resting and think about their relationship. She looked simply gorgeous, and he reflected how lucky he was that she had fallen for him. Why hadn't he seen her this way at university? He had joked when they went to the Knossos Museum that she looked like Queen Europa, but it was true. The vision of her sitting astride a big white bull launching into the waves was almost too much to comprehend.

They arrived back at the Chania house just after four. Charlie had to be woken, and in her semi-conscious state she had to be helped through the door and up to bed. He whispered in her ear, 'I'll wake you in an hour or two. Sweet dreams! Don't forget that Nikos and Melissa are coming round tonight with Maria to tell us the rest of their story.'

At the same time as Tom and Charlie were being driven back to Chania, the Rethymno police were bringing Tom's car back to their house. They had just passed the town of Georgioupoli when they were overtaken by a speeding 4 x 4 which rammed them in the side, pushing the car off the road and severely injuring one of the policemen. Later in the day, the 4 x 4 was found abandoned just outside Souda, with no indication as to who had taken it or why it had happened. It had apparently been hired the day before by some tourists, and the constabulary were following it up.

Two local police officers called round just after six to tell Tom about his car and ask whether anyone knew they had decided to go to Rethymno, and why they might have been targeted. Apart from Maria and her family and their regular police escort, George and Stathi, he could think of no one. The officers thanked him and advised Tom that they would tell their guards to be doubly vigilant; he advised them to do the same. This concerned Tom, and he thought he ought to tell his father, not forgetting the fact that there was a good chance that their car had been written off.

'Hi Dad. It's Tom. Can you talk?'

'Are you OK, son? You sound worried. What's wrong?'

'Well, it was really strange. Charlie and I went to Rethymno to the wine festival and because I had had a bit of wine, our police escort offered to drive us back to Chania whilst two officers from Rethymno took our car back to our house. But on the way, our car was rammed and both police officers were hurt, one seriously. Chania police have told us it looked like a deliberate attempt to damage the car and injure the passengers. Of course, if I hadn't had a bit to drink, that could have been us.'

There was a pause before Neville responded. 'Are you sure you're happy to continue your stay?' he asked. 'It seems a bit odd I must say. Why would someone want to target you? Do you get the impression that the police are taking the matter seriously?'

'Yes, they are. It did get me thinking I must say, but yes Dad, I think we're OK to stay. I'll talk it through with Charlie when she wakes up.

'Well, if you're sure,' said his father. Tom could tell by his tone of voice that he was not convinced, but Neville decided to leave it there for now.

'We've got Nikos and Melissa coming around again tonight and Maria is cooking us all a Cretan banquet,' said Tom. 'It should be good.'

CHAPTER 32

The Papadakis story continued

❧

'Hello, Nikos. Come on in. Welcome, Maria and Melissa,' said Tom. 'Charlie is just upstairs . We've been out all day at the wine festival.'

'Charlie does not need make-up,' said Maria. 'She's beautiful as she is.'

'Have you had a good day in Rethymno?' asked Nikos.

'Well, the visit to the town was fabulous, but we had a bit of an adventure on the way back.' Tom told him about what had happened, playing it down a bit, as Charlie had been asleep when the police had called.

'You didn't tell me about that, Tom,' said an anxious Charlie.

'You were fast asleep, and they only left shortly before our guests arrived. We'll talk about it a little later if that's OK.'

Sensing that Tom didn't want to make a meal of it, Nikos just said, 'Well I hope the police find out what it was all about quickly. Not a pleasant thing to happen.'

'Can I get you something to drink? Beer, wine, water?' Charlie asked, still looking a little sleepy.

'You've caught the sun today,' said Melissa. 'It will be the wind. Crete is known for it and on a hot day, it can easily catch you out.'

'As I found out!' Charlie said, smiling.

Maria had been to the house earlier and prepared a wonderful feast of true Cretan food.

'I think we should eat first,' said Tom. 'I've had a fair bit of local wine, so I need something to line the stomach. And the smell from the kitchen is extremely enticing!'

After the meal, they sat in the lounge. Nikos said. 'Where did we get to?'

'You were telling us about your grandfather Ioannis and his son Theodore being taken away,' Tom reminded him.

'Ah, yes. You may remember I told you about a shepherd called Aegeus who lived up in the mountains with his family and flocks. He helped the British soldiers set themselves up in a cave and provided them with lots of food and clothing. So did many of the villagers, but it was a long walk up from the village. You remember me mentioning Christina, Theodore's sister? She became a runner, taking messages to the resistance and the isolated British army units. She became very friendly with one of the soldiers. Not long after Ioannis and Theodore had been taken away, they came back on one of their days off and the whole family packed up what they could carry and disappeared up into the hills and into hiding. When they didn't report back to the labour battalion, the Germans came looking for them in Manolas and in the area surrounding the village. That was when they found Aegeus, who had been reported to them by an informer as a member of the resistance. They tried to take his bull and he went crazy. He killed two of them with his bare hands before he was clubbed and taken prisoner. But for that the village paid a terrible price.'

He paused for a moment, obviously in some emotional discomfort. He sipped his beer and continued, 'The Wehrmacht arrived in numbers. They surrounded Manolas and gathered the whole community in the square. They selected twenty people they wanted to execute, then lined them up and shot them by firing squad. Then they looted every house, taking food, jewellery and animals. Although Aegeus lived up in the mountains, the nearest village to where he lived was Manolas, and that was enough for them. So twenty villagers were murdered in cold blood. Not long after, there was an attack by British soldiers on an army compound in the village with the help of some of the villagers. There were many deaths of German soldiers, so the Germans came back again and shot as many as they could find, setting fire to the whole village – something Cretans would never forget. This year is the seventy-fifth anniversary, so feelings will be running high.'

'That's truly terrible,' said Tom. 'Thank goodness your family escaped to the mountains in time.'

'Nikos still feels the pain today, as you can see,' said Melissa, taking his hand in hers. 'Although his grandparents survived the war, they were never the same apparently. And their daughter Christina, well that's another story for another day.'

As they were leaving after an enlightening and emotional evening, Tom said to Nikos, 'I spoke to my father earlier about the killing of the German tourist and he told me that the night club bouncer who had been detained on suspicion of involvement had told the police that Hercules was the murderer. But he wouldn't tell them anything else. My father asked if that meant anything to you?'

'Well, during the war the shepherd I mentioned called Aegeus thought he was the reincarnation of Hercules because of his massive size and strength. My grandfather visited his home high up in the mountains and saw many items to do with Hercules, including a full-size bust. He and Costas, the leader of the Manolas resistance cell, thought it was odd, but then Hercules is a hero to many Cretan people, even if he's a mythological figure. But that was seventy-five years ago. I can't think of anything or anyone relevant to that name today.'

'Thank you, Nikos,' said Tom. 'I think it was just on the off-chance that you may have known something. And thank you Maria for cooking us such a lovely meal. You will make someone a wonderful wife one day.'

He realised afterwards that this was a tactless remark, knowing what her feelings were for him. He just wanted to call her back and say sorry, but the moment was not right. He knew that Charlie would take him to task over it.

CHAPTER 33

The SOE arrives, 1941

It was eerily quiet, with just the gentle sound of the lapping of waves on the shore. A single beam of light shone for a couple of seconds from up in the hills, pointing out to sea, then nothing. A minute or so later, it was repeated. This brought a response; the sound of an engine from a small craft approaching the bay. It was a Cretan caique, identified by its two sails on a single mast, a common type of vessel in the Greek islands.

A light appeared again and three men appeared coming down from the hill to the beach, two Cretan resistance fighters and a British officer. There were regular German patrols on mules on the south coast of Crete, so this small bay was chosen as it was thought to be almost impossible to access from the surrounding countryside unless you were familiar with the area. The two Cretan fighters were local, so they knew exactly how to get to and from the beach without attracting any attention. A small dinghy was launched from the caique and four men came ashore. It then returned and equipment was loaded onto the dinghy to be unloaded onto the beach. There was much joy from the Cretans, who gave over-excited kisses on both cheeks in greeting, as this was the first time armed SOE (Special Operations Executive) agents had been sent to Crete. They were greeted by Lieutenant Penrose, who shook them warmly by the hand, introducing them to Yiannis Pappas and Georgias Koladis who had accompanied him down to the beach.

'These men will take you up to a monastery where the Abbot is very friendly,' Penrose said. 'They've prepared a room deep underground for you to use as a base. You will then be introduced to the resistance leaders in the area. There's a mule to carry the supplies – they just have to make sure he doesn't start bellowing. Good luck to you all. I'm going back to Mersa Matruh on the caique which brought you here.'

'Bon voyage,' they said to Penrose as they headed quietly off the beach and up the cliff-side.

It was tough going, the mule stumbling with every other step, but they hit it with a stick to keep it focused on the job in hand. It was carrying a heavy load of weapons, ammunition and medical supplies, but these animals seemed capable of carrying vast loads. Yiannis and Georgias spoke no English, but the SOE officers all had a smattering of Greek, so communication was possible, although it was not easy because of the men's different dialects.

After half an hour, they rested. There was a small stream

trickling down the hillside towards the beach, and from it they were able to top up their water bottles. Everyone in the party smoked, so Yiannis showed them how to hide the glow in case there was a German sentry up on the hill.

The four men were all British SOE agents, dressed in typical dark Cretan clothing with heavy moustaches and turbans on their heads. Their mission was to co-ordinate activity against the occupiers with local resistance groups in the White Mountains. Another part of their brief was to link up with any British and Commonwealth soldiers who had opted to stay behind. They had been told that there were at least two established resistance groups in the White Mountains, and these were to be their first targets.

The trek up to the monastery, with Georgias leading the way, ended just before daylight. One of the SOE officers, Captain Andrew Parker, asked why the monastery was so high up in the mountain. Georgias said with a broad smile, 'to be nearer to God!' The building was of considerable size and had been founded originally in the fifteenth century. The outer walls of the square compound contained the fathers' accommodation, with windows looking inward to the central courtyard where the church was located.

To ensure that their arrival was as discreet as possible, Yiannis led them to a shepherds' croft in a neighbouring olive grove. In the floor was a hidden hatch which opened up to reveal a secret tunnel which led directly to a basement of the monastery. Clambering down into the tunnel with all the equipment was a major challenge, especially without making a lot of noise.

Closing the hatch behind them, they entered a narrow, dark passage with steps leading down to a secret hiding place well away from the resident fathers. It was cold and damp in the room, even though it was the height of summer, but they felt reassured that the Germans would never find them, unless they were betrayed by one of the fathers or a member of the resistance.

On the orders of the Abbot a fire had been lit in the centre of the floor to give them some warmth and for cooking, but the smoke had to exit somewhere. Georgias pointed out to them a narrow opening which led out to the cliff-face and had been used in times of religious persecution. It was here that the smoke would escape. That was fine as long as some bright sentry did not wonder why smoke would appear to be coming out from the side of the cliff.

Georgias and Yiannis left, saying they would return the following day, which would give the men time to rest and settle down. The officer in charge, Captain Andrew Parker of the 11th Hussars, told Yiannis that they must not mention the existence of the hidden men to anyone, but that help was on its way. He was aware that Cretans tended to get very excited and it would be all too easy to inadvertently 'spill the beans'. This mission had been well-planned and was not to be put at risk by someone failing to keep his mouth shut. They assured him that they could be trusted.

When they had left, Andrew said, 'Henry, can you get the radio set up so we can start communicating? We've been told there's a fully trained and experienced operator hiding in the mountains called Simms and he must be one of the first we contact. He's broadcast a couple of times at around nine in the morning, so that should be a good time to make a connection. It's almost that now, so we'll wait until tomorrow. He will be crucial. Right, let's get something to eat, then we can crash out and get some sleep.'

They were woken by the sound of gunfire in the middle of the afternoon and realised that it was coming from the escape opening in the side of the cliff. Parker crept down with his binoculars and looked out to sea, where he spotted a caique being strafed by a Messerschmidt 109. On the face of it, it looked like an innocent boat and was not returning fire, but the fighter had set it ablaze and there was nothing Parker could do but watch. Two fishermen jumped into the water, but they were a long way from shore and there was little chance that they would survive.

Returning to their sanctuary, he realised that they had not eaten since the night before on the boat. He explained to the others what the gunfire was all about and suggested that they should relight the fire and get the beans and bully beef heated up.

It was early evening by the time they had got the weapons and ammo sorted ready for the following day. Parker hoped that someone would be there early to get things rolling. The bells in the monastery were ringing for evening prayers, a comforting sound. They lit a candle and settled down for the night.

The resistance in the early days following the invasion

was somewhat chaotic, with communist and non-communist factions vying for supremacy. The resistance, formed after the invasion, had brought together islanders of all political persuasions to help the population by boosting morale, supplying information and distributing food, which was in increasingly short supply. They were also there to do what they could to undertake operations against the Germans. But personalities and egos were beginning to come to the fore, and sadly some individuals were beginning to put their personal attitudes and feelings above the more important issue of helping their fellow Cretans.

The Cretan resistance worked closely with the British almost from day one, and the British formed many cells throughout the island, mainly in the mountains. Attached to these cells were Cretans who tended initially not to have any involvement with the main resistance organisations, but worked closely with British SOE agents. One such cell was the Manolas group led by Costas and helped by Aegeus the shepherd and the Papadakis family.

Like his sister Christina, Theodore had become a runner between the resistance groups. They often carried messages over vast distances in one of the most mountainous regions in Europe. Their parents were obviously nervous about the risks involved, but were hugely proud of what they were doing. Manolas, being equidistant from the coast at Chania and the south coast of the island, become a pivotal location for the distribution of messages. Ioannis and Katina had made the decision to hide out in the hills, not far from where

Aegeus the shepherd lived. Costas brought the messages from Manolas to the Papadakis family. They then set off on their tasks. Very young and fit, they covered hundreds of miles with only the occasional scare from the Germans. Heading up into the mountains was dangerous territory for the invader, who had decided that there was a serious risk of ambush from the andartes, so they would only venture out in numbers. This made it easier for Christina and Theodore to spot the enemy.

Christina arrived at the hiding place in the monastery an hour after sunrise with instructions from Georgias and Yiannis to guide the SOE officers to the cave where Sergeant Bob Neame and his group were in hiding. Captain Parker was astonished that this slight and attractive young lady with the darkest eyes he had ever seen had run over twenty-five miles without breaking a sweat.

'Please follow me, just bring your light weapons and leave everything else here,' he said. My instructions are for just the senior officer and his assistant. The others are to stay behind.'

Parker and Lieutenant Henry Morris introduced themselves. Christina acknowledged them with a smile, and they told the two remaining SOE officers not to attempt to make contact by radio as they would get there in the next couple of hours. Strapping on their pistols, they filled their water bottles and set off, trying hard to keep up with their extraordinarily fit guide.

CHAPTER 34

Chania, 2016

೪

It was after ten o'clock when Nikos, Melissa and Maria left. Tom and Charlie sat back with a glass of wine, thinking about everything Nikos had said.

'Well,' said Tom. 'After hearing that story, I'm not sure about going to Manolas. There'll be so much sadness there. On the other hand, Maria's parents will be upset if we don't. I've got tomorrow mapped out, so maybe we'll do Manolas the day after if that's when they are holding the seventy-fifth anniversary remembrance. It will mean a lot to the Papadakis family. Are you OK with that?'

'Sure,' Charlie said. 'You know, weren't at your best with that remark to Maria. You know what she feels for you.'

'I know,' he replied. 'It was thoughtless. I'll apologise and make it up her.'

'Not too affectionately, I trust,' she said. 'Anyway what's on the agenda for tomorrow?'

'Are you OK to go on with the holiday? I felt that that strange incident unsettled you a bit.'

'Yes, I think it did.'

'You must say if you would rather pack it in. I really would understand.'

'We have the police looking after us, so I'm sure it will be fine.'

'OK,' said Tom. 'I quite like the idea of going to somewhere where we could have the place entirely to ourselves. Kastelli on the far west coast has a couple of beaches near the town where we can swim undisturbed. And if we get fed up with that, there are some thousand-year-old ruins close by. Our new hire car should be here in the morning. Sound good?'

At that moment Tom's phone rang. It was his father.

'Hi Tom,' said Neville, 'I've been in touch with our Consul in Heraklion just to confirm that the police are taking the matter of your car seriously. They're convinced it was deliberate, but they have no idea why it was done. So now there are two unexplained happenings which are bound to give us, and you, some concerns. Did you ask Charlie what she thought?'

'Yes, I did Dad. She's a little nervous, but she wants to carry on. I think if the police weren't here to look after us it would be a different story. By the way, I did mention the Hercules issue to Nikos, but apart from some connection during the last war, there was nothing to help.'

'OK son, thanks for that. But if at any time you want to change your mind, just let me know and I'll get the arrangements made.'

Tom turned back to Charlie and told her what Neville had said. 'Still happy with the decision to stay?'

'As long as I can go skinny dipping again,' she said. 'I've always wanted to do it and this holiday has been the perfect setting.'

He laughed. 'Two things to worry about there,' he said. 'One, the police will be watching, and two there are crabs here called vagina crabs. Guess where they might end up?'

'What? You are kidding me!' she said.

'Yes, I am actually.'

She leapt across the settee and hit him playfully with a cushion before kissing him passionately on the lips.

'Enough of that,' he said. 'We've got clearing up to do. And wear something under the apron, not like the other night!'

'Oh dear. You're becoming such a bore!'

CHAPTER 35

Interrogation, Manolas, 1941

Ⓢ

The moans from the cellar were horrifying. Some of the villagers had been hearing them on and off for two days. Aegeus had been brought down from the mountains in chains by four men and had been locked in the cellar under the Mayor's house. A patrol had entered his farm and had started killing and taking his life-stock. Aegeus had gone berserk and killed two German soldiers with his bare hands before at least half a dozen more jumped on him, pinning him to the ground. They clapped him in irons and it was certain that he would be executed, but the Wehrmacht wanted to get any information out of him before he met his end. He had been secured to a table flat on his back with leather straps around his neck, body, arms and legs – eight in all. Realising just how strong he was, they broke his arms and legs with an iron bar. But even with these injuries and the massive pain which went with it, he was still refusing to give in.

After two days during which they had failed to elicit a single word from him, it was obvious that they would get nothing from him, and they did not yet have a 'truth drug' in their armoury, so the Captain decided to abandon the interrogation and execute Aegeus in the centre of what was left of the village after German engineers had blown most of it up. All the remaining residents and others from the neighbouring countryside were ordered to watch the execution as a warning. Aegeus was tied to the trunk of an old olive tree. He was unable to stand, so they tied him by his head, chest and legs. His wounds were horrendous, and bones were sticking out of the flesh.

But his courage was undimmed. He raised his great head as the firing squad levelled their rifles and shouted with all his might, 'I am Hercules, hero of the Cretan people. You have broken my body, but never my mind. I will live on to haunt you for the rest of your lives!'

And with that, eight rifles each fired a single shot.

News of Aegeus' terrible death reached Neame in the cave. He had been a great friend to the British soldiers and they wanted to revenge the execution. But they would do it at the right time; there was no point in rushing in and risking their own and other lives in the process. That time would be come soon.

CHAPTER 36

To the rescue, June 1941

❧

Although it was still early in the morning, the temperature was already heading towards twenty-five degrees. Morris and Parker were exhausted just trying to keep up with Christina as they headed for the cave. Even by army standards, they were not used to walking at such a fast pace over rough ground such as this, and it was very hilly.

Christina asked them to stay low. She gave the sign as they approached and Fletcher, who was on lookout, waved them in. Neame came out of the cave to welcome them. He felt that for the first time in quite a few days something positive was being done about taking on the might of the Wehrmacht. The responsibility he had felt since assuming command of the group weighed heavily on his shoulders, but now at least he could share it a little with these officers. After all, he was only an NCO.

Parker sat on the hay-covered floor and was offered some water.

'Thank you. I need it after that. Christina is obviously an extremely fit young woman and she set quite a pace. Now, I am Captain Andrew Parker of the Hussars and this is Lieutenant Henry Morris, Black Watch. We're pleased to meet you Sergeant. Well done for keeping this group together after being left behind. The evacuation was a bit of a shambles.'

Neame did not wish to get into a debate with an officer over what had gone wrong. 'Welcome to our humble abode, sir,' he said. 'Christina has been our main contact with the group in the village of Manolas. But she also carries messages as a runner to other resistance groups in the White Mountains. So does her brother, Theodore. Sadly, we have lost our other main contact, a shepherd called Aegeus. He killed two German soldiers and in revenge the Wehrmacht shot many of the residents and blew up much of the village. I'm afraid he was tortured and executed. As far as we know he gave nothing away. Our W/T operator Simms managed to make contact with North Africa to explain our position here. I presume that's why you have come to this part of the island.'

'Yes, we were informed that there was a unit in this area. Our job is to get the groups working together to create difficulties for the Germans and to keep their men tied up here so they can't make a nuisance of themselves elsewhere,' said Parker with a wry smile. 'What do you know about local guerrilla groups? Are there any other British troops about here?'

'To be honest, the best person to ask is Christina,' Neame replied. 'She regularly gets around the mountains, and with Costas, the local mayor, they know just about everything there is to know. Shall I ask her to come in?'

Christina was sitting on a rock with Fletcher when Neame asked her to join the men.

'Please sit down, Christina. How is your English?' Parker asked.

'Is OK I think,' she replied. 'It has helped much to meet with Sergeant Neame and his men.'

'What can you tell us about the Cretan resistance groups in this area?'

'There are three close to our village of Manolas. They are on, how you say, a plateau and high up in mountain. At Omalos, Samaria and Leivada. I will not give you names but I will take you there when safe to go.'

'Thank you, Christina. But perhaps you could please walk a little slower next time!' He smiled. 'Sergeant Neame mentioned Costas, should he accompany us as well?'

'Sorry, what is accompany?' she asked.

'Oh, sorry. Come with us.'

'Yes, I can arrange. He will be pleased you here.'

Turning to Neame, he said. 'I'm sure you will be delighted to know that there is a job for you. We have been told that there are around twenty of our soldiers being held captive in a compound near Manolas. They would be very useful to us if we could get them released before they are taken to Chania for shipment to prisoner-of-war camps in Greece. But we want this undertaken quickly, so, Sergeant, please leave a few at the cave including Simms, and hit this compound early one morning in the next couple of days when the Germans are half asleep. Then we will begin organising some sabotage with the help of our Cretan friends. You OK with that?'

'Can't wait sir. It's been difficult for all of us sitting here doing nothing but eating, sleeping and cleaning and re-cleaning our weapons. The men will be very keen.'

'Right then,' Parker said. 'Christina, do you have a good map of the area?'

'Not with me. If I found with one, the Germans will suspect me. I will ask my brother Theodore to bring one. He is good boy. We are living in hiding with our parents in mountains not far from here. My father escaped from a forced labour camp, so we had to leave village quick. After I speak to him, I will go with Costas to the other villages and tell them you here to arrange meet with all three together. Better that way as the PMK, the name they call themselves, have many who wish to lead, if you understand. Much politics. You will tell them and they will listen. They are good people who want to help with food and information for the people but the war against the German soldier needs British to lead.'

'We understand, Christina, and thank you. We'll return to the monastery and wait for you to let us know when you've arranged the meeting,' said Parker. He was deeply impressed by the way she seemed to be in control of the situation. Her knowledge and her English were going to be invaluable.

'Sergeant, we'll wait here with you until the map appears to discuss the action plan.'

'OK sir. Do you mind if Christina and I have a private chat before she leaves?'

'Of course not. We'll get something to eat. We brought a few provisions with us from the monastery which we can share round. How have you managed so far?'

'Well, Aegeus, the shepherd who was executed, used to bring us supplies, but now we have to rely on the villagers for help. Is there any chance of supplies from Africa by plane or boat?'

'They're being organised as we speak and Simms should receive a message soon. Weapons and ammunition will also be on their way, as well as medical supplies. The resistance will be needing some as well as you.'

Neame took Christina by the arm and walked up the hill away from the cave. Parker watched them in mild surprise.

'Something going on with those two, Corporal?' he asked.

'Not for me to say sir,' was Weeks' reply.

Once Neame and Christina were out of sight, she lay back on a rock. 'I do not want problem with us and your men but I do want to be with you, Bob,' she said. 'But it is so difficult with all these people to see us. I cannot relax and enjoy. Can you forgive me if we wait? I want you to be my first, and my last.' She took his hand and placed it high up between her legs. 'Can you feel how much I want you, Bob?' she said.

'More than you will ever know, but as you say we must wait. This is not the place or the right time, but the time will come, and soon.' They began kissing passionately, but were interrupted by the sound of approaching footsteps and a discreet cough.

High up in the sky, an eagle was circling looking for movement on the mountainside. Lunch was all it had on its mind.

When Theodore arrived later that afternoon with the map, Parker took Neame aside. 'You could say it's none of my business, but it is when men's lives are at risk,' he said. 'Sergeant, you need to have your mind totally on the job. I do understand that when you're in the presence of a pretty young woman and you're a long way from home, you may get distracted, but it's important to keep your mind on what you're here for. Got it?'

'Yes, sir,' replied Neame. 'As you say it's tough, but I will always do my job, one hundred percent and nothing less. We have already made some important friendships with the Cretan people, and that's crucial to our success here. This girl just happens to be part of it, a very important part. There's no one in the resistance who knows what she knows. We need her.'

Neame and members of his team, plus others who had subsequently joined, left the cave just as first light was lifting the early darkness. Yiannis had come to act as their guide, taking them down the mountain towards Manolas. Neame followed him, with Corporal Weeks bringing up the rear. At five-thirty it was just about light, with a mist still hanging over the mountain top. They had a march of around an hour ahead of them, all downhill over rocky paths. There were sixteen of them, lightly armed, although Lance Corporal Butler was carrying a Bren gun with Fraser as his number two. Neame carried four grenades and a sidearm. The rest had their .303 Lee-Enfields and bayonets. Ammunition was in good supply, thanks to their action in storing plenty of it at the church on the way to the attempted evacuation.

It was remarkably quiet. They could hear the distant sound of the bleating of goats and sheep up on the hillside, disturbed by the soldiers as they passed, but everywhere else was silent. There was a pall of smoke ahead of them, but no clues as to what was creating it.

They passed some cottages which were obviously occupied, with a few sheep, goats and chickens in evidence. They steered clear of any larger habitation and Theodore's map proving to be invaluable, even though the date on it was 1935 and it bore the stamp of the local school.

As they came out of an olive grove, they hid behind a low stone wall to survey the scene in front of them. Neame looked through his binoculars at the farm buildings where he had been told that the men were being held, but he could see no sign of them. He signalled to Stevens to creep forward to find out what was going on. There was sign of life in the compound with some Germans going about their daily ablutions, but where were the men being held?

This compound was a former farm, belonging to the Mayor's house in Manolas where the Oberleutnant and his staff were living. Here there was a small platoon from the Bavarian Mountain Regiment, along with their mechanised transport and a few mules. Stevens managed to crawl forward to a point where he could see the main farmhouse and some ancillary buildings without giving away his position. There was a dilapidated barn to the rear and he observed a German sentry standing outside, indicating that this could be where the British soldiers were being held.

He withdrew, keeping himself as low as he could go. At one point a German lorry came down the road from the village towards the compound. Stevens kept absolutely still, thinking the truck had come to pick up the prisoners. Whilst the risen dust from the lorry was still floating in the air, he made a hasty retreat back to where Neame and the group were waiting.

'Sarge,' he said quietly, 'I'm sure the lads are being held in the barn at the rear, but that truck has come to collect them I think.'

'How many Germans do you think are there?' Neame asked.

'Probably about twenty, maybe a few more.'

Turning to the machine gunner, Neame said, 'Butler, set up the Bren in the gateway of the stone wall. That will cover anyone coming at us from the compound entrance. Gwinnett and Todd, you go to the left, Fletcher and Stevens to the right – deal with the sentry and get the prisoners out. I'll go forward with Baird. The key is to get the men away quickly up the hill under covering fire. Baird, that's your job. You know the way. Butler, only open fire when you know that we have been spotted. Right, any questions?'

The men split up, running low. Fletcher and Stevens reached the barn without being seen by the sentry, and Fletcher despatched him silently with a knife. As they opened the barn door, Stevens shot in and signalled to the prisoners, who were all sitting cross-legged on the floor, to follow him. Taken completely by surprise, they did what they were told.

Meanwhile Neame had taken up position just outside what had been the cookhouse, where most of the Germans were tucking into breakfast. Covered by Baird, he threw two grenades in and slammed the door shut. As the prisoners came pouring out of the door a burst of rifle fire came from the far side of the farmhouse, and Butler immediately opened fire with the Bren gun.

Baird yelled, 'This way, and be quick about it!'

They ran for their lives, with bullets flying everywhere. Stevens went down clutching his leg. 'I'm hit!' he shouted, grimacing with pain.

Neame ran up to him with Baird and they grabbed him by the upper arms and lifted him between them. Then they ran as fast as they could back up the hill. Sweating profusely, they passed one of the prisoners, who was lying on the ground, shot through the throat. The Bren gun was still giving covering fire, but Gwinnett and Todd were now giving crossfire, allowing Butler a brief opportunity to withdraw. When they were confident that Butler had left with the precious Bren gun, they stopped firing and retired themselves.

Almost immediately, Todd fell with a bullet in the back. Gwinnett, realising that his partner was badly hurt grabbed his rifle and ran at a zigzag up the path, followed by Weeks, who was covering their withdrawal. Butler continued to pour fire down over Weeks's head into a few pursuing Germans. He saw that the main building in the compound was ablaze from Neame's grenades.

Although totally exhausted from the climb, the men kept going. It had taken an hour to get down to the compound, but it was going to take much longer to get back to the cave, because of the steep ascent and the need to carry Stevens, who was in great pain. But the group was now nearly forty strong, and some of the rescued British soldiers took it in turns to carry him. It was with relief that they heard that some Cretans had attacked those Germans who had followed them up, and not only stopped them but inflicted some casualties.

Neame knew the Germans would not take this lying down. They would send spotter planes up to locate the retreating Brits and gather forces to hunt them down. They would now start taking the Cretan resistance seriously, and more reprisals were inevitable. The German Commander had publicly stated that ten Cretan citizens would be executed for every dead German. But he knew that would not stop the Cretans killing this hated and aggressive enemy. They would take what the Germans threw at them, but they would hit them back just as hard, without warning.

As they approached the cave, Corporal Weeks ran forward to alert those inside. He ordered them to cover the returning party whilst they got their breath back and Stevens could be attended to. They were reasonably confident that they had shaken off the Germans following them, but could not afford any mistakes. The cave was plenty big enough for their enlarged party, and the prisoners were delighted to be out of German hands but worrying what would happen to them next. The enemy would guess roughly the direction they had taken, but the Cretan resistance would certainly distract them for the time being.

'Right,' said Neame. 'We have some new members of the team who need to be looked after following what they've been through. But above all, we must keep our heads down for a while. No fires. No one outside unless essential, and only in the dark. It's vital to keep the cave entrance covered with branches so it won't be seen from the air. There are many of us now in the cave, so those who have been rescued will need to make their way with Yiannis to the monastery once they've rested up for a while. If Christina comes, she must take a message to Parker at the monastery about the firefight and the success in rescuing the captives, and to expect them tomorrow. I feel that Costas may be visiting us soon, as I'm sure it was his men who helped us out. Now, let's see how Stevens is.'

Dark came and all was quiet. Weeks was taking responsibility for the watch, as he could see that Neame was all in. He had led a textbook raid and to come away with only two casualties and one prisoner killed was almost a miracle. On top of that, they seemed to have killed around ten of the enemy.

'Simms, are you able to contact the monastery?' said Weeks. 'I would rather keep radio messaging to a minimum because the Germans will be using tracking devices, but we may have to if Christina doesn't arrive.'

'Yes Corp, I can. But I'll await your instructions.'

At around ten o'clock, a familiar whistle was heard. Fraser, who was on point duty a little way down the hill, called out 'Halt! Step forward and identify.' He kept his .303 pointing at the sound, but was soon relieved to sat that it was Christina hurrying up the path.

'Hello Christina. Good to see you,' Fletcher said.

'Is Bob OK?' she asked.

'Yes he's fine, but he's dead to the world.'

'What does that mean – he is hurt?' She looked very concerned.

'No, just an expression. He got back so tired that he went straight to sleep. He was worn out.'

A smile of relief spread over her face. She pushed the bushes aside and went into the cave. She was met by Weeks.

'How is Bob?' she asked.

'He's tired out, so we'd better leave him till later. He did say that if you came, could you go to the monastery and tell Captain Parker that the mission was a success? Tell them one prisoner was killed and two of our men were injured, one believed to have died. They released twenty-three prisoners from captivity, and they are now here and need to be moved on, so they'll be arriving tomorrow with Yiannis. And he wants me to tell you that he was very grateful for the help from the resistance. Were they from Costa's group?'

'Yes, but they had two men wounded, and I'm sorry to say that they were executed by the Germans. A sad day, but they were pleased to have killed five. They worry now what the Germans will do.' She looked at Neame, sound asleep. 'I will go now straight away to the monastery,' she added.

CHAPTER 37

The resistance takes shape, 1941

As soon as the German forces arrived in Crete, initial planning meetings began to take place all over the island to put resistance groups in place. Patriotic Front, National Liberation Front, communists, democratic republicans, monarchists – groups were formed by all of them, and in the coming days, personalities started to come to the fore. It was obvious from the outset that no single leading figure would be accepted throughout the entire island. The Cretan people had taken a hard knock, and whilst they had given the intruders a bloody nose, the main initial reason for setting up the resistance groups was to support the people under occupation.

It was obvious from the first few weeks that a time of great deprivation was coming. Food was already being taken away from the mouths of the Cretan people by the occupying army. Here the people in the mountains would become vitally important, as the Germans did not approach this part of the island in the early days with any degree of confidence. It was dangerous territory to the invader. He could deal with the mountains at his leisure, once the coastal regions and the major towns and cities had been secured and under tight control. What the Cretan people had done to the invading army on the first day would not be forgotten in a hurry.

Communication with the Allied forces in Egypt and North Africa was quickly established. Allied soldiers who had been left behind liaised with the Cretan resistance groups on the island, who then both contacted members of the SOE who were coming by boat to the southern shores. A bond of trusting friendship was built up between British and Cretan people, one which led to one of the closest guerrilla partnerships of World War Two.

It was not long before a system of runners was established throughout the island, so that the British were well informed as to what was being planned. Although there were occasional acts of independent sabotage, they were by and large well co-ordinated. And when large supplies of weapons and ammunition started to arrive by boat and by airdrop, the Cretan fighters became a force to be reckoned with. They were quite content to be led by British officers. Harassing the enemy in order to contain large numbers of German soldiers on the island was one of the principle objectives.

The attack by Neame's unit on the compound at Manolas was one of the first acts of aggression after the initial landings. A direct result was the execution of five innocent men from the village. A notice was posted by the Germans that should there be any further attacks on German soldiers, dire consequences would occur. Irrespective that these acts were in contravention of the Geneva Convention and constituted a war crime, they became common practice by the Wehrmacht all over the island. They instigated a scorched earth policy, burning and destroying towns, villages and religious establishments. Even monasteries were looted and ransacked. Everyday life became intolerable. Fear, hunger, poverty and lack of freedom of movement tormented the people. Basic foodstuffs were almost impossible to afford, particularly in urban areas. But the Cretan people were strong, mentally and physically. Instead of kow-towing to the Germans, many took to the mountains, living in appalling conditions. Here they were safer and stronger because the Germans feared what might happen to them if they were found by these isolated pockets of armed civilians, with the help of the British. Word soon got around that should any of the invaders be captured, they could expect no mercy.

Christina returned to the cave from the monastery with Morris and Parker following, this time at a slightly gentler pace. They wanted to know all the details of the action to release the British prisoners. There was now a fairly good size unit which would soon be on its way off the island by boat to North Africa. They were urgently needed elsewhere. None of Neame's platoon opted to go with them. Stevens was in better shape, thanks to medication which the SOE officers had brought to the island. It was a clean wound, but he would have to stay off the leg for a couple of weeks.

'That was a first-class operation, Sergeant,' said Captain Parker. 'Well done. We've advised Cairo of the success of the mission and they're sending a gunboat to pick up the prisoners. I have recommended to headquarters that you receive some recognition for your leadership, but quite how that will be seen when you are here in an unofficial capacity remains open to question. I understand that your men have decided to stay, which off the record I think is commendable. I did include in my report how well the Cretan people seem to value working with the British. In the meantime, I recommend that you don't stay too long in one place, as you'll be discovered sooner or later. We'll work with you and other groups to co-ordinate future operations. Please be ready to move Sergeant, just in case Jerry gets a whiff of where you are. Ask Christina if she would lead us back to the monastery. That will remain our base for the foreseeable future. It's not so easy to find your way when you don't know the terrain, so in the dark she will be invaluable.'

'Did you hear what the Captain said?' Neame asked Christina.

'Yes, I did, and of course I will guide them back. Yiannis left some time ago.'

When they were out of earshot of the others, Christina said, 'I am so proud of you Bob, for what you did. It has given Manolas some hope and that is so valuable at this time. It has caused the village to scatter, but our people will forever value your friendship to us, and me in particular. I hope this doesn't mean you will be leaving.' She was looking tearful. 'My parents are suffering severe hardships, my brother is not well and you are the one bright part of my life. If you must move camp, make sure you find me again.' She discreetly grasped his hand, holding it tight.

'Don't worry Christina. I will find you wherever you are,' he replied. 'I would love to stay here forever.'

'Do you really mean that?' She looked up into his eyes.

'Yes. Yes, I do.'

The following day, Neame decided that they should leave the cave. The decision was made with some regret, as they felt safe and warm there, but it was dangerous. They knew the Germans were scouring the countryside for them, and there was always a danger that someone would let the cat out of the bag. The cave brought back memories of Aegeus who had found it for them, but it was time to move on.

Before Christina left for the monastery, Neame had asked her to ask Georgias or Yiannis to suggest another cave at least an hour's walk away, and Yiannis had come early to guide them to one. He asked Yiannis to tell Christina and Costas where they were heading, but no one else. The walk was hazardous, and they had to keep a wary eye open for spotter aircraft and locals wherever they could. The Germans were expert in getting information out of people they caught.

The men took it in turns to carry Stevens on a hand-made stretcher. He was on the mend and had opted to stay, rather than go with the others. Simms and Butler also needed help

carrying the heavy radio equipment and the Bren. This was
when they needed a mule. Yiannis did a superb job, not only
of leading them but in helping wherever he could. It took
quite a time, stopping to rest and take in water. It was very
hot again, with no let-up and very little shelter. Any trees
on the mountainside tended to be small, with little foliage,
and they were constantly on edge and on the look-out for the
dreaded German spotter plane.

It was mid-afternoon when Yiannis took them off the
beaten track, sliding down an escarpment where a large
aperture opened up. Neame's first thought was that this was
perfect. With brushwood over the entrance, it would never
be seen from the ground or the air. It was slightly hazardous
getting Stevens down on the stretcher and unloading all the
equipment from the slope into what was a huge cave, but
once there it soon became their new home.

Yiannis got ready to leave, saying he had been told that
there was a small group of soldiers on the run and he would
bring them the following day. Neame thought they would be
most welcome, but he had heard that there were Germans
about dressed as English soldiers, so they would need to be
checked out carefully. Yiannis said that he would bring food,
wine and cigarettes at the same time.

Meanwhile more SOE officers were starting to arrive from
North Africa, swelling the numbers ready to take the war with
the Cretan resistance to the enemy. Additionally, seventeen
more British Commonwealth soldiers had been found by
civilians sheltering in the mountains and sent with Yiannis

to Neame's group, with a few going to the monastery. They all checked out. This was just the start. Dozens of agents in the Allied secret services were infiltrated onto the island, setting up wireless stations, gathering intelligence and organizing sabotage attacks. The battle was well and truly on.

CHAPTER 38

Kastelli Beach, 2016

❧

Tom heard a toot on the horn and looked out of the window to see that a shiny, brand-new hire car had arrived, courtesy of the police.

'We have taken care of all the paperwork, Mr Richardson,' the police sergeant said. 'Will you please make sure that you stay in sight of the escort car. George and Stathi are with you again today. We still don't know what the incident was all about, but we can't afford to take any chances. Where are you heading for today?'

'We thought we would go to Kastelli, which I believe is off the tourist trail, and then head for Manolas tomorrow,' said Tom.

'Please just keep a look-out,' said the officer.

'Come on Charlie!' Tom shouted up the stairs. 'The car's all loaded and ready to go.' When she arrived in the hallway, she was dressed ready for the sun and sand with no make-up, hair tied back in a bun, a tight T-shirt, shorts and sparkly flip-flops . He kissed her full on the lips and said, 'That's well worth waiting for. Good enough to eat!'

She punched him playfully. 'Thank you, kind sir! It's all yours, you know.'

He didn't know what to say, so he just grabbed her by the hand and headed for the car.

It was a straightforward drive from Chania to Kastelli, the westernmost town in Crete, following an interesting coast road for around an hour. At the southern end of Kisamos Bay, Kastelli, a small, unaffected town with a pretty little harbour, was away from the tourists, which was what they both wanted. They parked up in the square, keeping an eye on the unmarked police car, which parked about fifty metres behind them.

'Do you know what I would like to do?' Charlie said to Tom. 'See that sign over there? It says there are boat trips to Balos Beach. Can we find out what that's all about? I would love to be out on the water and get taken to a quiet unspoilt beach. What do you think?'

'Sounds good to me, but we'll have to tell George what we're doing. Let's find out about it first.'

It was just what Charlie was hoping for. A beautiful old wooden pleasure boat with about twelve people on it was heading for the beach, and it was a boat where she could lie on the fo'c's'le soaking up the sun. They boarded the boat, while George and Stathi were happy to follow in a smaller craft, commandeered from the coastguard in order to give Tom and Charlie some space.

As they glided through the waves, she lay back facing the sun, taking it all in. They were heading for a beach about twenty minutes from the harbour, complete with their escort. To Charlie, this was the stuff dreams were made of. She could see the mountains rising majestically behind the town with the sky a deep azure setting off the remains of snow still on the horizon. They were the only passengers alighting from the boat, as the other tourists were going to visit an ancient fortress further along the coast.

The boat with the police on board pulled up on the sandy beach a few minutes later.

'We would like a little privacy please,' Tom said. 'Do you mind sitting over by the quay whilst we wander down to the far end? You'll still be able to see us.'

'No problem, sir,' Stathi said with a smile and a wink. 'The boat returns at four, so we'll see you then. Have a nice time.'

Charlie and Tom took off their trainers and walked hand in hand along the sand, dipping their feet in the sea. 'This is heaven Tom,' said Charlie. 'Soft sand, beautifully clear water, warm, quiet and just about no one else around. Where is everyone? Are you coming for a swim?'

'You bet. I'll race you!' Tugging off his shorts and T shirt, he was running down to the water when Charlie overtook him, completely naked. 'You can get arrested for that!' he shouted as he chased her. They both fell into the waves together, laughing.

Charlie grabbed him from behind, putting her hands around Tom's waist. Reaching down, she put her hand inside his trunks and said, 'This is what I want, right here and now.'

He turned and pulled her off her feet and with her legs wrapped around his waist, he entered her. With a soft moan, she said, 'Now, fuck me hard, now!'

Afterwards he carried her out of the water and they collapsed on the sand, exhausted.

'Wow, that was pretty special,' Charlie said, wiping some sand from his face. 'I think you and I have found each other on this holiday, and it's rather nice.' Kissing him lightly on the lips, she said, 'Let's get a drink and have some lunch, and then maybe a little sunbathing. I'll expect you to oil me all over!'

After an alcoholic lunch they both had a nap, which was very welcome. The ship's hooter woke them as it approached the landing stage and Tom and Charlie hurriedly packed their beach gear and ran back, waving to the police, who were making their way to their boat. The wind had got up as often happened in Crete, making the sea a little choppy, but it didn't spoil the day one iota.

When they arrived back in Kastelli, the one thing Tom needed more than anything was a long cold beer. They found a harbourside café where they could sit outside under a colourful umbrella. He looked across to where their car was parked and noticed that a giant swastika had been sprayed on the driver's door. What the hell was that all about? Leaving Charlie at the table, he walked over to the police car and told them what had happened. George took a photo and told Tom he would report it at the station. More upset for Charlie, he thought. He would speak to his father out of earshot of her when they got back to Chania. It was starting to get a little unsettling.

Much as Tom hoped that Charlie wouldn't notice the swastika, it wasn't going to happen. She saw it as soon as she walked across the road. Putting her hand to her mouth in shock, she said. 'Oh Tom, who would do a thing like this? You don't think it has anything to do with our car being rammed off the road?'

'To be honest Charlie, I don't know. I couldn't see any other cars damaged. Let's get back to the house. Let's not it spoil our lovely day.' He put his arm around her.

Later he called his father.

'Hi Tom, is that you? Is everything OK?' Neville asked.

'Well, not really Dad. When we were out at Kastelli today, our new hire car got sprayed with a large swastika.'

'What the hell were the police doing whilst this was going on?' said Neville angrily.

'No, it wasn't their fault Dad. They were making sure we were OK on the beach. They have been very good and diligent.'

'OK, I take it back. What about Charlie? Is she upset?'

'Yes, she is. She's made of strong stuff. We're having some super days, but they keep being spoilt by something unpleasant. I'll talk to her, but I think we'll go where we have planned to go tomorrow, that is Manolas, and then call it a day. Perhaps we can stay for a few days with you.'

'No problem Tom. I'll get Helen to book your flights for

the day after next and email you the details. I'll speak to our Consul in Heraklion to find out what the hell is happening out there.'

'Thanks, Dad. I do appreciate that. If Charlie decides to stay a while longer, I'll let you know, that is if we can change the flight booking.'

'No problem Tom. Being an ambassador has its advantages – sometimes!'

CHAPTER 39

Organised resistance, 1941

❧

After Christina had escorted the British officers back, it was nearly midnight before she left the monastery and headed for home. She wasn't concerned about the dark, as she knew the way backwards. What Bob had said to her had given her such a lift. She didn't think for a moment that he was even remotely thinking of staying on the island with her; it seriously had not occurred to her. She still couldn't quite take in what he had said.

It was a light evening after a very warm day, and she could hear all the night-time noises which she remembered from her childhood. Becoming a runner for the resistance had taken her out of her village environment to meet people from many parts of the world, but of course, this wasn't by choice. The war had forced these people on her and her homeland. Many were welcome. Some were not.

Her parents were living in an old stone farm building which had been empty for decades. They had chosen this austere existence to avoid arrest by the Germans, and had made it as comfortable as circumstances would allow. Ioannis and Theodore had escaped from the forced labour and moved up into the mountains with Christina and Katina, knowing full well that for him and his son, staying at their house in Manolas would have meant almost certain death. What could have happened to his wife and daughter didn't bear thinking about. Going back to the village for food was a problem in case they were recognised, so they had chosen this very isolated existence, meeting up only with other Cretans who were living the same kind of lifestyle. Food for them all was a problem, but they pulled together as one.

Ioannis had had some military experience with the Cretan Territorial Army before the war, so his knowledge would be invaluable to the resistance groups in the area. He met up secretly with Costas and others, the meetings arranged by either Christina or Theodore.

Christina crept in through the door so as not to disturb anyone, but the family were always awake when either she or Theodore, or both, were out on missions. Whilst the Germans were reluctant to head into the mountains for fear of ambush, they were content for now with this status quo if the resistance did not cause them problems. Fortunately for both Christina and her brother, their missions as runners tended not to be down in the urban areas where there was a greater risk but liaising between the cells higher up. That was all about to change with the arrival of Special Forces.

There was still a little warmth left from the fire in the middle of the floor where the whole family slept. Christina was soon feeling sleepy from her long exhaustive day. She fell into a contented sleep, thinking of her Bob.

Her father gently shook her awake at first light. Costas had come to their house early with an important message to be delivered.

'Sorry Christina, but there's an urgent message to take to Sfakia. Are you OK to carry it out?'

Christina yawned and stretched. It took her a while to come to after a very hard and long day the day before.

'Yes Papa, that's fine. Just give me a little time to prepare myself.'

After a rather meagre breakfast, she set off. It took her just over two hours to arrive at the hideout where Fortis, the local resistance leader, was holed-up. A temporary home had been built between two huge boulders with cypress branches as a roof and shrubs hiding the entrance. It was very well concealed and just a short way up from the beach.

Fortis was a formidable sight in his Cretan breeches and boots, a black shirt and a turban with a magnificent set of whiskers. He never went anywhere without a cigarette dangling from his lips, a constant habit which had stained his whiskers.

He greeted Christina like a long-lost daughter. 'How are your parents, Christina?'

'They are as well as can be expected, living as we do up in the mountains,' she replied. 'I'm not sure how we will cope when winter comes.'

'You have a message for me?' Fortis asked. Christina turned away to retrieve the paper hidden in her underwear, and handed it to him. 'Oh, it's lovely and warm,' he said cheekily. There was another man in the back of the hut, but Fortis suggested that she shouldn't ask who he was as he was obviously British. There was a wireless transmitter in the hideout, but the signal was not good.

'I'll have a reply to go back to Costas,' he said. 'Please give me a few minutes. I'm sure you could do with a rest. I have a little coffee, if you would like some. Don't look so surprised – it's one of the perks of being near the coast when the boats come across from North Africa.'

'Oh, that would be a real treat, thank you,' Christina replied.

After a few minutes, Fortis returned, saying, 'We're getting very low on supplies. We must get in touch with Cairo to parachute some food and medical supplies. I expect Captain Parker will need some as well, so please take this message to him. And there's the one for Costas.'

Feeling a little refreshed but still tired from the previous day, Christina set off, but this time it was all uphill, and it was exceptionally hot again. By the time she had reached the monastery, she was badly in need of a rest. Captain Parker came out to meet her.

'You look all in. Come into our luxurious basement,' he said, smiling.

Walking down the steep steps into the cool air was a huge relief. This was where the fathers had paced for hundreds of years. It led into a dark smoky area which was home to a large group of men, all British except for one Cretan of indistinguishable age who was smoking a huge pipe.

'This is the team – you'll have met a few of them before,' said Parker. 'Help yourself to some water, it's cold and there's plenty of it.'

'Thank you. I have a message for you from Fortis in Sfakia.'

She passed it over, and he asked her, 'Have you heard any other news?'

'Only that a senior British commander is arriving by submarine and he's due to arrive shortly, but I don't know where or when. Which is just as well, it is better that I do not know too much.'

Two nights later, the most important British officer to arrive in Crete since the invasion, Lieutenant Colonel Harry Wright, came ashore in a rubber dinghy from one of Her Majesty's Royal Navy submarines. After landing on the beach at Chora Sfakia, he was quickly introduced to Captain Parker, Costas and Ioannis Papadakis, and with an escort from Neame's group, he made a fast exit away and up towards the White Mountains. The landing party had also brought some supplies, which were unloaded from the mule and stored at the monastery to be distributed as deemed appropriate by Morris and Costas. Wright immediately impressed the men, having arrived dressed in Cretan clothes as a shepherd, and he was fluent in Greek; he had communicated with Ioannis as they climbed. This single asset would make him highly popular with the Cretan resistance and make dialogue so much easier, cutting down the possibility of mistakes.

'Tell me Parker, how are all the resistance groups communicating with one another?' he asked. 'I'm led to believe that there are at least six major groups on the island with many other smaller cells. How do they all know who's doing what?'

'Until we have W/T units with the main groups, we have to rely on runners to take messages from one to another,' Parker replied. 'Ioannis' son and daughter are both runners and they cover hundreds of miles. They are very fit of course but it is a dangerous job, never knowing when they might run into a German patrol. Neame's group has a very well qualified radio operator who is proving invaluable.'

Turning to Ioannis and speaking in Greek, Wright thanked him for what he and his family were doing to help both the British military and the Cretan resistance, and assured him that he had arrived to pull all groups together with a campaign of co-ordinated action. He asked that this news should be sent out with care to all units and said that a meeting would be essential in the coming days. He also explained to Ioannis that it was crucial that only one runner per region was used, to keep the chances of an interception to a minimum.

'My daughter is at Captain Parker's base in the monastery at present and I will ask her to deliver a message to the three groups in the mid and south west part of the island,' said Ioannis. 'My son can head to the north and north west. They will then organise others to get the news to the rest of the island. Will you write the message in Greek? Then it will be taken very seriously by all parties.'

CHAPTER 40

Chania Police HQ, 2016

❦

There was consternation in the Chief Inspector's office. 'Sergeant,' he shouted. 'Get in here, now!' He stood up from behind his desk, clearly incandescent with rage.

'I have just had a very difficult phone call from the British Consul in Heraklion demanding to know what the hell we are doing about these so-called attacks on our ambassadorial guests,' he stormed. 'First their car is attacked, even if they weren't driving it at the time, but two of our men were seriously hurt and now their car, whilst under our watch, has been damaged with unpleasant graffiti. This is bad news for us. The British are good friends of Crete and we certainly don't want any difficulties, particularly with British and German visitors here during the seventy-fifth anniversary of the invasion. That would be the worst possible scenario. I want you to get every available man on the case. Have we any further leads about the death of the young German tourist?'

'Not really, sir,' answered the sergeant. 'We have questioned the Cretan club bouncer who was the one who said that someone called Hercules had committed the atrocity, but he would and could not tell us more. We are none the wiser, I'm afraid.'

'How can he just come out with this without anything to back it up? Have we got anything to tie him in with the murder? Does he have a firm alibi? Is this guy known to us?'

'He said he was working in the club all night with a colleague, and this was confirmed by both the colleague and the manager.'

'Do you think there is any possibility, sergeant, that these events are in any way connected?

'I cannot see it, sir,' he replied. 'What would drunken German youths mouthing off about Cretan people have to do with two English people holidaying on the island? It doesn't make sense.'

CHAPTER 41

A kiss among the rocks

❧

Yiannis explained to Christina where the British group were in hiding and told her she was making her first journey. It was new territory for her, but she was excited to be on her way to see them. She was startled when an ibex ran out of the scrub to her left, and she had to take a big breath before starting off again.

It was an arduous journey to the hideaway, which was higher up in the mountains than their previous home. Fortunately it was still only a couple of hours away from the Manolas area. The cave was so well hidden that she had trouble finding the entrance. She kept on repeating their secret whistle every ten minutes or so in the hope that someone would appear. After what seemed to be an eternity, she saw a British soldier appear from behind a large rock, and he immediately recognised her.

'Christina,' he said. 'You're a sight for sore eyes!'

She was not sure exactly what that meant, but the fact that he smiled as he said it surely meant that she was welcome.

'You are the first to visit our new headquarters. Bob will be very pleased to see you,' he said with a slight grin.

Hearing voices outside the cave, Neame appeared. Letting protocol dictate his manners, he greeted her with a handshake, which she returned with a knowing smile.

'Hello Christina, can we offer you some refreshment? A glass of water perhaps? We are a bit short of anything else,' he said.

'That would be very welcome,' she said. 'There are two messages here for you, one from Captain Parker and another from the new officer who arrived two days ago.'

Taking the letters from her, Neame went outside to read them, with Christina following. All the group knew of their friendship by now, and although not all of them agreed with it, they had huge respect for Neame as a leader and a soldier. It was he who had got this group to the point where they felt that Cairo had accepted and recognised their existence as a fighting unit. They had earned that respect.

Sitting on the rocky hillside in the shade, he read both messages and paused, needing to take it all in. The first was from the new CO on the island, to introduce himself and advise Neame that a meeting was being arranged with the resistance leaders and he was requested to attend. He would be told when and where shortly. The other was from Captain Parker, telling him that an air drop was taking place the following evening at midnight, and saying he would be told the location by Georgias early in the morning.

He turned to Christina and took her hands in his.

'I can't stay for long, Bob,' she said. 'I have to get the Colonel's messages to Costas and the other resistance group leaders in the west.'

It was a journey of around thirty-five miles, which was going to take her a couple of days. Neame put his arm around her, and she nestled her head on his shoulder.

'Oh Bob! How I would love to just spend a day with you without having all your men around or me having to rush off on a mission. It seems so unfair,' she said.

'Well, if it wasn't for this war, we wouldn't have met,' he replied. 'In the past few weeks you have made me realise the need for what we're doing here to help your people rid themselves of the dreaded Germans. At the same time, I have fallen for a girl hook, line and sinker, as we say in England. That means absolutely and totally.'

She raised her head and kissed him passionately on the lips.

'That's all I wanted to hear Bob. You are mine, all mine.'

Realising it was unlikely that they would see one another for quite some days, he whispered, 'We'll make time somehow soon, I promise. Just take good care of yourself, you mean the world to me.'

He kissed her gently on the lips and she left to go back towards her home.

There was low cloud when she set off. She couldn't believe

what Neame had just told her, and everything else went out of her mind. He had been so gentle with her that it filled her with supreme happiness. There was just one thing missing – the chance to be together, on their own – but that would come.

It was a humid day as Christina headed down towards the family home. Removing her headscarf helped her to cool a little with the help of the gentle breeze. She had a sheep's bladder filled with water over her shoulder and in her waist bag, some goat's cheese, olives and bread. But above all, she had a huge smile on her face. Bob had always made her believe there could be a future for them together, and now even more so.

As she headed back towards her home she felt utterly exhausted, having covered something like twenty miles in a day. She passed the cave where Bob and his men had originally sheltered. It did not just remind her of him but of Aegeus, who was so missed by his family and by the people of Manolas.

When she was close to home, she passed Father Pavlos Voskakis sitting astride his mule. He was dressed in a black robe and smoking his pipe, which had discoloured his wonderfully long white beard. He was a man of God and a man of the people.

'*Geia sas*, Father. *Ti kaneis?*'

'Ah, Christina. I am well, thank you. It is such a pleasure to see you. I assume that I am not supposed to be seeing you!' he said with a wicked smile.

'I would be grateful, Father, if you would not mention our meeting to anyone.'

'I am not seeing you, but please, we miss your family in our destroyed village. Are Ioannis, Katina and Theodore well?'

'They are as well as can be expected in the circumstances,' she replied.

'Ah, a most correct but uninformative answer, Christina! You will not find Costas in his home, which of course has been requisitioned by the Germans, but in the cottage just outside the village on the road to Chania. God speed.' He kicked the mule to move him on.

It was worth checking that all was safe before approaching Costas' new home, so she watched from the walled olive grove up the hill. After fifteen minutes, all appeared to be clear. The back door was ajar, with chickens running around. At least they hadn't been requisitioned as well.

She called quietly through the door and Costas immediately appeared, pulling her gently in. 'Shh,' he said putting his finger to his lips. 'A patrol is in the area and they mustn't see you. What have you got for me?'

She took the letter out of her clothing and passed it to him.

'A new British commander has arrived with a brief to bring the resistance groups together, and he speaks Greek,' she said. 'He is trying to arrange a meeting, so there is a proposed date and place planned and I have delivered copies to the other resistance cells in the area. This is good news for us all. There are planned parachute drops of arms and ammunition, as well as radios to help communication. At last we can take the fight to the Germans and vindicate those who died in our village.'

'Thank you, Christina. You are doing a wonderful job.' Kissing her on both cheeks, he added, 'Take care of yourself, and pass my regards to your parents.'

She said farewell to Costas and headed off out of the village and back up towards the mountains. It was a long haul, but her love for Bob and for her country was only heightened as she took in the beauty of the surrounding countryside. She passed a flock of goats and waved to the shepherd, wishing him a good day.

It was at least a two-hour walk until she reached her next letter drop, and she needed to stop and take a drink of water. Looking down into the valley, she saw pillars of smoke and the sound of gunfire. All she could work out was the it was to the north of the island between the mountains and the sea. She could only imagine what carnage was taking place. The Luftwaffe were strafing the area.

She suddenly felt the need to hasten her journey; she knew that the sooner the Cretan resistance met with the British Colonel, the sooner they could work together to do something about these barbaric soldiers.

CHAPTER 42
Chania, 2016

'Shall we go out tonight, or stay in and cook something tasty and local?' Tom asked Charlie.

'I'm sorry about these little upsets, Tom, but they've unsettled me. It's not knowing what it's all about I suppose. Let's pop into the town and treat ourselves to some nice fish, if the market has anything left. If tomorrow is to be our last full day, and we've promised Nikos and Maria that we'll visit Manolas, we must make the most of tonight as we'll be busy getting ready to leave tomorrow evening.'

'Good plan.'

He grabbed her by the hand and they left the house, letting the police officers know where they were going before they set off.

'I shall really miss this pretty little town, Tom,' she said as they walked down a narrow, stepped alleyway. 'Without the difficulties, I have felt very happy here, the people are so friendly and welcoming. And for you and me, it's been very special. I keep thinking about all that time at uni when I fancied the pants off you and you didn't see it! And what will happen when we get back home? Will you still want to see me then?'

He laughed. 'You try and keep me away! I must have been blind. I chased lots of girls without any great degree of success and there you were all the time, waiting for me to make a move.' Looking at her full in the face, he threw his arms around her, saying, 'Anyway, we can't look back now, only forward, together.'

She felt like dancing all the way into town. All the concerns of the past few days were suddenly a million miles away.

'Come on lover boy, let's get this done, then it's down to the serious stuff,' she said with a twinkle in her eye.

Tom remembered a stall down by the harbour where his parents had bought fresh fish in the past. Thankfully the stallholder was still there, but just packing up.

'E, *pou to psari!*' Tom said. '*Ine fresko to psari sou?*'

'You English?' he asked.

'Ah, thank goodness,' Tom said. 'My Greek is not good!'

'I understood you well. You asked was my fish fresh? On the table, no! But in my cold bag, yes. I have lovely *lithrinia*, red sea bream. Beautiful baked in oven or on hot grill. Special price for you my friend.'

Tom wasn't going to argue. It was a bargain and the fish was easy to cook, so even he couldn't muck it up. A salad would be perfect to accompany the bream, so they stopped in the market and bought some rocket, cucumber, coriander, spring onions and tomatoes. Tom was in charge of the fish and Charlie the salad.

'We're in for a real treat,' Charlie said. 'Can't wait! And there's a nice bottle of white chilling in the fridge.'

At just after seven the doorbell rang. Charlie opened the door to see Maria standing there.

'Hello Charlie. I just stopped by to see how you are getting on and whether there's anything you need.'

'That's very kind of you Maria. Tom!' she shouted through to the BBQ grill on the rear terrace, 'Maria's here.'

He came through, wearing a pink apron.

'Hey, I like that,' Maria said with a huge smile.

'Hi Maria. Good to see you. Can I get you a drink?'

'No thanks Tom. I just wanted to make sure that you were OK. My mum and dad were keen to make sure all was well.'

'Yes, all fine, but we have decided to leave the day after tomorrow,' Tom said.

This clearly came like a bolt out of the blue. Completely taken by surprise, she said, 'Oh, I thought you were staying until next week!'

'That was the idea,' Tom said, 'but there have been a few unexplained things happen which have worried us a bit. The killing of the German tourist, our car being wrecked and then our new car having a swastika drawn on the door. All a bit unsettling.'

'I am so sorry Tom, and for you Charlie. It has spoiled your holiday. That is not what we want for our visitors, especially the English. I expect your father is watching events with interest?'

'Yes, you could say that.' Tom gave a wry smile. 'The Consul here was on the receiving end of a phone call from Athens. And I think it was him who persuaded my father that it would be best to cut it short. We're going to Manolas tomorrow, as we promised your mother and father, and then flying back to Athens for a few days before heading back to the UK.'

'Such a shame,' said Maria. 'I will miss you both. Hopefully we'll see you both here again. I'll bring you round a picnic tomorrow morning before you set off. You'd better get to your fish Tom, before it burns!'

She turned and walked away. As she headed away from the house, she was desperately thinking of ways she could get Tom on his own, just to show him how much she wanted him.

At the end of a very relaxing and tasteful meal, Tom had hardly finished his last mouthful before Charlie was dragging him up the stairs.

'You're in for a night to remember,' she said chuckling. 'Get in there and get your kit off. You've got work to do!'

CHAPTER 43

Maria out on the town, 2016

❧

Maria had arranged to meet Hans and Johann at the Athenian, a night club in Chania. The last time she had met them she had ended up on the beach drunk and having sex with both of them. The thought excited her. If she couldn't find a way to have Tom to herself, she would make sure that he knew that he was not the only guy on the island for her. And after hearing that Tom was leaving earlier than planned, she felt a bit down and was in the mood to have some fun.

The proprietors were relaxed about what went on at the Athenian, and Maria certainly would not be telling her parents where she was going, as the club's reputation was not squeaky clean. She told her mother that she was meeting a few friends for a drink, and her father shouted that she must be home by 11.30. A heavy drinking session and maybe some drugs were high on the agenda. She had experimented with dope in the past, but the boys said they had some cocaine and she was keen to try it, if a little apprehensive.

They arrived at the club and met up with her friends. Soon the noise from the disco began to penetrate her brain, and the combination of heat, alcohol and music led them to a quieter corner where Hans reached into his pocket for the foil package. Maria talked about the English couple she was helping whilst they were on holiday in Chania, while trying hard not to think about Tom leaving. She didn't want to appear bitchy about Charlie, but she did mentioned that they were visiting Manolas the next day as guests of her parents while attending the seventy-fifth anniversary of the invasion.

The drink and dope had made her more than a little indiscreet. When she said that Tom's father was an ambassador and his girlfriend Charlie looked like a goddess, the boys realised who she was talking about.

'We saw them at Knossos,' said one of the lads, Johann. 'They were being treated like a king and queen. The stuck-up bitch was lording it about, with him pretending to be Hercules. Makes you sick.'

'Come on,' Maria said, 'forget them, let's get snorting. I want to try it.'

It wasn't long before she was feeling extremely sexed up, and the image of Tom flashed through her mind. Christ, she thought, if he were here right now, he wouldn't know what day of the week it was. She would show that English bit of skirt what the man she loved was missing.

While those hazy thoughts were going through her mind, the two German lads were leading her out towards the beach, where within moments she was being taken by them simultaneously. She would certainly not be home by 11.30.

CHAPTER 44

The long-awaited air drop

In daytime, the Omalos Plateau was one of the prettiest places in Crete. Wild flowers grew plentifully in the fertile soil, and the surrounding uplands brought shelter to the plain. The plateau was chosen as the location for the first of the parachute drops for supplies coming in from Egypt. Simms had received the radio message two days before and had informed Neame, who had in turn advised Captain Parker. It was felt that the British soldiers should act as a reception committee and should not involve the resistance until they were sure it was going to work. Also, more importantly, it was crucial that word did not get out that it was taking place.

Parker took Neame and Corporal Weeks aside and explained what would be needed. 'When we operated these drops in the desert, we used kerosene in tin cans to create a drop zone,' he said. 'They last long enough for the pilot to see what he's doing. So we need the kerosene and cans without the resistance getting wind of what we need them for. Any ideas?'

'Well,' replied Neame, 'our only options are to ask Ioannis or Costa – they can both be relied on to keep quiet. They don't need to know what we need them for.'

'Right, can you arrange that, but we need them for tomorrow night.'

'Christina is due here today. We'll ask her to see what her father says. We know she can be trusted.'

True to Christina's word, a mule carrying the goods arrived just after lunch the next day led by Theodore. She arrived with him, which was a pleasant surprise for Neame. Parker, who had stayed in the cave the previous night, was so pleased that he almost did a highland fling.

'Well done you two,' he said. 'Brilliant work!' Calling Neame over, he told him that each can needed a taper so that they could light the kerosene safely. He explained this to Christina, who suggested that her petticoat could be torn into strips. 'That's perfect, but are you sure? It won't be easy to replace.'

'My mother is very resourceful, it will not be a problem,' Christina replied.

With the drop due at ten, the teams split into pairs and left for the plateau in plenty of time. There would still be a little light left when it came, but they needed to spread out in a wide area, each pair being at least fifty yards from the next. Captain Parker would organise the positioning and Neame had asked if it was all right for Christina and her brother to stay with them.

'Considering all that family does for us, it's the least we can do,' said the officer.

Neame teamed up with Christina, and Theodore went with Corporal Weeks. That made twelve pairs in total, ready for the Captain to give the signal to light the cans.

It was a very apprehensive Neame who found himself lying in the wild flowers next to Christine. The excitement of the air drop was one thing, but the hypnotic aroma of the flowers was increasing his desire for her. He buried his face in her hair, not needing to say anything; they both knew that this was the moment. They were far enough away from the next pair not to be heard, if they were careful. And the plane wasn't due for thirty minutes. His hand reached down and parted her legs.

She whispered in his ear, 'I'm ready for you Bob. This is my first time. You must please teach me what to do.'

Afterwards, he lay looking at her for some minutes with a smile of blissful contentment on her face. Whispering so the others couldn't hear, he said, 'That was the most beautiful of moments, Christina. I shall remember it for always.'

'It was for me too, Bob, but I am bleeding a little,' she said.

'Don't worry, that is normal the first time. Hasn't your mother explained it to you?'

The thought of telling her mother what had happened rather dampened the sense of complete fulfilment she felt at this moment. She would have to deal with that another day, but for now, she knew he was truly hers.

There was a rude awakening when they heard the sound of engines from the south, and Parker flashed his torch to indicate that they should all light their tapers. Neame was quick to recover from his moment of passion, and within a minute, all the kerosene cans were alight. The Dakota aircraft was coming round again, flying high enough to miss the mountain tops and ready to drop down to three hundred feet above the plateau to release the canisters. The first pass sent four hurtling to the ground, the second another five, and with a waggle of his wings the aircraft was gone into the darkening night.

It was impossible to carry all the containers in one go, so some were well hidden to be collected the following day. The mule was put to good use, and by midnight the team were back at the cave, well pleased with the mission.

Now the war could well and truly be taken to the Germans.

CHAPTER 45

The White Mountains, 1941

❧

The venue for the resistance meeting was well chosen. It was an old schoolhouse, long since unused, high up on a plateau among the mountains. It was perfect, because nobody could approach within at least half a mile without being seen.

Lieutenant Colonel Harry Wright was there with Captain Andrew Parker and two of his SOE operatives. Neame was also there, with Corporal Weeks. This was the first time the Colonel had met any of the main Cretan resistance leaders, and these were the four covering the western side of the island. He had often heard the description 'Cretan warrior', but that was exactly how they appeared. Politically, they seemed to come from all sides of the spectrum. Dressed almost entirely in black, they were wearing embroidered waistcoats, bandanas, leather boots, riding breeches and bandoliers of ammunition, and they all had impressive moustaches. He wondered whether there was a competition for the best moustache or whether it was a matter of pride as to who could grow the finest. Although small in stature, these men's physical presence was hard to ignore.

'Kalimera' said the Colonel to each in turn, shaking their hands. 'Thank you for coming. I can speak a little of your language, so I will continue in Greek, but please correct me when I am wrong.'

He spoke with a smile and his words went down well with the assembled leaders. They felt that he was not trying to be superior but was treating them with respect, and simply wanted them to come together to fight a common enemy.

'I have three of my friends here from an organisation called the Special Operations Executive, or SOE', Colonel Wright went on. 'We are all serving officers with the British Army, but we have been seconded here for special duties. I can speak passable Greek and my colleagues a little. I believe that Costas here from Manolas knows Sergeant Bob Neame and Corporal Weeks, who have been here since the battle, and this is Christina, who I think you all know. She has been a very efficient runner of messages between your units. Sergeant Neame very bravely attacked the German post in Manolas to release some British prisoners recently, which you all probably know about. I understand that members of Costas' resistance group joined in to prevent the Germans following Sergeant Neame's soldiers as they headed back to the mountain.' It was noticeable that Christina was beaming with pride at the mention of Neame's exploits. 'It was a very successful operation and the first time the Cretan resistance had worked alongside the British. And that is why I am here, to encourage both parties to plan a series of engagements against the enemy which are co-ordinated and well thought out. I understand that executions of civilians are already happening and we must be mindful of this when planning our actions. We want to do as much as we can to protect the lives of all civilians on the island, but at the same time to take the fight to the Germans.'

With that, their faces lit up.

'What we need to decide today,' the Colonel went on, 'is what supplies we need and where they will be distributed and securely stored. I need to know how many men and women there are under your command so we can judge how many weapons, how much ammunition and explosives we need. Then we need to identify targets, but these must be co-ordinated so we don't make problems for ourselves. And lastly, for now, we must keep any information to ourselves. There will be attempts by the Germans to infiltrate our ranks, which could be disastrous. I have been told that there are Germans dressed as British soldiers, so we need to be on our guard. Are we all agreed?'

There was unanimous agreement, but Wright knew that the Cretans by nature were an excitable people and after a few glasses of raki, tongues could become loose.

'There is a parachute drop due very soon, which we will distribute as soon as we can get started. A larger shipment will follow and this will leave Alexandria within a month. We will need you all to help, but our runners, like Christina and her brother Theodore, will let you know when and where the drops will take place, giving you twenty-four hours' notice. That is for security purposes. So, gentlemen, please give Sergeant Neame the numbers in your groups.'

'Sir,' said Costas, 'we are impressed that some of you are dressed like Cretans but there are some errors which we will correct, with your permission of course. Neame and his men are still in British uniforms, but we suggest that they change these. May I suggest that you all dress like Cretans. We can supply these clothes, but the moustache will be down to you!'

'Thank you, Costas. I think our uniforms will offer us no protection from the Germans irrespective of the Geneva Convention, so we will take your advice. And we will be proud to do so.'

With a lot of hugging and lighting of pipes, they drifted away back to their villages to wait for news of the drop.

As Christina and Neame left the meeting, she said to him out of earshot of the others, 'Is there any way we can have a little more time together, soon?'

'The Colonel will be asking for a runner to get the message out to the groups about the drop – hopefully there might be an opportunity then,' he replied. Taking her hands in his, he whispered to her, 'You mean so much to me Christina. I can't wait for all this to be over. But we must face it, it is going to be some while. We just have to be patient and grab every opportunity we can.'

She headed back towards home with Costas deep in thought. She couldn't help thinking about her own and Bob's future. Would he really stay with her when it was all over? After all, he had a wife and children back in England. There was the worry that he could be treated as a deserter, even though he would have done more than his bit.

As they passed by Costas's home, he said to Christina that he had secreted a couple of chickens there for her and her family. He went in to collect them, wrapping them in old newspaper. Coming back out, he said to her, 'I feel very positive about the meeting today. The British will give us some hope. They do seem committed to help and I like the Colonel. And that is not just because he speaks Greek.'

'Thank you, Costas. This will mean so much to our family. It is very hard up in the hills, but we are learning to go without so much. Bob has promised us a share of their supplies when the drop arrives.'

'Well, we couldn't do without you and Theodore running our messages. So, you need to keep well fed!'

She stuffed the birds into her backpack and set off towards her home. Her village looked so sad after the destruction caused by the Germans. There were not many houses left untouched, and she was desolate to see the emptiness; it wasn't just the people, but the stuffing had been knocked out of the place. Manolas had previously been a very close-knit community with everyone looking after their neighbours but now, with many of the residents executed and most of the rest going away to the countryside to live in whatever accommodation they could find, the village was practically empty except for the German garrison, the priest whose house had been saved, the civil policeman and a couple of dozen local people.

As she stood and recalled her childhood running through the streets, she failed to notice the German patrol which was coming up behind her.

CHAPTER 46

Christine taken: 1941

'Hey, you,' the Corporal shouted, 'what have you got in your bag?'

Christina did not answer straight away, so he grabbed it and pulled it off her shoulder. Finding the chickens inside, he said, 'where did you get these? They were supposed to be handed in.'

Feeling that the last thing she wanted to do was to get Costas into trouble, she said, 'I stole them. My family are desperately hungry.'

'Where did you steal them from? Because they will be in trouble and so will you. Your papers?'

'They are in the bag you are holding,' she replied.

He studied them for a moment. 'Ah, what have we here? Christina Papadakis. We will check this out, but if you are the daughter of Ioannis Papadakis and you have a brother called Theodore, who absconded from the labour camp, then you are an accessory and you're in real trouble. Come with us.' He pushed her roughly ahead.

Costas had watched the encounter with horror from the cover of an olive grove. He was seriously regretting offering Christina the chickens. Realising that there was nothing he could do, he crept away through the olives, heading for the Papadakis house to warn them of what was happening and to get Theodore to run to the cave to tell Neame. Christina knew an awful lot about the organisation. There was trouble ahead.

Running as fast as he could, Costas followed the well-worn path up to the Papadakis home. There was a little smoke issuing from a hole in the roof. Although this was an isolated position, he would have to tell them not to light a fire as a spotter plane would see it miles away.

Walking in through the open door, he shouted breathlessly, 'Ioannis! Ioannis! I need to talk to you straight away!'

Ioannis appeared; he had been chopping wood around the back. 'I heard you Costas. It's Christina, isn't it? I can see it from your face.'

'She has been arrested in Manolas for having chickens in her bag. It's all my fault because I gave them to her for your family. Then they asked for her papers and realised that she was a Papadakis, and they asked whether she was related to you and Theodore. She didn't answer, but they took her in. If Theodore is here, he must go straight away and warn the Sergeant what has happened. I will get a message to Captain Parker at the monastery. We have to let them know quickly, and you must move out of here as fast as you can.'

Ioannis gazed in horror. Terrified for his family, he was finding it hard to think straight. 'Ioannis,' said Costas, 'you concentrate on getting you and Katina away from here. Just take what you need and make sure you don't leave anything incriminating behind. I'll find out if there is room in Aegeus's cottage and ask his wife whether she would be prepared to shelter you for a short while. He had a hidden cellar under his house for such an emergency. Go!'

Costas left them and headed as fast as he could for the monastery. It was almost all uphill and a rocky and uneven path, and he was tiring rapidly; it had been a very difficult few hours and emotionally and physically he felt drained. He was not a young man, but he had to keep going. He also had to keep a sharp look-out for the enemy, either on the ground or up in the air.

As he breasted a ridge, he saw the sea on his right and the monastery high up in front of him. Even though it was getting late in the day, it was still very warm, and he had a terrible headache coming on as a result of dehydration.

As he approached the building, Father Pavlos was leaving on his mule.

'Kalimera, Costas. You should not be running in this heat, it is bad for your heart,' he called.

'Thank you for your advice Father, but the need is urgent. I need to see the British officers immediately.'

'Don't let me hold you up then, brother. May God be with you.' With that, the priest kicked the flanks of his mule and set off down the slope, puffing on his pipe as he went.

Costas rushed across the cobbled courtyard towards the shepherd's croft in the olive grove and into the secret door which led down to the underground cellar where the SOE officers were housed.

'Colonel Parker,' he said breathlessly, 'we have a big problem!'

'Take a seat, Costas, and get your breath back.'

'There's no time for that. Christina has been arrested by the Germans and she has been taken to their compound. She was stopped and searched. They found dead chickens which I had given her in her bag and then asked for her papers. It wasn't long before they realised she was the daughter of Ioannis. So, they took her in. But of course, she knows about us. We must get her out as soon as possible.'

'Then we must tell Sergeant Neame straight away,' said Parker.

'Yes. Theodore is on his way.'

Parker thought for a moment. He was concerned that Neame might act impulsively because of his relationship with Christina, putting her at risk as well as him and his men. He strapped on his side arm and said to Costas, 'I know you are tired but you must take me to Neame's cave now, so we can make a proper plan. We cannot do this via the radio, just in case.'

They set off at a trot, but the paths were rough and they had to go at a fast walking pace while keeping a wary eye open for trouble. It took almost two hours, but because Theodore had already given them the news, their arrival was expected.

Neame was in a state of shock. He could not believe this terrible news. They had known that the chances of something going wrong were high, but now that it had actually happened, he felt totally drained. This was the bravest of young women, and someone he dearly loved, the woman he was planning to live with when the war was over, and now the Germans had her.

He looked at the officer. 'We must mount a rescue mission,' he said. 'I will lead it.'

'I'm not sure that's a good idea, Sergeant. You have an emotional interest here, do you not, and that may affect your judgement at a crucial moment.'

Keen to overcome the Captain's objections, Neame managed to convince him that nothing would interfere with him doing a professional job. Because of the success of the raid to release the other British soldiers from the same encampment, Parker realised how important knowledge of the base would be to the success of this operation.

'Right, Sergeant, pick six of the best men in your command and my number two, Lieutenant Morris will accompany you. Costas, you get back to Manolas and alert your men that an attack will take place in the next twenty-four hours, but they must wait for our soldiers. There is too much at stake here to mess this up.'

Neame and Parker got together to work out a strategy to get Christina released.

'There are two ways to look at this,' Neame said. 'Either they won't be expecting anything because of the recent hit against them, or they'll be doubly alert because of her capture. My guess is the latter. And I think we should try and outthink them rather than go for a frontal attack, which might take them by surprise but would probably be bad news for Christina.'

'I agree, Sergeant. Did you have anything in mind?' said Parker.

'We could involve Costas and his group under the pretence of going into the compound to sell them some local produce. Or possibly, I remember Costas telling me that after the invasion they stripped some of the German bodies of their uniforms. If they still have them, we could gain access by arriving dressed as a German patrol. It wouldn't take them long to work out there was something not right, but it may be enough to do what we need to do. Quickly, let's see if Costas has left yet and ask him about the uniforms, and what he thinks about the plan.'

Costas was still recovering from the traumatic events of the day and was having some lentils and local wine with the British soldiers. Neame asked him what he thought.

'It would have to be in the daytime because German soldiers don't come out at night for fear of having their throats cut,' said Costas. 'It is possible. We have uniforms, though some of them are a little bloodstained.' He smiled. 'We also have their weapons, so they would look the part. I think it could work. We could be lying in wait to cover the withdrawal, but it would not be good for the people still left in the village. Their vengeance was swift and ruthless before, you remember what happened. And for the Germans, seeing their dead comrades' uniforms will just make it worse.' He thought for a moment. 'When the decision has been made, we must make the people aware to be ready to move away to the mountains,' he went on. 'Our job will be to help protect you and the people. It will be difficult, but we know the terrain. Christina is one of us and her knowledge is great, so we must do our duty. We need someone who can speak German.'

Parker chipped in. 'Morris has a passable amount of the language. So, are we all agreed?'

At the German base, two soldiers grabbed Christina by the arms and pushed her through the guardroom door.

'Name?' the duty corporal shouted.

'Christina Papadakis.'

'Your address?'

'I used to live in the village until you came and trashed our house.'

'You have not answered the question.' Hit her hard across the face, 'Now, again, where do you live?'

Still smarting from being hit and her anger rising with the taste of blood in her mouth, she realised that she had to keep control and think hard about her responses.

'I live in an old cow shed in the mountains,' she said.

'Well, that's a start. Are you going to tell me where?'

'No, I don't think so,' she replied.

'Ah, we are going to start playing silly games then. Why don't you want to tell me?'

'It's quite simple. Firstly, I've seen what you do to our

people – executing innocent women and children in what was our village until you came along. And secondly, I have lost one home because of you. I don't want to lose another.'

'I think it is because your father and brother are living with you and you know that we are after them. So, if you won't tell us, we will find a way of getting it out of you. Corporal, take her down to the cellar.'

CHAPTER 47

Maria's mistake, 2016

When Nikos arrived home from school, Melissa shouted to him from the kitchen, 'How was your day, Nikos?'

'Oh, pretty much the same as usual,' he replied. 'Except some of the older boys have been putting dodgy pictures on Facebook and the headmaster wants to clamp down on it before the police get involved. Not good for the reputation of the school.'

'Sadly, that's the age we live in,' said Melissa. 'There are many pluses and minuses with social media.'

Changing the subject, Nikos said to Melissa, 'Have you noticed anything different about Maria recently? Since Tom arrived, she seems to have had a personality change. At first I thought it was because Tom had brought Charlie with him and she was jealous. But I think it's more than that. And she was home very late last night, although I told her 11.30 at the latest.'

'Like you, I thought it was something to do with Tom,' Melissa said. 'The day he arrived, she came home desperately wanting to tell me all about him and how handsome he had become. But I think that feeling has turned to anger because she hasn't been able to develop a friendship with him, for obvious reasons. But in the last few days, with the anti-German march, she has not been her usual sparkly self. There is something else going on, I am sure.'

'One thing is for sure, we don't want any issues with the Richardson family,' replied Nikos. 'Not only is Neville a very important man but the income from looking after their house is important to us. School teachers and tour guides do not get paid much and we have a daughter who we hope is about to go to university in Athens. We need to talk to her and determine what this is all about.'

Maria got home just after six, throwing her schoolbag on the floor in the hall and going straight up to her room. Melissa could hear music thumping out and shouted up the stairs, but there was no response. She climbed the stairs and knocked on her door, but there was no reply. After a couple of seconds, she opened the door to see Maria sitting on the bed with her headphones on, looking at her laptop. She was obviously chatting to someone. Not wanting to start the evening off badly, Melissa scribbled a note to say that they wanted to have a talk with her. She nodded sullenly. What did they want with her now?

She did not come downstairs for over an hour. Nikos called her into the sitting room.

'We just wanted a chat because we've noticed that you haven't been your normal self for the past few days,' he said. 'Is there anything wrong?'

With that, she burst into tears.

'Come here Maria, what on earth is the matter?' he asked.

It took some time for her to recover her composure. 'I find it hard to talk to you about some things Dad. I need to talk to Mum. Don't be upset.'

'I don't care which of us you talk to, my love, I just want you to be your normal self.'

She kissed him on the cheek and went to talk to Melissa in the kitchen. 'I've been such a fool, mum,' she said, biting back the tears. 'I was so, so desperate to get somewhere with Tom. I think I have been in love with him for years, but when I saw him arrive, I was so smitten. I didn't know what to do. Charlie was so pretty, so assured and although I don't think they were lovers when they arrived, I'm sure that they are now. I knew I had lost him, and I was devastated. Then while all this was going on in my head, I met a couple of guys at the anti-German march. I got drunk with them and smoked a bit of pot.'

Melissa looked at her in fury. 'What did you say? You've taken drugs? Haven't we brought you up to know better than that?' She threw her hands up in despair. 'Maria, I am so disappointed! Your father will be beside himself when he hears what has been going on. How could you?'

Maria felt she could not possibly tell her mother what else had happened on the beach. 'I have to listen all the time to you both about what the Germans did in the war. I think I was just rebelling against it.'

'What are you talking about? Rebelled against what? How?'

Maria realised her mistake. Taking a deep breath, she said, 'The guys I met were German.'

Her mother gasped in shock.

'I can't believe you did that. You took drugs from a German?'

Maria at that moment realised just what this meant to her mother.

'If you tell me it went any further than that, I just don't know what I will do.'

Maria did not know what to say. She just sat there, with her head in her hands.

'I'm really sorry, mum. So sorry.'

There was a stony silence. Neither of them knew where this was going to go.

'I assume by your silence that the worst happened,' Melissa said. 'I just can't believe you did that. I don't know what your father will say. He will lose all reason. We must think very carefully how we handle this. It would have been bad enough with a couple of local lads, but Germans! It is the worst possible thing you could have done. The anniversary of what they did in Manolas seventy-five years ago is this week. I've just... well, I don't know what to think.'

Maria stood up and went to her room without another word. Melissa was left in the kitchen hoping that Nikos had not heard any of their conversation. She had to think hard about what she was going to say, and when.

When Nikos had finished marking some homework, he asked Melissa what the reason for Maria's change of mood had been. All she could think of saying to him was, 'It's a women's thing. Nothing for you to concern yourself with.'

CHAPTER 48

A rescue in the mountains, 1941

❧

Theodore, desperate to do something to help his sister, collected a mule from Aegeus's wife and visited Costas to pick up the German uniforms and weapons. He knew it would be curtains for him if he was found carrying the load, but he had no choice. He harnessed a cart to the animal and hid the outfits under a huge load of hay.

Being in the village was agonising for Theodore because he knew his sister was so close, yet so far. He waited till dark and set off, having wrapped linen around the mules' hooves so that the Germans didn't get wind of what was going on. Theodore could have carried out the journey blindfold, so many times had he run these hills in his youth, and in recent days running messages. It was a balmy evening, and once he had put Manolas far behind him, he could relax a little. It was all uphill and the mule seemed to relish the challenge, rather than being its normal cantankerous self. However, it was a long, slow haul, and it took the best part of three hours.

He arrived at the cave just as first light was showing. Bob Neame was awake and unable to sleep as long as the woman he loved was in such danger.

'Well done, Theodore,' said Neame. 'We will do all we can to get your sister out of there. Go and get yourself some food and try and get a little sleep. We will let you know when we will be setting off. You know she means the world to me too.' He smiled, embarrassed to be talking to his lover's brother.

Parker had stayed in the cave, and he took Neame aside. 'We've got the uniforms, now we need to work out a plan of action. Fortunately, these uniforms are all from the same unit, so arriving as a single platoon won't raise any suspicions,' he said. 'There is one officer's uniform and one NCO – the rest are privates, and they are from an infantry unit, which makes life a little simpler. Right, now for the method of deception.'

'I've got an idea, sir,' said Neame. 'We could take them off their guard by charging up at the trot and telling them we're after a group of partisans and need some help searching for them up in the mountains. Once they're distracted, we can get into the buildings whilst Costas and his men attack from the other side. With a bit of luck, I think it could work.'

Parker thought for a moment. 'Well Sergeant, I agree,' he said. 'I think it's a good plan. Hitting them at the right time is crucial though, possibly at lunchtime. But we need to talk to Costas first to get his approval. Speed is of the essence. I know he's worn out, but can we get Theodore to talk to him, rather than take him a message, outlining our plan and wait for an answer? Whatever happens, he must not get caught.'

It was an anxious wait until Theodore returned. He was exhausted, but he was able to tell Colonel Parker that Costas was in full agreement and would be ready to support them the next day at midday. They could only hope that Christina would be able to hold on until then.

CHAPTER 49

Safety concerns, Chania 2016

Tom's mobile rang at a very inappropriate moment, and by the time he had untwined himself from Charlie's long legs, he had missed the call. He noticed it was his father again. Not more trouble, he hoped. He called back in case it was urgent.

'Thanks for calling back, Tom. I spoke to the Consul in Heraklion as I said I would. He couldn't add anything remotely comforting, so the decision we took is sensible. I've emailed details of your return tickets, and it will be nice for you both to spend a few days in Athens with us. I'll send the car to collect you from the airport.'

'Thanks, Dad. We'll look forward to it. See you on Saturday,' said Tom.

Charlie had crept down the stairs, having put on a very sexy black and red basque.

'Gosh, where on earth did that come from?' he asked.

'Don't concern yourself with that. If it does what I think it will, it won't be on for very long!'

Tom wondered when he would ever be able to satisfy his beautiful partner's needs. Still, he reflected, you only live once.

CHAPTER 50

The cellar, Manolas, 1941

For Christina, it was a long night. The cellar was damp, the walls green with mould and there was no furniture, so sitting or lying on the floor was the only option. Sleep was impossible. She had not been given any food, and a cup of water was her only sustenance.

So many thoughts were going through her head. The protection of her family was foremost in her thinking, along with her love for her Englishman. She did not know that Costas had witnessed her arrest; she was just aware that at some time in the next twenty-four hours someone would realise she was missing. The German attitude to Cretan civilians following the landings where there had been a mass slaughter would not be too sympathetic. She could expect the worst, but she was adamant that whatever they did to her she would not let her family or Bob down. He was her future, and her family were her support.

There was no window in the room, and it was only when she saw a sliver of light appear under the door that she knew it was sunrise. She could hear people starting to move around upstairs and knew it wouldn't be long before someone came for her.

She heard the bolt slide back and the German Corporal shouted, 'On your feet. Come with me!'

He pulled and pushed her roughly up the stairs. They reached the guardroom, where she was pushed into a hard wooden chair.

'Now. What have you got to tell us? Co-operate and you can have coffee and a tasty breakfast. You really do not want to think about the other option. You have fifteen minutes to decide.'

She was having a job keeping awake, but after what must have been around a quarter of an hour, the door swung open and in walked the young Wehrmacht officer. He gave her a cold, intimidating smile.

'Now young lady, are you going the answer my questions or not?'

'It depends what your questions are,' she replied.

'Ah, silly games! You know very well what I want to know. I wish to know where your father and brother are, and I have a feeling that you know about the local resistance. So, I want you to tell me everything you know, or we will make you tell us.'

She stared him out, but kept her mouth firmly closed. He grabbed her by the hair and pulled out a large handful.

'Now, where are they?' he shouted into her ear.

With tears streaming down her face from the pain, she just shook her head. The Corporal came in and threw a bucket of water at her, knocking her to the floor. The officer then kicked her hard in the ribs, cracking some of her ribs. She yelled at the top of her voice.

'You are going to tell us in the end, Christina, so why not spare yourself the pain and tell us now?'

Doubled up in agony, she simply shook her head again.

'Take her back down to the cellar, Unteroffizier. Then I will start on her in earnest.'

They had taken a long table into the room and tied Christina flat on her back, secured by her wrists and ankles. For a time they left her, to give her time to worry about what was coming next.

It was perhaps two hours later that the officer returned. Without saying anything he forced a rubber tube down her throat, and then began to pump water into her stomach. He then sat upon her lower abdomen, which had the effect of pushing much of the liquid back up through her system and gushing out of her mouth. Christina struggled in panic, unable to breathe.

He got up, walked around and whispered in her ear, 'That's just for the beginning. We haven't really begun this yet.' He pushed his hand slowly up between her legs. She was consumed with fear. Then he walked out, slamming the door behind him.

It took her some time to start to regain a little of her inner strength and try to prepare herself for what might lie ahead.

They came back later that morning. She was not sure how much time had passed since they had left.

'Have you changed your mind yet, Christina?' asked the corporal. 'Are you ready to tell us now? Let me tell you what we will do if you don't answer our questions. We will break your fingers, one by one, slowly, and very painfully.'

She did not respond. The German held her left hand and cracked the middle finger. The pain was excruciating, but this time she refused to scream. She was not going to give them the satisfaction. When he broke the second finger, she passed out with the agony. The next thing she knew, they were bringing her round by throwing a bucket of water over her.

'This is very silly, Christina,' the officer said. 'A pretty girl like you being disfigured because of your loyalty to your family? So unnecessary. They will not be hurt; we just want them back in the labour camp. It is not in our interests to damage them in any way. Just tell us where they are, and save yourself more pain.'

She was almost out of it, scarcely hearing what was being said.

'Tell you what Unteroffizier, let's give her something to really remember the German occupation of this shitty little island. You can go first.'

With a hateful smile the corporal tore off her knickers and pushed his fingers hard into her. She kicked out in protest, but being tied down so tightly she knew it was hopeless. Then he climbed up onto the table and raped her. Tears of anger and pain came, but she would not scream or shout. In due course these bastards would get what was coming to them.

After what seemed like an eternity, she was untied and turned over before the officer took his turn to rape her, again and again. When he had finished, she slid off the table in a heap, not moving, just crying to herself inside, in secret. He walked away, grinning and buttoning up his fly.

CHAPTER 51

The raid, 1941

❧

Parker felt that Theodore should not be part of the rescue plan. He was too close to Christina and too young to think objectively, and from a selfish point of view, Parker realised the importance of this young man after Christina had been captured. Experienced runners like him were crucial to their future success.

Although it was nearly dark, Parker told him to go and tell Costas that the attack would take place at midday the following day. Then he was to go to the home of Aegeus, where his parents were hiding, to tell them of the plan to rescue their daughter. Meanwhile, Neame and Parker had talked to the men before organising the German uniforms.

'Firstly,' said Neame, 'Those of you who are wearing German uniforms must familiarise yourselves with the weapons. You must use these with precision, so practise operating them until you are perfect. There's a lot at stake.

I'm sorry you can't use the .303 and Brens that you are used to, for reasons which are obvious.

'Some of you are already familiar with the German base. The plan is to arrive there at speed and to pretend that we're chasing a group of Cretan resistance. Lieutenant Morris speaks fluent German, so when challenged he will tell the Germans of our intentions. This should distract them for long enough to allow Corporal Weeks, Gordon, Johnson, Fraser and me to go around the back in the hope that Christina will be where I think she is being held. At the same time, Costas will launch a second front with his group to cover our retreat, in the hope that they don't open fire and hit our men, particularly those dressed as Germans. They've been told that our German uniforms will be marked with a yellow circle on the front and rear of our belts. Hopefully, the Germans at the base won't be suspicious, but we can't take any chances. Any questions anyone? We have to get this right – not only to save Christina, if we're not too late, but because they must not find out about Costas and his cell and other groups in the mountains. Right, let's get the uniforms sorted.'

It was late by the time the briefing had finished, and Neame checked out each man to make sure they were all one hundred percent ready for the off in the morning. Parker had warned them that the Germans would not take this lying down and would pursue them back up the mountain. Those staying behind at the cave would be ready to ambush anyone following, with Costas harrying them on the way. The Wehrmacht in Manolas would be nervous about going too far away from their base without significant forces to support them, so that would give the British and Cretan fighters time to disperse after the operation if it was felt necessary.

During the night, a message was received from Cairo SOE Headquarters. They had been advised of Christine's capture and had immediately realised that the whole resistance network in Crete was at risk should she talk under pressure. Parker had been told in confidence that there were only two options – a successful rescue, or to make sure she didn't talk. He imparted this information to Morris, but he could not tell Neame in case it affected his decision making. Parker's instruction to Morris was to watch for the outcome of the rescue bid and deal with it as required. Not very comfortable for anyone.

It was light very early, and in the cave they could hear morning bells being rung somewhere down in the valley, calling people to prayers. This was also the call for the soldiers to get ready for the rescue, and to get some breakfast under their belts. It had been a restless night for most due to their thoughts about the coming day and the heat from many bodies in a confined space. Stevens had recovered enough from his wound to get a porridge of sorts prepared, the flavour enhanced hugely by local honey. 'You should never fight on an empty stomach,' Parker had told them the night before.

The oats had been soaking overnight and the porridge tasted really good, giving the men vital energy for the fight. Those who were not taking part lent a hand with the equipment, while the wireless operator sent a coded message to advise SOE in Cairo of the impending operation. Neame had posted three sentries at vantage points around the cave to ensure that their security would not be compromised. There had been a couple of Storch reconnaissance planes sweeping the area in the past couple of days, and it was crucial that nothing was identifiable from the air which would alert the enemy.

They planned their departure for 8 am. The group wearing German uniforms were to take a northerly route and approach Manolas from the west, whilst the smaller detachment of soldiers in British attire would take a different route and come in from the south. Costas and his andartes would cover the east, allowing the rescue party to head north following the rescue attempt. Lieutenant Morris was leading the 'German' contingent, with Neame taking charge of the rescue party.

Captain Parker took Neame aside. 'Good luck, Sergeant,' he said. 'I know what this means to you. Your responsibility is the safety of your men, whilst the release of Christina is the target of the exercise. I trust you to prioritise your thinking in the correct direction. You understand?'

'Yes sir, of course,' said Neame.

Shaking him by the hand, Parker went on, 'When you return, you must ensure that you give the correct call so the welcoming committee will know it's you. There's a chance that there will be Brits, other Brits dressed as Germans and some Cretan andartes all returning here at the same time, with the possibility of Germans coming up behind. Just be alert to all potential scenarios.'

Neame, as a seasoned professional, took all this in his stride.

The group dressed as Germans went off wearing their jackets inside out, so as not to appear at a cursory glance to be either German, British or Cretan. There was a slight mist which would help their cover. As they descended from the mountain over the rough ground of scrub and rock, they spoke not a word, all deeply immersed within their own thoughts, and Lieutenant Morris had to remind them to stay alert. They kept as far as possible away from habitation, and at one point they saw Neame and his small team away in the distance breasting a high ridge. After a short distance they heard goat bells, but if the shepherd saw them, he certainly did not appear.

Neame stopped in a position which gave him a clear view down to the village of Manolas. His thoughts were everywhere. What if... There was so much going on in his head, but as a professional soldier he knew he had to concentrate hard on the job in hand. There was too much at stake. Ever since arriving in Northern Greece, Neame had been under all sorts of different pressures, but nothing like what he was feeling right now. He could see palls of smoke rising from the compound, and he suddenly felt very sad that Christina was there somewhere, but he was comforted by the fact that he was so close to her.

'It won't be long, my love,' he murmured. 'I'm coming for you.'

Like a sign of good fortune, a bird of prey was picking up

the thermals and soaring to great heights, searching for a tasty breakfast.

Crouching behind a stone wall in an olive grove, Neame checked his watch. The sun was high in the sky and the heat was intense. So were their emotions. They had agreed to co-ordinate their attack at midday with the 'German patrol', having now turned their uniforms the right way round, arriving at the gate at twelve noon precisely. Neame and his group moved around to the rear of the compound whilst Morris was distracting the sentries with their ruse. Costas and his group were to wait unseen a little way up the hill to offer covering fire as Morris and Neame retreated from the German encampment.

From his position, Neame heard Morris's group approach at a slow trot. The sentry shouted, 'Halt! Who are you and what are you doing here?'

'Stand to attention when you address an officer!' snapped Morris. 'I am Oberleutnant Heimann from the 16th Company of the 4th Battalion and we are chasing some resistance who attacked one of our convoys carrying supplies and weapons. We need some support urgently – who is your commanding officer?'

Looking chastened, the sentry said, 'Please stay here Herr Oberleutnant. I will send for our commander to speak with you.'

'Be quick, it's urgent!' shouted Morris after him.

Meanwhile Neame had slipped round the back unseen, and after clambering over a wall he was starting the search for Christina. From the hillside using his binoculars, he had seen an officer and an NCO come up some steps out of a cellar. As they crept round the back of one of the two barns, Neame could see a guard posted outside the door. Neame had his knife ready. The only other German they could see close to where they were was an unarmed private in shirt sleeves bringing water up from the well. Weeks nodded to Neame to indicate that he would take one, and Neame the other. Part of their early training was how to take on the enemy with a knife, but this was for real. He wasn't sure how he would feel, but he had a job to do.

Meanwhile a lot of shouting in German was coming from the other side of the compound. It was a good time to act. Weeks came up behind the private and simultaneously pushed his knife in under the rib cage and his hand over his mouth to stop him screaming. Then he tipped him into the well. As this was happening, Neame threw a small stone to make the guard turn the other way, and then drew his knife across the man's throat from behind. He caught the man's body as it fell and dragged it out of sight.

Then the firing began. There were single shots, machine gun bursts and grenade explosions, with bullets ricocheting everywhere The raiders had been rumbled; he would have to get into the building now to try and find Christina. Leaving Fletcher and Gordon out of sight just inside the door, he and Weeks rushed down the ancient stairs into the cellar. There were only two rooms; one was a store with farming equipment, while the other was empty apart from a table and what looked like a heap of clothes in the corner.

'No more, please,' a voice said.

It was very dark and Neame's eyes took time to acclimatise. 'Christina, is that you? It's me, Bob.'

She started sobbing loudly and Neame bent down and took her in his arms, stroking the damp hair away from her face. 'Shush, my love,' he said gently. 'We must get you out of here. Can you stand?'

'I cannot,' she said weakly.

Giving his Sten gun to Weeks, he said, 'Here, I'll put you on my back and we'll make a dash for it. You'll soon be safe, I promise.'

Although there was still work to do, he felt relieved that he had got her out of that hellhole. As he lifted her onto his back, he thought he could feel the tension in her body start to dissipate. The need to get her to safety was acute. She was holding him tight around the neck and telling him through her sobs how much she loved him. He had a job to hold back his own tears, realising just how much she meant to him. It was painful to think about it – those bastard Germans, what had they done to her? The Gestapo were known to be brutal with their prisoners. He would get his own back for this. Christine's bravery knew no bounds, and apart from anything else he had a duty to get her away. But she was obviously in poor shape.

Nodding to Weeks, he carried her out of the darkness of the cellar and up the stairs as quickly as he could, thanking

God that she was slight in stature. Neame's two men waited outside the door in the crouch position ready to cover them if they came under attack, and as soon as they were out Neame and Weeks sprinted as fast as they could across the compound in the direction of Costas and his men, who were waiting on the hillside. Neame could tell from the noise that Morris was engaged in a rear-guard firefight with sustained bursts of heavy gunfire. Weaving to the left and right, Neame and Weeks reached the olive grove stone wall. This gave them a period of temporary respite, allowing Neame to get his breath back and make sure that Christina was all right. Talking over his shoulder, he said to her, 'Hang on my love. Not far to go now.'

Corporal Weeks tapped Neame on the shoulder, indicating that the German fire was being directed away from them, giving them a chance to get away up the hill. Neame told Christina to hold tight, and they set off again, weaving from left to right and making good progress.

They were just coming up to an old tumbledown cowshed when Neame suddenly went down as though he had tripped on a boulder. Christina fell heavily to the ground beside him, gasping with pain. Hearing Christina's cries, Neame stuttered, 'Sorry, my love.' He was trying to get up, but he seemed to find it impossible. He slumped back down again and was silent.

'Bob, are you OK?' said Weeks in an anxious voice, but there was no reply. Fearing the worst, he turned him gently over. Blood was pouring from a bullet hole in his neck.

Neame opened his eyes and looked across at Christina lying on the ground. He squeezed her by the hand and smiled. Then he closed his eyes and was still.

Weeks gathered a motionless Christina up in his arms and ran towards Costas who, seeing that Neame had been hit, stood up. 'Do not let even one of these scum escape!' said Costas. 'They will pay the price for what they have done to Manolas.'

They charged down into the compound with a surprised Morris giving them covering fire, rather than the other way around. No quarter was given. When the attack was over, there were three British dead, two of them in German uniforms, while six Cretan andartes had also died. Not one German remained alive, except a few who had run away.

Morris immediately commanded those remaining to head back up the mountain as fast as they could. Leaving the British dead behind was a tough decision, but the Germans would be aware that they were wearing British dog-tags, so he hoped they would be given a proper burial. Christina was safe, for now, but she was in a bad way, mentally and physically. She would be traumatised by the terrible ordeal she had been through, and devastated by the loss of her Bob. She would surely be scarred for life. Costas had survived and covered their rear just in case as they headed back, but the German retribution would be severe. His view was that they should hit them hard again in a different part of the island so that the Germans would not regain the initiative, and this would also take their minds off vengeance for the killings in

Manolas. But that was for another time – once they had got well away before the alarm was raised.

They took it in turns to carry Christina and to help the wounded, whose injuries were thankfully superficial. Morris gave the signal of approach, and several British soldiers came running forward to help. Colonel Parker was there to greet those returning, and he was told straight away about the death of Neame and the two others. Seeing Christina, he ordered her to be taken straight into the cave, but he knew she would need the help of the fathers at the monastery. He ordered Theodore to run there to get help from the other SOE men and to bring a mule to get her to the monastery, supported by a strong escort. The priority was to treat her physical injuries, not all of which could be dealt with by a military man, then to treat the wounded and get a brief from Morris about what had happened. He also knew that they might have to disperse until the heat had died down.

Costas came up to Parker and thanked him on behalf of Christina and his andartes for the brave actions of his men. He suggested that they should make contact immediately with one of the other resistance cells to divert attention away from Manolas and the hunt which would inevitably follow. Parker agreed wholeheartedly with this idea, saying he would send two of his SOE officers to help.

After attending to Christina, the medic took Parker to one side. 'She's in a bad way, sir. I'm no psychiatrist, but she is severely traumatised and she's been injured and badly beaten, and my guess is that she's been raped as well. She will not talk, and of course Neame being killed trying to save her is yet another burden she has to carry. It may be too much. We're going to get her to the monastery where the fathers can bring her some peace. Maybe that is as important as anything else at the moment.'

'I would support that, sir, as long as they understand that they must not let the Germans take her under any circumstances, because that would be the end for her. As far as we are aware she gave nothing away under torture in Manolas, but I couldn't guarantee her holding out a second time.'

In the days that followed, the German vengeance was terrible. The senior officer arrived in the village square and stood to address the villagers as he had when he had first arrived in Manolas, in the sidecar of a motor cycle.

'You were warned after the last attack that should it happen again you would be severely punished. The German army had twenty-one soldiers killed in the attack, so two hundred civilians will be executed, and your village will be razed to the ground. Manolas will cease to exist. Carry on, Sergeant.'

The village itself had almost emptied of people and livestock, knowing full well what was coming. Those who were left, mainly the elderly and infirm who had been left in Manolas after the original executions, were taken out and shot by firing squad. Seventy-one people were shot down in cold blood. The rest had dispersed away up into the mountains where they would be helped by the resistance as best they could. Every dwelling except the mayor's house was flattened and a notice erected to say that the same would happen to any other community which chose to challenge the laws of the Wehrmacht. The Germans then went to the neighbouring villages to find and execute one hundred and twenty-nine more.

CHAPTER 52

Airborne retribution, 1941

When the news spread about the annihilation of Manolas, the anger of the ordinary Cretan people knew no bounds. They had met the invader months earlier with a ferocity not seen before anywhere in the world from a civilian population since the start of the war, and they were not going to take it lying down. Such was their anger that many of those who had moved away up to the mountains got word to the resistance that they wanted to do something to hit back, and quickly.

Costas met Neame's group, who were now led by the SOE officers Parker and Morris, to decide a course of action and bring to book those who had carried out the inhuman slaughter. Lieutenant Colonel Harry Wright, guided by Theodore, went to the cave where the meeting was taking place. He announced himself to those who had arrived, some of whom he already knew, and speaking in Greek, he brought some calm to the situation. He had sensed that they were all for storming off at a tangent and would get into worse trouble, leading to yet more reprisals and executions.

He started by asking for quiet, and said a prayer for those who had died in the action to save Christina. He praised both the Cretans and the British and especially Bob Neame, whom he would be recommending for an award for his bravery. When he had finished speaking everyone stood to applaud, even the more warrior-like of the resistance fighters, who were puffed up with pride and trying hard not to shed a tear.

After a short pause, he said, 'We must act with intelligence so we don't bring the wrath of the whole German army down on our heads. I suggest we find a way to hit those responsible as hard as possible without putting any more civilian lives at risk. When we know who was behind this latest atrocity, we will take action against them, from the most senior officer downwards.'

Wright could tell by the men's body language that they wanted instant reprisals of the most bloodthirsty kind, but he could also see that some of them were thinking things through. There was much talk among themselves, with Costas taking the lead, but he was struggling to pacify the more vociferous members, who obviously wanted a mass killing.

After half an hour of talk and a few glasses of raki, Colonel Wright stood up to make a suggestion.

'Men of the resistance, I have a plan which would set out what we wish to achieve, and that is to take an action against those responsible which will not directly threaten more innocent civilians. It will also send a clear message to the

Germans that we have the will and the power to hit back.'
He took a deep breath and looked around at the faces of the
fighters. 'This may not be the action which some of you here
want, but please listen to what I have to say and then think
about it before making any rash decisions. We will find out
which regiment was responsible, and when we know for sure
their location, we will organise a bombing raid by the Royal
Air Force to cause them maximum destruction. We can
identify the target for them and use our powerful transmitter
to liaise with the airfield in Egypt or Libya on timings.'

He could see immediately that this was not what they
wanted to hear, but Costas stood to speak for them.

'Colonel, the men here, by and large, are desperate to take
the enemy on, face to face, as the German execution squad
did with our families, ' he said. 'But we will consider what
you say because you are an intelligent man and you will have
considered all angles. And we sincerely believe that you are
here in the best interests of the Cretan people. Please give us
a little time to consider what you have suggested.'

The debate continued for some while, with many a loud
opinion expressed. It was obvious that they were not all going
to all agree with Lt Col Wright's plan, but eventually Costas
rose and Wright asked for quiet to let him speak.

'Colonel, all here agree that something needs to be done,
and quickly,' he said. 'Most of us agree that your suggestion
is the most sensible. So, we will go along with it, but with
the proviso that it does not stop them taking co-ordinated
action against the occupier after the raid. The sabotage will

continue and if German soldiers get in the way,' he ran his finger across his throat, 'they will be dealt with.' After a pause, he continued, 'One other thing. They feel that in order to be taken seriously, one of the Germans responsible needs to be executed immediately.'

'I am afraid that we British cannot be party to the killing of an unarmed person, German or not,' the Colonel replied. 'But of course, if one of your Cretan soldiers decided on that course of action, and we knew nothing about it, then that is your decision, if you understand what I am saying.'

There were smiles of agreement and nods of understanding.

'But remember, the Germans have publicly stated that they will kill ten civilians for every German soldier who dies. Is that what you want?'

He had only to look at them to know that they were more than prepared to take that risk.

Surveying the smoke-filled cave, the Colonel said, 'Thank you all. We need to identify the culprits, the regiment and which battalion was responsible – Costas, can you deal with that please, and then we will meet again in three days here at 12 noon. Then we will strike.' He thought it a good moment to mention some other news. 'The British are sending more officers in the next few days along with an airdrop of weapons, including many automatic guns.'

This brought wide grins from the members present. They had lived all their lives with rifles in their homes, mostly of antique vintage. Guns were part of the Cretan way of life, and the prospect of more .303 rifles and automatic weapons was music to their ears. The meeting broke up with the resistance leaders leaving in different directions so as not to attract any unwanted attention.

These were dark days on the island. The only light on the horizon was the arrival of more SOE officers and air drops by Liberator bombers from Egypt. The supplies were starting to arrive in ever increasing volume, including substantial quantities of explosives. The co-ordination of the resistance groups by SOE was crucial, as each group demanded more and more of everything, so SOE needed to control these groups and know what the supplies were going to be used for and what actions were being planned. The boundaries were not clearly defined, and jealousies were commonplace.

Three days after their first meeting, the men reconvened. The importance of the meeting was obvious, with Lieutenant Colonel Wright in attendance along with Parker and Morris, and the air was tense with expectation. Dressed as Cretan resistance fighters, carrying knives and side arms, the men were eager to know the detail of the forthcoming raid. Costas had the information they needed.

'The regiment involved with the Manolas killings was the 85th Mountain Regiment, commanded by Major Treck,' he said. 'There were two other officers directly involved, Hauptmann Reinhardt and Leutnant Schlauer, along with Unterfeldwebels Heidrich and Dittmer.'

'Thank you, Costas. Where is the regiment based?'

'Their headquarters are in Chania, but there is an outpost at Vaphe where this battalion is stationed.'

'Right,' said Wright. 'We need to find someone who knows the outpost in Vaphe who can tell us how many men are there and whether they leave their post in the evening, because I feel that that would be the best time to hit them. We will have to work out how to light a pathway towards the target, as we do for arms drops. Parker, will you take care of that please? This must not be discussed with anyone outside this room. We are already hearing about the Germans recruiting informers.'

'My Colonel, no one will say a word and if we find any informers, we will know exactly what to do with them,' said Costas.

Antoni, a leader from the Plantanos region, stood and spoke. 'There is a schoolteacher in a village close to us who we suspect of passing information to the enemy. We could tell him that there is about to be a raid, but a long way from Vaphe. If they follow it up, we will know for sure that he is an informer and deal with him. That will kill two birds with one stone.'

'That sounds like a good plan. Everyone agree?' There was much nodding of heads before Colonel Wright spoke again. 'Captain Parker will co-ordinate the raid. Good luck to you all.'

Antoni went with all speed back to his village. He arrived just after mass, when members of the community were leaving church to take a drink in the local bar. Only home-made liquor was available, except for a few bottles which had been hidden from the Germans. They would not last long.

He spotted Levtheri, the schoolteacher, and Antoni with his co-leader at the next table. They talked purposefully about a possible raid and where it would happen, loud enough for him to hear what they were saying. After a few minutes, the teacher got up, nodding to Antoni as he left. They felt he had taken the bait.

On returning to the SOE cave, Wright got Simms to send a message to Cairo requesting an urgent air strike and explaining why it was vital to support their operations on the island, without giving the game away at this stage as to where and when it was required, just in case Jerry was picking up the transmissions. Wright's reputation at Headquarters was high, so it was accepted that if he thought it was essential, it would get support. However, the RAF in North Africa was at full stretch and all that was available was a squadron of Beaufighters based at Mersa Matruh, which had been converted to become maritime rocket-firing attack aircraft. While slow and heavy, the Beaufighter packed a big punch, as many of Rommel's ships sailing across the Mediterranean had discovered. A message was received stating that 252 Squadron was available to make the attack in two nights' time and final details would be required in the next twenty-four hours. A 'message received and understood' was sent back. Parker set to work on preparing the approach; he had received a crude sketch from Costas of how the village and outpost were laid out, prepared by a relative of his from Vaphe. Although the German outpost was away from the village, it was suggested that those living close by should discreetly move out of the area until after the attack.

At just before midnight, the British soldiers, with members of Costas's group, were in position ready to light the approach flares at three minutes before the time when the Beaufighters were expected to fly in from the south. Simms received a coded message at 11.57, indicating their imminent arrival. As agreed, the flares, arranged in an arrowhead formation pointing at the building, were lit. The tension was evident, with everyone straining for the sound of the approaching aircraft.

At a signal from Parker with his torch, the men swiftly withdrew from the area. Four aircraft came in low, the first going in immediately to attack. Everyone heard the whoosh as it released its rockets, followed by a sudden flash and explosion as the outer wall of the building was seen to crumble. Parker could see figures running from the building. Then the next attack hit home. This one hit a petrol bowser, which blew up, showering blazing fuel over the running figures.

The third aircraft scored a direct hit, and the whole two-storey building fell in on itself. The adjoining buildings also caught fire, causing many small explosions from stored ammunition, and dense smoke covered the area.

The last aircraft dropped a thousand leaflets telling the Germans why the raid had taken place. It read:

BE WARNED. This raid by the Royal Air Force was in retaliation for the illegal killing of innocent civilians in Manolas by the 85th Mountain Regiment. Any further such atrocities will be avenged in the same way. You have been warned. British HQ, Cairo.

One German soldier who was not killed in the raid had been found the day before with his throat cut. Investigations had started. The same fate had happened on the same day to the schoolmaster in Plantanos. No one in the village was surprised, and the Germans did not investigate.

CHAPTER 53

Manolas, 2016

❦

Tom reached over and planted a kiss on Charlie's shoulder. 'Come on beautiful, it's time to rise and shine,' he said.

'You rise and I'll shine!' she said, grinning back at him.

'You cheeky devil. Didn't you get enough last night? I heard Maria come in earlier. I hope she brought something in for breakfast, I'm starving.'

He went downstairs into the kitchen to find a note saying, 'Sorry couldn't stop. Might see you later. Fruit with fresh yogurt and orange juice in the fridge and coffee brewed. Maria X.'

Charlie came down, dressed and ready for the day. 'You're looking gorgeous this morning,' Tom said. 'But much as I love you walking about without a bra, we are going to Manolas today and the mood may be a little sombre, because it's the anniversary of the German invasion. Perhaps something a little more discreet?'

'Point taken,' she said. 'I'll cover up a bit today. But I guess it will be another hot day.'

'I'll just go and tell our police escort where we're going. Can you get some fruit and yogurt in a couple of bowls? But the first thing I want is a cup of Maria's delicious coffee.'

It was a glorious day and Tom had suggested to Maria the day before that they should meet her parents in the village café at eleven. There was to be a short service of remembrance at midday, the time at which the Germans had committed the atrocity on this day in 1941. Although it was going to be a sad occasion, Tom was looking forward to seeing this place he had heard so much about. He wanted to walk around the area and go up to the mountains which Nikos had described to him in such detail.

They walked out into the bright sunlight, smartly dressed as a token of respect. Tom felt his father would approve. Charlie looked the epitome of a Greek goddess, and he felt very proud to be with such a beauty.

As he unlocked the car, he noticed that the police had managed to remove the offensive graffiti, which was just as well, considering the circumstances. They headed inland towards Alikianou, very pleased to have air conditioning on full blast. They certainly did not want to arrive damp and sweaty. The police car stayed at a discreet distance behind. It was a relaxed journey with hardly any traffic apart from the occasional donkey, tractor or tourist bus. Nikos had said that the ceremony would just be a local affair and should not attract too many outsiders, if any.

The road sign for Manolas appeared, partially covered by a mule which was using it as a scratching post. The road was narrow and they could see that the village square was busy, so they left the car in the shade on the outskirts, with the police car pulled up some thirty metres back. They walked into the village hand in hand, smiling at the villagers they passed. The café was immediately facing the square and Nikos and Melissa were waiting for them. They seemed so pleased to see them that Nikos almost knocked over his chair in his excitement to greet them.

'Tom, Charlie – welcome to our village! I call it that because that is where we both come from, where our parents still live, where Maria was born. We feel very much at home here.'

Melissa gave Tom a kiss and Charlie a big hug.

'Maria not here today?' Tom asked.

'No, she was not well last night, so she decided not to come,' said Melissa.

Tom thought this was strange, as she had come to the house that very morning. 'That's a shame,' he said. 'Hopefully we'll get to see her before we head off tomorrow. She has looked after us very well.'

'What can I get you to drink?' Nikos asked. 'A beer, Tom? Or something lighter? Charlie?'

'I'll just have a nice cold diet coke or similar please Nikos,' replied Charlie.

'I'd like a Greek coffee please,' said Tom.

The café was buzzing with people, and cigarette smoke

hung in the air. It seemed no one here took too much notice of regulations. If they wanted to smoke, they smoked. Nikos and Melissa introduced them to people they knew, and everyone seemed pleased to see them there. The only people in the café apart from locals were a couple of tourists sitting with their backs to them; they looked as though they had been hiking and had stopped to cool down.

'Everyone seems so nice,' Charlie whispered to Melissa.

'Yes, we feel very much a part of this village. In fact, we're going to come back here when Maria has gone to university. It will be more of a journey for both of us to get to work, but it will be worth it.'

So far it felt like a day of celebration, but Tom knew that part of the day would not be so happy.

It was almost midday when a slightly overweight but handsome man with a wonderful moustache and a smart sash stood up and asked for quiet.

'My friends, we have an important ceremony to carry out today,' he said. 'We will lay a wreath at our war memorial to our friends and neighbours past who were brutally murdered seventy-five years ago, at this spot, at this time. Then we will place a wreath in memory of a hero of ours, Sergeant Bob Neame, an Englishman who died saving one of our own from the hands of the Germans and did so much for our village. We have also decided to name a street in Manolas after him. The priest will say a few words to honour those we remember. Please follow me.'

Tom, quite shocked by what he had just heard, said to

Nikos, 'I remember you telling me about an English soldier, but I didn't realise his death meant so much to the village.'

'Oh, yes Tom. Because if he hadn't rescued our aunt, Christina Papadakis, from the Germans, they would have almost certainly made her talk, and she knew everything about the resistance here. They had already tortured and raped her. He is a true hero to this village, and he'll never be forgotten.'

These words made Tom think about all the times he had visited Armistice Day services with his father back home, when he had never really thought about one individual, just of the thousands who had given their lives. Somehow this moment made it much more personal and moving.

'You must tell me more about it Nikos, after the ceremony,' he said.

They were the last to leave the café apart from the two tourists, who seemed vaguely familiar.

With everyone standing in a semi-circle around the memorial, the Mayor read out the names of the villagers who had perished on that terrible day in July 1941 and those who had died during the rest of the conflict. The priest, Father Constantis, then said prayers. After a period of silence, and many tears, they moved to the memorial to Bob Neame, a simple plaque embedded in a dry stone wall facing the square.

'We particularly remember this man today,' said Father Constantis. 'On this day seventy-five years ago, Sergeant Neame decided to stay and fight here to help the Cretan people against the invader. He could have left to go back to his regiment, but he chose to stay. While he was here, he fell in love with one of our own people, a young woman called Christina Papadakis. She was at the time a runner for the resistance, taking messages, with her brother Theodore, between our resistance groups and the British soldiers up in the mountains. She was captured and tortured to give them information, but she held firm. Sergeant Neame led the mission to rescue her, and he got her out successfully, but he was shot while getting away, and sadly he died from his wounds. Many lives were saved here because of this man's actions. We are pleased that our good friend Nikos is here today and that he has brought friends from England to witness this occasion. I will now invite them to lay the wreath in memory of their brave countryman – Sergeant Bob Neame.'

With tears streaming down his face, completely overcome with emotion, Tom walked up with Nikos and bowed his head in honour of Sergeant Neame. The whole crowd burst into rapturous applause, with everyone crying and throwing their arms around one another. It was a deeply moving moment. In the crowd Charlie and Melissa were both crying, and Melissa was saying, 'I wish Maria could have been here.' Then, she thought to herself, maybe not. Particularly after last night's episode.

Just to dampen the atmosphere a little, the two tourists shouted from the back of the crowd, 'Where's the barman? We need another drink.'

It was only then that Tom and Charlie realised that they were German.

The café owner had laid on a superb spread and invited everyone to help themselves. All the old wartime stories were aired, not for the first time, and much drink was consumed. Tom and Charlie sat down with Nikos and Melissa. They had inadvertently become the centre of attention because they were British and guests of the Papadakis family, who were highly respected in the village. Everyone wanted to buy them drinks.

To many people's annoyance, the German tourists started to help themselves to the food. They were stopped only when a giant of a man from the village went up to them, took their piled-up plates away and told them the food was for villagers and guests only. They were by this time more than a little drunk, and started to get aggressive. At that point the big man picked them both bodily up and took them outside, dumping them on the square.

'Who on earth is that?' asked Tom. 'I've never seen such a huge man.'

'You remember I told you about a shepherd called Aegeus who helped the resistance and the British during the war, and was executed by the Germans?' said Nikos. 'That is his grandson. He still lives in his grandfather's house up in the mountains, and like him he believes he is the reincarnation of Hercules. He is immensely strong, but he is also a very kind person who will do anything for anyone. He would not stand any nonsense from trouble-making Germans, and certainly not today of all days.'

When the excitement had died down a little, Tom said to Nikos, 'Now, you were going to tell us the story about Christina.'

'Yes, it is a story of valour, love, hate, sadness and vengeance. Christina became a really important part of the resistance around here, and a symbol of defiance. Her father Ioannis was a true villager. He lived with his wife Katina just outside Manolas, up towards the mountains. She helped her father when the British first arrived, because she could speak a little English. When the British started sending people here, they made sure that they could speak a little Greek. But as you will have realised today, she fell in love with Sergeant Bob, as he was affectionately known, and after his death, she had a baby. No one was ever sure if it was Neame's or whether it was the result of the rape whilst she was held by the Germans.'

'That is so sad,' said Charlie, who had listened to the story intently. 'What happened to her?'

'When she realised that she was pregnant, bearing in mind the terrible ordeal she had had at the hands of the Germans, she spent some months recovering under the protection of a monastery. Later, she went to live with the wife of Aegeus, as her parents and brother were in hiding in the mountains. It was Aegeus' wife who delivered the baby. Sadly, because of the injuries she had suffered, she haemorrhaged during the birth and died. There was nothing they could do to save her. Aegeus's wife brought up the baby boy as her own. There were not too many questions asked, as some thought the baby could have been Neame's.'

Tom could see Charlie's eyes welling up with tears, for the second time that day. 'I don't think I have ever heard anything so sad,' she said. 'So what happened to the baby boy?'

'He survived and was brought up with the two sons of Aegeus and his wife. They bred livestock when the war ended, including some prize bulls, which seemed synonymous with a family who believed in the story of Hercules. He is seventy-four now and married with children and grandchildren. When he was told the story about his mother, he was asked if whether he wanted to know his true parentage, but he said no. It was enough for him to know that he had brown hair, the same colour as his mother's lover, Bob Neame.'

CHAPTER 54

Missing person, Manolas 2016

Tom felt deeply sad about what had happened here all those years before, although he was also proud of the part Britain had played. 'Why don't we go for a walk up towards the mountain to see where all of the events took place that Nikos has told us about?' he said. 'It's a lovely day, after all. Perhaps you could show us, Nikos?'

'Of course, I would be delighted to,' he replied. 'I'm sure Melissa will come too. We can call in and see my parents – they would be delighted to meet you.'

It was obvious that Charlie had found the ceremony far more emotional than she had ever imagined. This was not her war, or her country, but it had deeply affected her.

'Before we go, I would like to talk to the people here for a few moments,' she said. 'Everyone seems so nice and welcoming. I won't forget today in a hurry. It's been very special. But first I am just going to use the toilets.'

'They are just round the back of the café,' said Nikos. 'I am sorry, but they are a little basic.'

Tom watched Charlie disappear around the corner of the building, then turned to Nikos. 'It's been a very emotional day Nikos, but we're very pleased we came,' he said. 'Your people went through some really bad times, and of course they went on for another four years. It is right to remember what happened.'

'Maria has a slightly different view of things, being from a younger generation, the same generation as you,' said Melissa. 'But I hope she will continue to remember as we do. It is not about hating the aggressor. It is simply important not to forget the terrible events which took place.'

They waited several minutes for Charlie, but she did not return. Eventually Tom said, 'Charlie's been gone a little while. Melissa, would you mind just seeing if she's OK and hasn't locked herself in?'

When Melissa came back, she said, 'She's not there, the toilets are empty. I couldn't see her anywhere.'

Slightly concerned, Tom went outside with Nikos. 'You go one way and I'll try the other, just to see if she has gone to do a little sight-seeing,' he said. 'She did say she wanted to talk to some of the local people.'

When they met back at the café again a few minutes later, no one had seen any sign of Charlie. Tom tried her mobile without success, as the calls went straight to voicemail. It occurred to him that the police officers might have seen her, so he walked down to where their car was parked. He found them under an olive tree, asleep. Waking them up, he said, 'Have you seen my girlfriend? She hasn't walked past?'

Obviously extremely embarrassed, the sergeant said, 'I'm sorry sir. It was very hot so we were sitting in the shade waiting for you.'

Trying to control his frustration, Tom said, 'Don't worry about that now. She went to the toilet at the back of the café, and she didn't return. You know what she looks like. Please help us to find her. Now!'

There was now some real concern as to where Charlie might have gone. It was totally out of character for her to wander off without saying where she was going. Someone said they thought they had seen her with a bunch of wild flowers in her hand. Where could those have come from?

It was now the middle of the afternoon and extremely hot. Volunteers from the café who had heard what had happened were offering to join in the search, but after two hours, there was still no sign of Charlie. Tom was beginning to realise just how much she meant to him. He did not want to alert his father, but if she did not show up by five, he would have to. He was mystified by Charlie's disappearance, and he was now getting extremely worried.

Given that an ambassador's son was involved, the Honorary Consul in Heraklion was alerted by the Chania police in the patrol car, worried that something untoward might have happened on their watch. Although the Consul was in the middle of a meeting, he left immediately and contacted Tom's father from his office. Neville phoned Tom on his mobile.

'Tom, it's Dad,' he said. 'I've just had a call from the Consul about Charlie. What on earth is happening?'

'Oh, so sorry Dad. Charlie has gone missing in the most inexplicable circumstances and no one has seen her for nearly three hours. We were in Manolas when it happened. Dad, I'm really worried for her, she means the world to me.' He was having a real job trying to keep his emotions under control.

'Were the police not with you?' Neville asked.

'Yes,' replied Tom, 'but they were asleep.'

'What? I can't believe that. I'm getting on to the Chief of Police in Chania right now.'

'What we need is more help to find her Dad. Giving them a roasting won't help.'

A few more hours passed with no news. There was a deep hush everywhere with no sound of livestock, vehicles, nor even birds. Tom kept thinking about what Charlie had said about talking to the local people. Had she been invited to someone's house? Surely she wouldn't have done that without coming back to tell him? Each time he bumped into someone, they would shake their heads as if to say 'sorry, there is no news'. Villagers were still out searching, walking the fields, looking in farm buildings and knocking on doors. Reinforcements had arrived from the police in Chania. By evening there must have been almost a hundred people searching for Charlie.

The light was just starting to go down when a shout went

up from beyond the mayor's house. 'She's here!' It seemed she had been found by a couple of local volunteers.

Tom rushed to the scene as fast as he could. At first he was held back, as the villagers wanted to save him from the sight that awaited him. Charlie was lying partially clothed on her back under a cypress tree in a field of cattle. A white bull was standing over her, snorting, as if to offer her protection. But it was too late; she was clearly beyond help. She was naked from the waist down, and wild flowers had been scattered around her body. Tom could not take in what had happened.

Then he saw that a book had been left beside her body. He looked at the title: *The Rape of Europa* by Lynn Nicholas, a book about Nazi activities during the Second World War. That title brought a terrible wave of guilt. It was he who had invited her to come on holiday, and it was he who had kept comparing her to the Greek beauty Europa. Yet he had done nothing to protect her against obvious threats. And above all, he had never told her how he felt about her. He began to sob, and the tears just kept coming.

Inevitably, all hell broke loose on the island when the news of Charlie's terrible death was announced. The Diplomatic Service in Athens and Crete were involved. Politicians blamed the police for their incompetence. A full-scale police investigation got under way. After interviewing most people who were in Manolas that day, it became clear that the prime suspects were the two German tourists who had got drunk and been thrown out of the café by the grandson of Aegeus. But the motive was not clear. The media in Germany were blaming the Cretan police for using the German suspects to divert attention away from the earlier murder, with which their investigations had made no headway. People on the island immediately began to think that there was a connection between that murder and this horrific crime.

When Tom was told about the manner of her death, he remembered where he had seen the two German tourists before. It was at Knossos, when the tour guide had described her as resembling Queen Europa, and again, briefly in a bar in Chania. But why? It didn't make sense. The story of Europa came to him – the white bull, the flowers, making love under the cypress tree to Zeus, the bull in human form. Was that what the German pair thought would get them noticed?

The description of the two men was emailed to the airports and every police station on the island. The suspects were picked up the next day, still high on drugs and hiding under an upturned boat on a beach near Chania. Under questioning in the presence of a solicitor, the pair admitted that they had been asked by a young Cretan girl who they had partied with to give the couple a 'hard time'. The motive was jealousy, but the drink and drugs had turned a 'hard time' into a horrendous and murderous act.

It did not appear that Charlie's death was linked to the earlier murder. The tourist had opened his mouth too wide about the Cretan people during the war, and someone had taken exception to it. He would be found one day, although not soon enough for the German media. The two tourists were charged with aggravated murder, rape and attempted murder with a vehicle. They would stand trial in the capital, Heraklion, the date to be announced.

When all the formalities were over, Tom went back to Athens to the bosom of his family for a period of quiet solitude before trying to pick up the pieces of his life. He knew he would have to return to the island for the trial, but first he had to visit Charlie's parents in Harrogate. It would be the most difficult journey he had ever undertaken. His mother and father had offered to accompany him for the funeral. He knew that was something he would not be able to handle on his own.

For Maria, the terrible death of Charlie felt like the end. She had shamed her family, driven astray by drugs and alcohol, and given herself to two German boys who had initially seemed normal but had turned out to be hard right-wingers. She had hardly known them. She had also told them in a drunken moment all about Tom and Charlie and how she was jealous of Charlie and even, in a rash moment, she had wished her harm. She had had no idea that it could end up so tragically. All along the man she had really wanted, ever since they had been young children, had been Tom, at it seemed that at one time he had wanted her. While Charlie was there, obviously in love with him, it wasn't going to happen. Now she was dead, and there was a chance that Maria would be charged with being an accessory to murder. Certainly she now had no chance of ever getting Tom for herself.

With her honour lost and disowned by her parents, Maria was in complete turmoil. Even her grandparents, Stelios and Lalika, both in their seventies, were so shocked by the events which unfolded that they closed up their house to everyone except Melissa and Nikos and became virtually isolated in Manolas. There was no one Maria could turn to for help. She had to make her own decision.

Seventy-five years before, Christina had gone to live a lonely existence in the mountains after the shame of her illegitimate pregnancy, and now Maria felt that this was what she must do too. She needed time, to reflect and to heal. The home Aegeus the shepherd had lived in was empty and a ruin, but she could be content there and visit the monks for absolution when the time was right. If the police decided to prosecute her, she would have to deal with that. Fortunately, such was the pain she had suffered inside that her friend Roussos had spoken to his Commander to ask for leniency.

As that long, lonely winter set in, Maria discovered with mixed feelings that if she had been pregnant, she certainly was not now. She began to do her best to devote herself to a life of simplicity, isolation and solitude.

One morning a warm spring sun appeared over the valley, making her feel for the first time in months that she might be turning a corner. She strolled out into the sunshine to pick some wild garlic to make soup. As she did so, she saw that a visitor was ambling up the track towards her. He was tall, young and well built, and there was something familiar about him.

She shaded her eyes to see more clearly, and her heart began to thump furiously.

It was Tom.

Postscript: 1953

❦

At the same time as Queen Elizabeth II was being crowned in front of huge crowds in London, a well-dressed middle-aged English woman wearing a floral waisted dress alighted from an ancient bus which had arrived in the village square in Manolas. She had come from the Commonwealth War Graves cemetery at Suda Bay, where her husband had been interred after the war. Dabbing her brow with a handkerchief because of the heat, she walked into the local café and ordered a coffee. She sat quietly in the corner for a while before asking if anyone knew what had happened when the Germans came in 1941. The waiter asked her what in particular she wanted to know. She replied that her husband been left behind on the island after the invasion and had stayed to fight alongside the resistance.

'His name was Bob Neame,' she said, 'Sergeant Bob Neame. I understand that he died here. I'm his wife, Pamela Neame.'

'Sergeant Bob!' said the waiter with a big smile, knowing immediately who she was referring to. 'You are most welcome to our village, Mrs Neame. Your husband was a hero to us. He died trying to save some members of the resistance. He is remembered over there – that plaque on the wall. Fresh flowers are still placed there every week in his memory.'

Mrs Neame stood thoughtfully for a moment. 'I was only told by the authorities that he had died fighting the Germans. I knew nothing more except that he was awarded the Military Medal for gallantry here on the island. It has taken me all this time to find the courage to come here to find the truth.'

'I had better find someone who can help you,' said the waiter.

Costas, who was still the mayor of Manolas, was sitting quietly outside smoking a cigarette and had noticed the stranger alighting from the bus. The waiter whispered in his ear about the Englishwoman. Costas stood up rather hesitantly, knowing all too well what had happened in 1941, and walked across and introduced himself.

'Good morning, madam,' he said. 'Welcome to our village. The waiter tells me that you are here because of Sergeant Neame. He is well known here. As his wife, you must be very proud of him.'

Costas was wondering whether to tell the whole story or whether to keep the truth about Bob Neame and his relationship with a Cretan girl secret. He wanted Bob to remain, in her eyes and those of her children, a hero for his part in the war.

'May I get you something?' he asked.

'No thank you very much,' said Mrs Neame.

He took a big breath and began to give her a carefully edited version of the events of the summer of 1941. 'Now, the handsome Englishman we all knew as Sergeant Neame…'

Because that, he felt, was all she needed to know.